HEIRS AND ASSIGNS

HEIRS AND ASSIGNS

Marjorie Eccles

This first world edition published 2015
in Great Britain and the USA by
SEVERN HOUSE PUBLISHERS LTD of
19 Cedar Road, Sutton, Surrey, England, SM2 5DA.
Trade paperback edition first published
in Great Britain and the USA 2016 by
SEVERN HOUSE PUBLISHERS LTD.

British Library Cataloguing in Publication Data

Eccles, Marjorie author.
  Heirs and assigns.
  1. Police–England–Shropshire–Fiction. 2. Murder–
  Investigation–Fiction. 3. Family secrets–Fiction.
  4. Great Britain–History–George V, 1910-1936–Fiction.
  5. Detective and mystery stories.
  I. Title
  823.9'2-dc23

ISBN-13: 978-0-7278-8528-9 (cased)
ISBN-13: 978-1-84751-633-6 (trade paper)
ISBN-13: 978-1-78010-691-5 (e-book)

All Severn House titles are printed on acid-free paper.

Severn House Publishers support the Forest Stewardship Council™ [FSC™],
the leading international forest certification organisation. All our titles that
are printed on Greenpeace approved FSC certified paper carry the FSC logo.

PART ONE

ONE

The whole idea is ridiculous, of course. Ida knows she shouldn't have come. It always unnerves her, returning to what she still regards as home. But if Pen has decided to throw a birthday party for himself – even a sixtieth, for heavens' sake! – no one is going to refuse to attend. Verity, in fact, had come down to Shropshire for it a week ago and today has unwillingly driven over to Wolverhampton to meet her mother off the London train.

'You're looking peaky, Verity.'

Without replying, she had glowered darkly at her mother (brittle and glossy, too old for pencilled eyebrows, long red nails and a shingle). Her mouth is still set in a sulky line half an hour later. She is usually a competent driver, in contrast to the incompetent way she presently chooses to conduct the rest of her life, but today, Ida can only be thankful she hasn't had to drive down from London with her. The twenty-odd miles to Hinton Wyvering, close to the Welsh border, have not been without their terrifying moments, and Ida's nerves are frayed. But at least they've managed to get so far without actually squabbling, mainly because Ida has kept her eyes closed for most of the way. She doesn't want to talk anyway. Communication with Verity lately is too exhausting and she has enough on her mind without that.

To give herself time to consider, she has shut up for two weeks the little business she runs from the front room of her Chelsea house and has spent most of last night and all of the train journey here turning over the offer to buy it. Not by any means generous but amazing to have received one at all in the present climate, and she is on tenterhooks lest it might be withdrawn. Money is tight everywhere, even ten years after the end of the war with the Germans, and the exclusive designs she sells are expensive, to say the least, and therefore only affordable to the select few. An additional worry is that old Millie Wainwright, a woman with magic in her fingers when it comes to fashioning a model hat, has just announced her retirement. 'I'm sorry, I don't want to leave you in the lurch, Mrs Lancaster, but my hands are getting that stiff I can't hardly hold a needle. I shall miss the money, but I reckon I can manage if I'm careful with my pension, God bless Lloyd George.'

Ida would have welcomed retirement herself. She is tired – tired of selling hats, tired of flattering customers, tired of keeping up appearances and, most of all, weary of trying to make ends meet. Verity is not interested in millinery – or anything outside of herself it seems, not even nightclubs, jazz or rackety young men in fast cars, as the daughters of Ida's friends all seem to be. But even if Ida does take up that offer and sells the shop, she will still be left without enough of what she considers it possible to live on.

They eventually cross the river bridge and begin the steep ascent to Hinton. (No one local ever bothers with the Wyvering part of its name.) Over the centuries, endeavouring to escape the endemic flooding at this point, dwellings have crept further and further up the hill and now form at the top what the residents call a town, although really it's not much more than a large village. The road, Nether Bank, twists tortuously upwards through a huddle of ancient cottages and forgotten little by-lanes, with Verity taking the bends at a speed that makes Ida's stomach lurch. Guardian angels must be watching over them for they suffer nothing worse than Ida's crocodile-skin dressing case toppling on to the suitcases stacked behind the front seats.

As the porter had stowed these into the little second-hand Austin Seven Ida had been nagged into buying for her daughter, Verity had rolled her eyes. 'Crikey, Mother! How long do you intend staying for? It's only Uncle Pen's birthday party.'

A birthday party, at his age. What is Pen thinking of? He is a widower, his wife having died many years ago, he is childless and has no one to please but himself, but Ida sees no reason why anyone, even a man, should announce to the world that they are sixty years old, especially when their sister, who is only two years younger and has so far managed to conceal the fact quite successfully, has been invited to join the celebration. An invitation that has come out of the blue but which, in the circumstances, can't be refused.

Ida belatedly regrets that spontaneous remark she'd made on seeing Verity drooping colourlessly on the station platform. It was perhaps tactless – though undoubtedly true – but the subsequent glances she throws across the car now suggest that looking peaky isn't the only thing she finds unsatisfactory about her daughter. She sighs, frustrated as usual. The child only looks so lumpy because she slouches and takes no trouble with her clothes; she's naturally pale but scornfully refuses to use make-up, and her quite acceptable features are marred by a disagreeable expression that seems to have become permanent lately. Which is foolish. When she was a child she'd been the apple of Pen's eye but lately, like everyone else, even he is growing impatient with her. 'Your Uncle Pen never could stand sulks,' she remarks unwisely.

Verity throws her a look of distaste but Ida is examining her *maquillage* in the mirror of her enamelled compact for any smuts collected on the train journey and doesn't see it. 'Why don't you say what you mean, Mother – that it isn't in any of our interests to upset him?'

'That was an unnecessary remark.' Ida snaps her compact shut. But it's nothing she hasn't thought herself – and said too, on occasions. They are coming to the top of the hill where the road divides and they turn, leaving the town on their left. Half a mile further along, just past the ruins of a small hill fort that masquerades under the name of castle, built to repel long past Welsh raiders, the motor takes another unnerving swing, narrowly missing a pedestrian with a small white and brown terrier on a lead. 'Verity!' she shrieks, clutching her hat. Then, as the car straightens, she adds, 'Who was that?'

'Who?'

'Didn't you even *see*? That man and his dog stepping out from under the trees? They nearly went under the wheels when you threw the car to one side like that.'

'Oh, he's nobody – and I wouldn't have needed to swerve,'

says Verity through gritted teeth, 'if my passenger hadn't been taking my mind off my driving.'

In a stiff silence they drive along the ridge of the hill until they take an abrupt turn between stone gateposts and career down the drive of Bryn Glas.

There's not much trace now of the green hill after which the house – originally, long ago, a manor house, thereafter a farm and now a house again – is named. It is built on a sort of natural plateau in the hillside and the drive ends on this sizeable flat area, where excavations of the red sandy soil have formed a weird lunar landscape. Ida takes the appalling mess to be the creation of this much talked of garden, where none to speak of has ever previously existed as far as she remembers. It's being undertaken by a woman who used to work with the famous garden designer Miss Gertrude Jekyll, and who doubtless wears the same sort of men's hobnailed boots as that lady is reputed to wear, and possibly breeches as well. It seems to Ida that her brother doesn't intend letting his enforced retirement curtail his enthusiasm for mad ideas, although making a garden is unlikely to turn the sort of profit his other brilliant schemes have generated over the years, making him and Llewellyn Holdings worth more than all the rest of his family put together. As the car skids to the front of the house, the door is flung open by the beaming host himself, and Ida steps out of the car, thankful to be still alive, and allows Penrose to embrace her.

Concern about the garden project is put to one side. Most things – and most people – recede into the background when Pen Llewellyn appears on the scene, though he is not particularly impressive to look at, no more than medium height, muscular, not handsome but with a thick crop of white hair and bright blue eyes. Despite the heart problem he has, he looks the picture of health today, as he invariably does. 'Welcome to Bryn Glas, sister dear.'

TWO

Claudia Llewellyn is beginning to think this journey will never end, near as they are to their destination now. The warmth from the portable heater having long since expended itself, she is frozen, despite being wrapped in furs. And hungry. It's beyond her why they couldn't have travelled in a civilized manner from London by train, like her sister-in-law, Ida. But, although in other respects Theo is cautious to the point of parsimony in her eyes, he loves this expensive motor car with a passion not extended to much else, and Claudia is not a woman who finds it expedient to argue. Besides, he makes this journey regularly to visit his brother and enjoys every minute of it, or so he says; driving long distances apparently helps him to think. Presumably that's what he's been doing for the past four or five hours: for the most part of the journey he has been absorbed in a deep, lawyerly silence, his brow furrowed like a melancholy bloodhound's, the space between himself and his wife filled with the sense of a controlled, inner rage.

Claudia is a tall, lazily elegant woman, statuesque, with heavy, bronze-coloured hair which she wears unfashionably long, drawn back to a coil at the nape of her neck. Her clothes are classic, ageless. This doesn't mean she's out of the swim, indeed she has more social aspirations and expensive tastes than are useful to Theo in his career. But she has no need to follow fashion: she creates her own simply by being her rather beautiful self. She doesn't mind being thought singular, having at heart a disdainful disregard of lesser beings whom she thinks not as clever as herself, or as well dressed, or who have the misfortune not to be the child of a baronet. An impoverished one, unfortunately, who'd had barely enough money to keep himself solvent, never mind enough to leave to his only child. This party to which she and Theo have been invited – or should that be commanded? – and having to mix with all these Llewellyns, isn't her cup of tea. Who are they, after all, but descendants of petty Welsh landowners who had fortuitously found themselves in years gone by to be sitting on a coal mine or two? Four generations later they've sold up any shares they ever had in those mines, left the coal pits and the echoes of past exploitations and present consequences behind. Neither Pen nor his brother have ever been within spitting distance of extracting coal from the bowels of the earth. Pen, before the heart attack which has caused him to retire to an allegedly quieter life, was a property developer and Theo practices law.

Pen has returned to spend the rest of his life, rather than just the odd weekend, in their childhood home here in Shropshire. Quietly, so he says. Claudia wouldn't put money on that. Nor does she altogether believe Theo when he says he enjoys his visits here, especially those he's made of late. Although the scare over Pen's health has caused concern, Theo would really like to leave this town, and in particular Bryn Glas and its past, behind for ever. But needs must.

The drive to the house is little more than a dirt road, its potholes, when they occur, hopefully filled in with stones, rubble and gravel. It's mercifully short, though downward-plunging, before it reaches the level ground by the front door. From the back of the house, where the garden continues to slope more gently towards the cliffs above the river far below, the view to the distant hills, via a patchwork of green fields and red earth, is spectacular, very lovely in spring but not at its best on a gloomy late afternoon in November. Here at the front the old timber-framed house crouches, long and low. Instead of coming back to this shambling old ruin, Pen could have bought a good modern house in which to retire . . . with a ready-made garden, Claudia thinks, horrified at the ravages evident as they sweep to the front door.

In fact, the house is by no means a ruin, only to Claudia's way of thinking, but it's still an old farmhouse, despite the installation of modern plumbing and a hot water heating system that even so isn't quite up to it at times. There are rooms all over the place, dark corners, ceilings too low for tall people and floors at different levels, cunningly situated to trip the unwary. In spring, and especially in summer, its cool, shadowy interiors are welcoming, but this dark and melancholy heel of the year brings

out the worst in the house. Its low roofs and oak panelling are
sombre and absorb the light, the stone floors, however well
polished by Mrs Knightly, seem to breathe damp. To give him
his due, Pen will have attempted to counteract this by having
huge roasting fires made up in every room, the lamps lit earlier
than strictly necessary. And yes, the inside is brilliantly lit, there
are people moving around, a look of conviviality. Pen's famed
hospitality, though the party isn't until Saturday. It isn't Pen who
comes out to welcome them however, but someone they have
not expected to see, not in a million years.

'Huwie,' says Theo, as he gets out of the car at last, schooling
himself to hide his initial shock and delivering a brotherly slap
on the shoulder. The years have not improved Huwie. His mouth
has a downward droop, his hair no longer falls in the boyish flop
over his eyes that appeals to ladies, but is greying and receding
fast. The once attractively rumpled air has gone and he now looks
merely seedy. His fifty-shilling suit has sitting-down creases at
the crotch and is shiny at seat and elbows. Beside him, Claudia's
saturnine husband, for all his long, mournful face, his furrowed
brow, has presence and authority: Theo is tall, dark, well dressed
and obviously prosperous.

Pen, Theo and Huwie. Three brothers, same parents, same
upbringing. So different.

'Well, well, back to Bryn Glas after all these years then?' says
Theo to his younger brother, summoning up heartiness as they
go inside.

'When Pen invites,' Huwie replies, 'who can refuse?'

THREE

After three months, Carey had been expecting that returning
home to Hinton would be akin to entering a time warp.
But of course events haven't stopped. As she pays off
Swayne's taxi, she sees Dr Fairlie's car further along Lessings
Lane. May Grimley's baby arriving? Life, birth and death have
continued much the same while she's been away, of course.

Mrs Tansley's curtains twitch, as usual. The children are still chalking hopscotch squares on the flagstones. But Number Three has evidently gained a new tenant at last; its peeling front door has been repainted a startling, fire-engine red and there are new curtains, white with scarlet poppies. What will Hinton have to say about that? She hears the Grimleys' door slam, pushes her key into the lock and hurriedly gets herself and her luggage indoors. She's not ready to face Gerald Fairlie just yet.

There's a bright fire burning in the grate of the room that serves as both living room and kitchen and a warm, delicious smell issuing from the oven in the old fireplace range. Someone has left bread and milk, eggs and butter, and she doesn't have to guess who: she had left her keys with Anna. The lamp on the old-fashioned little dresser has been lit, helping to hide the dreariness of the room. There is also a bottle of wine on the table, places set for two, and two glasses. Not from Anna, this. She rarely drinks anything stronger than tea, copious amounts of it during the work she's doing on Pen's garden. A competent woman, Anna, calm and quiet. In her late fifties, she is still running her small business as a garden designer, besides running her home and being an excellent cook. Nor will the wine be from Carey's friend, Kate Ramsey. Wine is not something a young war-widow can afford. She has left a small posy of autumn leaves and berries in a pottery vase on the table and a note saying she'll be around tomorrow.

So who has left the wine? And two glasses? Which guest is she to expect?

Ten minutes later, having dumped her suitcases upstairs, washed her hands and face and changed from her travelling clothes, Carey goes downstairs again, makes a cup of tea and collapses into a chair by the fire. It's a strange homecoming, and despite the signs of welcome she feels the silence and a loneliness she hadn't been prepared for. She would almost welcome the sound of her mother's stick banging on the bedroom floor . . . Well, no, she's deceiving herself. To her shame, she has felt more relief than sorrow since her mother died, though by then she was at the end of her tether and everyone has told her repeatedly that she more than did her duty. It's no secret that Muriel Brewster was neither a patient nor an appreciative invalid, whom

Carey had nursed for thirteen years, ever since leaving school. She'd been querulous and demanding and, as Carey knows, often cruel in private.

'You should've married Jimmy Bickerstaffe while you had the chance, before he got himself killed. He'd have left you nicely off,' was an oft-repeated strain, to which Carey had been determined not to seem shocked, though she was. Jimmy Bickerstaffe had been killed in the very last desperate throes of the war, fighting for his country. She hadn't been much more than eighteen then, and still felt unbearably saddened when she thought of him and how much he'd wanted to marry her, though she could never have loved him in return.

'Too choosy, my girl, that's you. And now you won't have the doctor, either! What's wrong with him? He's a lovely man.'

Gerald Fairlie was indeed. Likeable and kindly, if a little dull. Hard-working and conscientious, a heart as big as his large frame. He'd been a tower of strength during those last few exhausting years with Muriel. There is in fact little or nothing wrong with him – just not enough that is *right*. At least not for her, Carey.

'Well, being a doctor's wife isn't for everybody, I'll grant you that,' Muriel had droned on. 'So what about Pen Llewellyn, then? Play your cards right there and you'll be in clover.'

'Mother, stop it. Stop it! He's old enough to marry you!'

Muriel cackled at that, but even she knew when she'd gone too far, though she hadn't been able to resist a parting shot. 'You have another think. Better an old man's darling than a young man's slave.'

She'd been a ridiculous, nasty-minded old woman. Pen had been no more than good-natured, giving up time to sit and play cards or dominoes with Muriel in order to give Carey an occasional break. He no more wanted to marry Carey than she would have considered marrying him.

Well, no more taunts now, anyway, no more of the demands which might have sucked her life away, had she let it. Muriel had been a creaking and complaining gate for years, but in the end cancer had claimed her. Now, refreshed and on the brink of a decision about her future, Carey is just back from a long stay in Paris with her friend Monica who has a rich French husband and a large and noisy family. The children had cried to see her

go and Monica had said, 'You've such a way with children,
darling. Must you go just yet?'

'It's time for me to leave anyway, and this invitation . . .'

The surprise invitation from Pen had perhaps been a signal that
her lotus-eating should end. It was a birthday party invitation,
where the Llewellyn clan would apparently be assembling in full
force. Pen was not so fond of his relations that he got them all
together very often – and to invite her, Carey, and forty other
guests as well . . . it must be important to him. It was time to
make the break anyway. Otherwise, she might have been tempted
to stay in Paris and put off making decisions on how to spend
the rest of her life. About which there were not many options.
Nursing? Certainly not, she'd had enough of *that*. A nanny? She
did like children, especially Monica's, but not enough to look
after them as a vocation. Teacher training? Secretarial work? No
appeal there, either. But at last, faced with the stultifying prospect
of spending her life doing any of those things, an idea had begun
to take root. She would sell the little house and its contents, to
none of which had she any attachment, only too many sad
memories. The sale wouldn't bring in much, but enough to travel
somewhere for a while. There was nothing – nor ever would be
– for her in Hinton, she thought with a plunge of sadness. And
afterwards? Afterwards could take care of itself. Suddenly, excitement had filled her and she'd felt a taste of what it might be like
to be free. Free to take charge of her own life at last.

It had all seemed so easy, viewed from a distance. But now,
coming back . . . She is beginning to dither again, and knows it.

She gives a start as there is a knock on the door. The brisk
rat-tat doesn't indicate Anna. It isn't Anna, it's her son, Jack
Douglas, whom Carey has imagined halfway across the world
by now. He laughs at her surprise, embraces her in a big, friendly
hug, overtopping her by a head, then stands back. 'You've
changed,' he says in surprise as he releases her. 'For the better,'
he adds, making her blush, and before she has time to reply he
hands her the envelope he's been holding. 'From Pen, via my
mother. We're all bidden to supper tomorrow – his family, you,
me, Ma and Doc Fairlie.'

'With the party so soon after? That's overdoing things a bit,
even for Pen.'

'Well, you know what he's like.' His eyes crinkle as he smiles. Brown eyes, like his mother's. Thick, dark hair like hers once was, too, but a bit unruly. He resembles Anna to some extent, though there is nothing remotely feminine about him. And where Anna gives out quiet and peace, the air around Jack always seems to vibrate with energy and purpose. He is confident, well educated, at home anywhere, with anyone. No dithering for *him*. He always knows what he is doing, where he's going, and drives straight for it.

'What are you doing here, Jack? I thought you'd be in parts unknown by now.'

'My gammy leg, curses be on it. It doesn't bother me in the least now but the medics aren't satisfied I'm ready just yet to risk another fall.'

Jack Douglas has followed something of his mother's professional inclinations and is now a botanist turned plant hunter. His job takes him away for long stretches at a time, to the furthest parts of the world, from the highest mountain regions of Tibet to the steamy jungles of South America, in search of rare botanical specimens to bring home to Kew Gardens, by whom he is employed. He would dearly love to finance an expedition of his own, but that prospect is so remote he knows it will never happen. Meanwhile, what he does is an exciting but sometimes dangerous occupation which satisfies his roving instincts and still allows him to work in the field for which he is well qualified, to gain satisfaction in contributing something to the developing and expanding knowledge of the plant world. He'll be off again the minute his doctors allow, but at the moment he looks, Carey thinks, slightly . . . preoccupied, is that the word? You can't always tell with Jack. Relaxed and charming, his nature has undercurrents that he rarely allows to show. Very likely, though, the prospect of his career being so long on hold is bothering him more than he's letting on. He was one of the daredevil fighter pilots in the Royal Naval Air Service during the war, had fought in all the war theatres and having miraculously come through without a scratch, it seems hard that this unlucky fall down a mountainside in China should have happened now.

'Oh, and Kate will be there too,' he throws out casually.

Jack and Kate. Kate Ramsey, ex-schoolteacher, around the

same age as Jack, early thirties, but already a widow. One of Carey's best friends, she is tall, her hair even fairer than Carey's own, she's athletic and has tremendous energy. An outdoor type, she loves tennis and long walks . . . Climbing mountains, no doubt, if she gets the chance.

'Well,' Jack says, 'aren't you going to invite me to share that hotpot my mother's left? The bottle's from me, by the way – I suspect you might have acquired a taste for wine while you've been in France.'

'Somewhat,' she admits with a smile. 'Thanks – and you'd be more than welcome to share.'

'Sit down and I'll serve. Don't argue – all this time on my hands has made me quite domesticated.'

'But no less bossy, Jack Douglas.'

'Organized, you mean. Come and sit down.'

She allows him to pull her chair out. He touches her hair and ruffles it. 'It's good to have you back, Carey.'

FOUR

Extract from Kate Ramsey's journal, written the following evening:

I should be getting on with my work, but important as that is to me and women like me, writing more of those letters seems wearisome tonight, in view of what has happened. Coming into my silent, empty house after the supper party, when Carey, Jack and his mother had left me after walking me home, was an anticlimax. I stood at the window before drawing my curtains, watching their receding figures along the dark lane until they had disappeared out of sight. Then, pulling the curtains together, my heart jerked painfully as I saw – oh, not again! – walking along the lane . . . my husband, who has been dead for more than ten years now. But as always, walking away from me, sidling in the shadows so that he was only half seen, a mere shadow that dispersed

in the headlights of Gerald Fairlie's motor car on the road
beyond the lane, as he, too, headed towards home. My heart
resumed its normal beat but I'm too wide awake now, not
ready for sleep. So perhaps bringing my journal up to date
and recording the supper party at Bryn Glas might banish
ghosts and even ensure my dreams are just that, and not
nightmares.

Pen was in great form tonight. He's always at his best
in company. There were eleven of us – Anna Douglas and
Jack, Carey, myself and Gerald Fairlie. All Pen's family,
too – except, thank goodness, for those two supercilious
boys of Theo's that no one can stand, the younger, we
were given to understand, doing very well in his last year
at Winchester, the other a fledgling banker. There was also
the mysterious newcomer, the younger brother, Huwie.
The black sheep of the family, I gather, unheard of for
years and now appearing out of nowhere. Someone, who
even on a first meeting, I wouldn't trust any further than
I could throw him. Ida was there, of course, dressed to
kill, and Claudia, indolently beautiful, upstaging her, as
usual. And not least Verity, pale and sullen, pushing her
food around her plate, eating practically nothing. What is
the matter with her lately? Under that belligerent exterior
she's actually very pretty (might even be beautiful, if she
took the trouble) with thick, creamy white skin and eyes
of an unusual greeny-gold, thickly lashed. A full, sensual
mouth. Ida has no idea how to deal with her and I'm afraid
other people are becoming impatient with her, too. She
was always such a nice child. It wasn't until after her
parents' divorce that she started to be difficult.

Carey was looking well tonight. These few months in
Paris have changed her. She has lost that hopeless air of
being resigned to her fate with that dreadful mother and
found a new confidence. She looks different, too. A new
smooth haircut, very becoming, and a simple dress – very
French, a dark smoky blue and exactly the same colour as
her eyes. Gerald couldn't take his eyes off her. Poor Gerald!
I suppose she could do worse, but being a country doctor's
wife, even one so socially well placed as Gerald, won't do

for Carey. She has been desperately in love with Jack Douglas for years, though she believes no one suspects this. He won't marry her – or anyone, I think. Too much of a gentleman to leave a wife and possibly children at home while he's roaming the world – unless he can bring himself to give that up, which is as unlikely as it's unfeasible. He should give her the chance to make up her own mind, but he's blind, like most men, when it comes to matters of the heart.

The dining room at Bryn Glas is two small rooms knocked into one to accommodate the long, black oak table. It was supposed to be a friendly meal tonight, informal dress requested, but it was still a civilized occasion. Mrs Knightly, Pen's cook-housekeeper, had done us well with some of her good, plain food, excellently cooked. Candles flickered on the table's gleaming patina (the sort that's only achieved by generations of beeswax and elbow-grease and a succession of maidservants to apply it!) and on the huge chest, laden with heavy old silver, bottles and decanters, that serves as a sideboard. Wine glowed in old cut glass. The logs in the fire blazed and sparks flew up the chimney. It's a pleasant room; in the daytime, there's a view from the diamond-paned windows of the grassy slope down towards the cliff above the river; although the room is panelled in dark wood, there are gleams of sunlight brought in by way of new yellow silk curtains and cushions, and last night a copper vase of tawny and gold chrysanthemums. Uncharacteristic of Pen, not renowned for his imagination. Mrs Knightly? Absolutely not.

He is an excellent host. No one's glass was allowed to be empty and he kept the good-humoured conversation flowing, himself centre stage as per usual, though no one minds that because he's so entertaining. At some point during the meal he began reminiscing about the escapades he and his siblings had got up to when they were children, living in that house with their parents – climbing on the forbidden hill-fort ruins, scrambling down the equally forbidden cliffs to the river bank below the house to construct a makeshift raft which didn't work. He and Theo one day lighting a fire which had singed his trousers so they'd had to be pulled off before they burst into flames, and having to run to the house in his underwear, in full view of guests. Even Theo, not much given to smiles, added his share to the amusement. Mostly, it had been the two older boys who got up to mischief, it seemed. Ida, as a girl, presumably wasn't included in the more memorable exploits and Huwie, younger than the others by so many years, didn't appear to have done anything worthy of mentioning.

We were just about to leave the table when Pen tapped on his glass for everyone's attention. I had guessed there was something in the wind, with this impromptu supper party, and I wasn't too surprised when he went on to say he'd meant to make the announcement later, at the official birthday party, but Anna had persuaded him it would be more appropriate to tell the family first, without all those other guests, that they were to be married before Christmas.

It wasn't to be expected that such a statement could be made without causing surprise. Consternation even. A dropped bomb, followed by a small silence, during which Pen kept his eyes and his smile on Anna, Anna looked at Jack, and Jack met my glance with a look that said his mother had already told him. Then everyone began to talk at once. Smiles. Congratulations, slaps on the back, kisses. Looks that could kill. Pen calling for champagne. And then Verity, white as a sheet, pushing her chair back from the table and rushing from the room.

Ida looked alarmed and made an attempt to follow. 'I'll go,' I told her, and she seemed relieved to let me.

Verity had locked herself in the downstairs cloakroom. I knocked on the door and asked if she was all right. There was a mumbled answer which I couldn't make out so I waited a few minutes. The two of us have always got along, right from when she used to come and visit her uncle as a little girl and I was still teaching at the school. I like to think she looks on me as an older sister she can trust, but if that's correct, she hasn't seen fit to confide in me recently. Presently, the door opened and she came out, looking a little better. 'Something I ate,' she mumbled. Seeing that she'd eaten practically nothing, it was more likely to be what she'd drunk, though I didn't think that had been much, either. Shock at what she'd just heard? 'I think I'd better go straight up to bed, Kate.'

I thought she was probably right. She still looked rotten. She squeezed my hand and then scuttled up the stairs to the little room under the eaves which has always been 'hers'. I went to rejoin the rest of the party, assuring Ida there was nothing to worry over. She looked relieved and didn't ask any more.

By now Pen was standing with Anna's arm tucked through his. He looked a little flushed, but that wasn't surprising – the room had grown very warm with that huge fire and all those people. Gerald, however, seemed concerned and murmured a few words in his ear. Pen favoured him with a quizzical glance, but after a moment confessed himself rather tired with all the excitement and agreed that perhaps an early night was indicated.

'I'll come up and see you settled, old boy,' Gerald said. It seemed to be a signal for the party to begin to break up.

Living as I do in such proximity to Anna and to Pen, and having drawn my own conclusions some time since, the announcement hadn't really come as a surprise (those yellow silk cushions and curtains, after all, those prettily arranged chrysanthemums!) though I suppose to most of the others it was a shock. It's easy to underestimate a woman like Anna. She is a good woman, and a strong one, having very creditably brought up alone a son of whom she can be proud, while at the same time carving a career out for herself; no mean feat for any woman, however unfettered we now feel ourselves: as I know to my cost, we are still facing opposition at every turn. She and Pen will be good for each other. I believe it's not only friendship and understanding that exists between them, but genuine affection, so why shouldn't they marry? But of course, that's not the point as far as Pen's family is concerned. He is a very wealthy man and all of them, I suspect, live up to or well beyond their means, and the only thing they will be able to see is that this marriage will necessarily lower their expectations.

There's always the possibility that they might, in fact, have been sponging off him for years, though on second thoughts, I would actually doubt that. Pen is generous, in so many ways, but you don't amass a fortune like his by giving it away. He was hard-headed when he was in business and there is a strong streak of ruthlessness in him. He's used to getting what he wants and doesn't take it kindly if he doesn't.

I feel awfully glad for his sake that he will have Anna with him at the helm in the stormy waters I see ahead.

PART TWO

FIVE

Detective Inspector Herbert Reardon, his evening meal finished, with only half his mind on two down, three across, was pondering the kindest way to tell his wife that their weekend away was scuppered. It wasn't that Ellen would raise objections; she respected what he did, supported him and put up with his unsociable hours. She normally took it in her stride, with good humour, and got on with her own work.

Only this time he was silently cursing the circumstances, especially since it was the first time ever he'd been the one to suggest such a break. Holidays were for wimps, in his book. But Ellen had suffered a bout of shingles earlier in the year, a painful and debilitating condition which had left her very run-down. Before winter began in earnest, he'd promised her (following a heavy hint by her doctor) they'd have a few days in a great little hotel he'd been told about in the Cotswolds. The doctor suggested that good long walks, sightseeing that Reardon was prepared to endure for her sake and the reputedly excellent food at the hotel, would buck her up and put some colour back in her cheeks. He cursed the timing of this case. It would have been good for her to get away from here, especially just now. It had been a dreary month, and today a slanting grey rain had fallen all day long – not, admittedly, making the atmosphere appreciably worse. Sometimes, living in Dudley, you felt as though you were existing under a permanent pall of smoke. You didn't like it but you put up with it because you had to if you lived in the Black Country: its clattering, stinking, heavy industry was what kept it and its inhabitants alive. If you'd grown up with it, as he had, you mostly didn't even notice it. And at night you could always draw the curtains and shut out the night sky that was lurid with the flame and smoke from belching blast furnaces.

'Come on, what is it? What have you to tell me, then?' Ellen asked, pouring their coffee. He sighed and abandoned the crossword. He wasn't the only detective in this house.

'I'm sorry, love, but the Cotswold trip's off. Something's come up.'

Her face fell, but only momentarily. 'Now, why am I not surprised? Oh, well. Best laid plans . . .'

What had he expected? Temper tears and tantrums? From Ellen? She wasn't that sort. Small and composed, with a neat bob of brown hair, her calm, sensible and matter-of-fact outlook on life was what kept him going. You always knew where you were with her – or almost always. Very occasionally, she could be unpredictable, which brought him up short, never a bad thing. She could also make him laugh.

'I know, love, it's too bad, but we've got a suspicious death on our hands . . .'

He saw enough of the seamy side of life not to want to bring it often to his own fireside, or not the sort of muck he usually had to deal with. The interesting stuff, the knotty problems, that was different. It somehow took the weight off, discussing a case with someone who was a quick thinker and had – all right, admit it – a woman's intuition. She'd never let anybody get away with sloppy thinking and that helped to clear his own mind. But this case wasn't even particularly interesting in that sense; it was a foregone conclusion. In fairness she still needed to know why their short break was off. He explained about the elderly gent who'd been found dead in his bed the week before. 'He had a weak heart, so it wasn't altogether surprising, but apparently someone's decided they couldn't wait for nature to take its course. You know what it is, when money's involved – pots of it in this case, apparently. And that always brings out the worst in people.' It didn't do to take those sort of accusations too seriously as a rule, of course, they usually came to nothing, but this time a post-mortem had been ordered . . . 'The upshot being that it's landed with us. The local staff can't cope apparently.'

And probably glad not to, he thought. Urban policemen like himself joked that the policing of rural outposts was still nothing more than rounding up a few sheep-stealers and rabbit-poachers. Hanging 'em on gibbets at the crossroads, too, no doubt, if the unenlightened country plods could have had their way. Reardon laughed at the joke, but he still thought they weren't as much on the ball as they should have been. More and more of the larger towns were setting up a dedicated detective department, one they could rely on with no need to call in Scotland Yard to investigate major crimes. And that was where Reardon and his department had come in on this one, even though its detectives were so few in number there was little room for manoeuvre when anyone was off sick, or taking leave. The police in the area concerned had no such force and were short-staffed anyway, their inspector having fallen off a ladder while doing some home decorating. Fate had dictated that Reardon was the only officer available this weekend to answer their request for assistance, even if he wasn't, strictly speaking, in view of the time off he'd earmarked.

Having got the bad news off his chest he sat back, fingering the wartime scars on his cheek, something he still found himself doing when he was nervous, upset or just plain bloody annoyed about the inconvenience of police work, as he was now. Ellen's calm acceptance of a man with a face like a one-sided gargoyle had helped him to come to terms with it. She'd once told him briskly that it was only a scar, that it wasn't nearly as horrific as he imagined, even that it made his face more interesting, and whether he could allow himself to believe that or not, the idea that she thought he was giving in to self-pity had brought him up short. He'd never considered himself a handsome chap anyway and he was luckier than some poor devils – not gassed, or internally disabled, or trying to make a life after being left with stumps for arms or legs. His mind was still intact, despite the nightmares – and nowadays even they didn't happen so often.

'So where did you say this happened?'

He didn't think he'd said, but maybe he had. 'Hinton Wyvering, a back of beyond place somewhere in the wilds of Shropshire.'

She nodded. 'That's where my friend Kate Ramsey lives.'

'The schoolteacher?'

'Not any more. That private school where she taught German was progressive, enlightened enough to let her keep her job on when she married, but it was a different matter when the war came. Tolerance didn't extend to pupils learning the enemy's language, so she was asked to leave.'

This was one of Ellen's hobby horses – the unfairness of a woman teacher's contract having to end on her marriage. Those responsible didn't see it like that. After all, a woman's place was in the home, looking after her husband and children and not taking jobs from men, the breadwinners, wasn't it? Ellen herself had been forced to resign when she married. She now took what private pupils she could get and did occasional French translation work for a publisher. Occasional being the operative word for either. Both jobs were like that: irregular, sporadic, with no guarantee of a regular income.

Full marks to the school where Kate Ramsey had taught for not insisting on her retirement after her marriage, but however liberal, Reardon could appreciate that they wouldn't have dared to go against public opinion and allowed the unpatriotic teaching of the Germans' language when it came to fighting them.

'Couldn't she have taught something else, or in another school?'

'As a married woman?'

'I suppose not.'

'Well, as it happens, she did. With all the men off to war, and such a shortage of teachers, they were glad enough to bend the rules, to the extent that she was allowed to teach at Hinton Wyvering. But after the Armistice she was told they must "let her go" in favour of an ex-soldier. After all, they told her, she did have her war widow's pension! It was such rotten luck, her husband was listed as missing, presumed dead, only months before the end of the war. But poor Kate, I think she must find life hard on ten shillings a week.'

'But she must have found some other work, I presume? An educated woman like her?'

Ellen frowned. 'To tell you the truth, I don't know for certain. I haven't seen her for years . . . we've only exchanged Christmas cards and the odd letter, and I feel rather guilty about that. We used to be such friends.' She added thoughtfully, 'It wouldn't be like Kate to be idle.'

It was a shame about her friend, Reardon agreed, but his mind had moved on and he was already sorting practicalities in his mind. 'We may have to stay, Gilmour and myself, depending on what we find when we get there tomorrow – we'll need to look for digs, if there's anything of the sort in such a godforsaken sounding sort of place.' Theoretically, although it was a long drive, it wouldn't be too far to drive there and back every day for as long as the enquiry lasted, but it would be tedious and time-wasting, and in any case he preferred, always, to be on the spot. 'I'd better pack a bag.'

'I'll see to it.' She was looking thoughtful.

'With a bit of luck, we should be able to wrap it up pretty soon.' Which was possibly true, but didn't make him view the prospect with any more enthusiasm . . . Poor old devil, murdered in his sleep, with only his family as suspects. Straightforward enough, possibly, but whichever way you looked at it, it wasn't pretty. 'I'm not too pleased about all this, but you know how it is.'

'And I suppose Joe's not going to be too pleased, either, at leaving Maisie.'

Reardon rolled his eyes. His sergeant's wife was expecting their first child. He was like a dog with two tails, endlessly fussing over her though Maisie, sensible and practical, was perfectly well able to cope without all the flap. She was not far off giving birth now, and by this time Reardon knew a lot more than he wanted to know about swollen ankles, heartburn and a craving for bananas. Ellen's only pregnancy hadn't lasted much beyond morning sickness, and they'd never got around to announcing it, so Gilmour had no idea that all this talk brought back their loss, and the sad reminder that there would never be another. And Reardon wasn't about to embarrass him by telling him now. Since coming to work with him, his red-headed sergeant had shown himself to be a good detective – energetic, capable and even intuitive at times. But he hadn't yet learnt to be less thin-skinned, God help him, and he'd be mortified to know he was causing distress. Reardon, who hadn't forgotten what the prospect of becoming a father did to you, held his tongue.

He said to Ellen now, 'It's a damn nuisance for both of us but we'll fix up another weekend when I'll make certain I can't be called in.'

She said slowly, 'It might be easier than you think to find somewhere to stay in Hinton Wyvering. I might just be able to persuade Kate to take us in as paying guests, if I put it in the right way so as not to offend her.'

'Ellen,' he said warningly. 'No. Not you.'

'A few days in the country was what we were planning anyway, wasn't it?' she replied, widening her eyes.

'You've work to be getting on with, haven't you? That novel?'

'I'm well ahead, and anyway it's exceedingly tedious. The world might be better off if it never sees the light of day. You can take a letter to Kate tomorrow, let her know I haven't forgotten her. I'd really like to see her again.'

'You know what I always say about not bringing my work home with me. It'll be on top of us there, and I wouldn't want—'

'You wouldn't want me interfering,' she finished. 'And when have I ever done that?'

'Never,' he had to agree, but he felt she was up to something. 'The answer's still no. *No*, Ellen. I can't allow it. This is not something I want you mixed up in.'

It would probably have been more exact to say that he didn't want to have her welfare on his mind when he should be concentrating on the case, but that wouldn't wash with Ellen. 'I'll take your letter with me tomorrow, if you like,' he conceded, 'but that's as far as it goes.' He didn't point out that it could have been posted. It had occurred to him that if Kate Ramsey had lived and taught in the area for some time, she had in all probability known the victim. In any case, her knowledge of the place and its inhabitants could be useful.

SIX

The day had turned out bright and sharp, and Hinton Wyvering, closed for half-day, lay sleeping in the silence. Gilmour, not happy with the situation, was determined to be non-committal but Reardon liked what he saw. Little more than an overgrown village, strung out along a hill ridge, Hinton was rather picturesque, if a bit run-down. Unspoilt, as far as he could see. Tourists, or those out for a Sunday afternoon spin from the Black Country in their new motor cars, deterred by the state of an upward-twisting road promising little more of interest at the end than a bit of an old, ruined fort, would be more likely to take the route into Wales that skirted round the base of the hill. But presumably hikers – and maybe cyclists of the hardier sort – must make it to the top sometimes . . . what else would justify the existence of a cottage tea room offering refreshments?

Otherwise Reardon's guess had been right – among the scattered buildings, shops and houses, mainly half-timbered but pleasantly mixed with later architectural styles, there were no obvious signs offering bed and breakfast. The one public house, so tiny it possibly qualified for the smallest pub in Britain, could have been overlooked had it not been for 'The Fox' sign swinging outside. To seek accommodation there was patently not going to be an option. Otherwise, Hinton Wyvering was only provided with half a dozen or so shops, plus a corn-chandler's and a smithy to service predominantly country occupations. Not even a police station. The local nick was in Castle Wyvering, an altogether different town some few miles away, recently grown larger, known for its public school, and a real, if ruined, castle.

Reardon had called in at the police station there, where the sergeant in charge, a beefy man named Bridgstock, had received them with open arms, trying to seem reluctant to hand the case over but not succeeding in concealing his relief, while admitting that he and the few men who manned this station were a little out of their depth with a case like this . . . not the usual sort of crime in these parts, you understand . . . if indeed, it does turn out to be a crime. Reardon had given him a sharp glance which the sergeant didn't meet, but he was all prepared to brief them with the necessary details. Ready and almost too cooperative. Anxious to shunt off a case that Reardon suspected they might, with diligent policing, have actually handled without assistance – had it not been for the fact that the elderly victim, Penrose Llewellyn, hadn't been just any poor old pensioner. He'd been a local bigwig, a generous contributor to worthy causes, opener of fêtes. Well thought of. He had been instrumental in getting permission for the building of a number of low-cost houses just on the outskirts of Castle Wyvering, and had been honoured by having it named Llewellyn Crescent, after him. And no doubt he'd been on friendly terms with the local hierarchy, possibly the chief constable.

But then, proving himself no country bumpkin, Bridgstock had handed over a remarkably efficient file, including copies of the post-mortem results and the principal witness statements. What was more, it was beautifully typed.

Now, in Hinton, Reardon left Gilmour to park the official motor and after that to do some scouting around for any possibility of digs, while he went to make the first call, at Bryn Glas, home of the deceased. 'Oh come on, Joe, cheer up,' he said bracingly as he left his sergeant. 'Look on it as a nice little holiday and it won't seem half as bad.'

'Yes, I'm afraid it was because of me the police were called,' she said abruptly.

'Then I've come to the right person to put me in the picture,' Reardon said. 'But why do you say afraid?'

'It hasn't exactly made me very popular.'

Anna Douglas wore working clothes, breeches and a thick jumper: even in the present circumstances she wasn't neglecting the work on the garden she'd informed Reardon she was contracted to do. But she'd come readily enough into the house with him and suggested tea. 'Thank you, that would be very welcome,' he told her. 'We had an early start this morning.'

They carried it into a cupboard-like room, small enough to have once been nothing more than a larder or a pantry, but out of earshot of the girl who was preparing vegetables in the kitchen. They perched on rather uncomfortable stools, with their drinks on a space cleared of the garden paraphernalia that filled the bare wooden shelves. Mrs Douglas was, she explained, using the place as a temporary office while the reconstruction was going on. Photographs, sketches and lists were pinned to the wall; piles of what were presumably invoices, orders and the like, were stacked on a slightly wider shelf that served as a desk. Some of the papers were smudged with earthy finger-marks and all of them were weighted down with large pebbles. There were weatherproof garments on hooks and a row of gumboots on the floor beneath. A very small window overlooked part of the half-completed garden. 'It was never intended to be very grand,' Mrs Douglas had told him. 'That wouldn't be appropriate. But we've come across traces of what *might* be an Elizabethan sunken garden,' she'd added, looking doubtful. 'It's quite small and contemporary to when the house was originally built, long before it was a farm, so we'd meant to try and keep to the same spirit.' She sounded disheartened. 'Clipped box, you know, and a knot garden.' Whatever that might be. Reardon was no gardener.

They sat on wooden stools and her hands, cradling her cup, were rough and work-worn; she held it so tightly he knew she was more tense than she was trying to seem. 'Why did it take so long to contact the police, Mrs Douglas?'

After a while she said, 'I really should have spoken earlier, I suppose, only . . . well, it was so incredible, such an enormous thing to even contemplate . . . And one couldn't be sure, after all . . .' Her voice trailed off uncertainly, her unseeing glance fixed on something beyond the window.

Yet she didn't look like an indecisive person. She had a firm chin and a way of looking out of those wide brown eyes that said she saw a great deal, but would take her time to make up her mind about what it might mean. She was perhaps in her late fifties. Her dark hair was short and greying, she had a healthy tan and laughter lines at the corners of her eyes. He waited for her to go on but she seemed more intent on staring out of the window than talking. A huge round clock on the kitchen wall, visible through the slightly ajar door, tocked away the seconds, loudly. He prompted, 'So why did you make the call in the end?'

'I . . . It was difficult. They all think . . . after all, it was always there in the background, something that could have happened to Pen any time, with his heart. Though he neither looked nor acted frail. He had a cough that had bothered him lately, but you'd have put him down as good for another twenty years.' She stared down into her tea. 'Sorry, I'd better start at the beginning, hadn't I?'

The beginning didn't appear to mean the same to her as it did to him. 'The supper party . . . I'd persuaded him it would be better not to wait until the birthday . . . oh dear, that won't be making much sense to you, either.' She drew a long breath and began again. 'The twentieth was his birthday, you see. He would have been sixty, and he'd taken it into his head to throw a party, a biggish one. But we also arranged a small supper a couple of days before . . . just his family – they're all staying here, in the house – and a few friends. We – we had some news, the sort I'd persuaded him would be best to give them privately, rather than announce publicly at the actual birthday, which was what he'd had in mind.' Her chin lifted slightly. 'Pen and I were going to be married.'

'I see.'

'Do you? I don't know that anyone else did . . . or at least, not as we saw it. We didn't deceive ourselves that we were either of us exactly spring chickens, but we knew what we were doing.' Her face suddenly bleak, she was unable to go on for a moment. 'We've known each other a long time, Pen and I. From the time when I was one of the local children who sometimes played with the Bryn Glas children. But when we grew up, we both moved away and lost touch, as one does. Then, when my father died several years ago and his house passed to me, I had a sudden yen to come back – I can run my business just as easily from here as anywhere else. It's not as though it's all that demanding, anyway,' she added honestly. 'Pen had always used this house as a weekend retreat, for himself and any of the family who wanted to use it. When he was advised to retire because of his health, he came back to live here permanently, we got to know each other properly and a few weeks ago we decided to get married, but—' She broke off.

'No reason why you shouldn't, was there?'

'None at all, of course.' She swallowed. 'Look, I'm aware how this is going to sound but I'll try to be as honest with you as I can about what happened . . .'

'Take your time.'

When she went on it was in a more collected manner. 'The supper party didn't go on late. I think it had in fact been rather a strain for Pen. He'd warned me beforehand that his family were not necessarily going to be pleased. They'd be afraid it would mean they'd be cut out of his will, and he was right about their reactions. Oh, they all did their best to conceal their feelings, but there was a definite atmosphere after he told them what we intended. Gerald – that's Dr Fairlie, who was one of the guests – obviously saw this, too, and tactfully stepped in with a suggestion of an early night, for which I was very grateful. After that, we all dispersed – my son Jack and I, and the other two guests, a young woman called Carey Brewster and Mrs Ramsey.'

That was better than he'd hoped, Kate Ramsey being on visiting terms at this house. A useful contact, perhaps.

'I came in early the next morning,' Mrs Douglas went on, 'the garden's at the messy stage at the moment, as you can see, and I thought I should get my lads to do some clearing up before the party – not that we would have been spilling outside, in November, but I wanted to make it look a bit more acceptable if I could. I was very early and let myself in, but Mrs Knightly had just made Pen's morning tea, so I told her I'd take it up to him . . .' Her breath caught in her throat. 'This – this may sound like hindsight but I swear I knew . . . I felt a sort of empty feeling about the room before I – before I even went in and saw him.' For a moment, she closed her eyes. 'His cough had been bothering him quite a bit the night before and – well, with a heart condition like his . . . All the same, I couldn't understand it. He'd been tossing around in that bed like you wouldn't believe. I've been with him when he had an angina pain, and he would go quite still, afraid of moving almost, until his medication kicked in.'

'I can believe that.' You wouldn't want to thrash around much with such a pain. The instinct would be to keep still, surely.

'The pillows were all over the place and the blankets and sheets were in a turmoil. And he'd knocked his water glass over on to the carpet.'

'Trying to reach his medication?'

Again she fell silent, this time for fully a minute. 'That's just it. I suppose I wasn't thinking straight at that particular moment, but before I went to tell anyone else, for decency's sake I tidied him up a bit, smoothed the sheets and put the pillows in place. It was only afterwards, when I was thinking about how it had happened, I realized I couldn't remember seeing his capsules on the bedside table. I went to check and I was right, they weren't there. I found them in his bathroom cabinet, where he never kept them – not ever! He was supposed to put one under his tongue when necessary and he kept them with him – always. Especially at night, within reach. That was when I began to wonder . . . to wonder if someone hadn't put those tablets where they were so it would look as though he'd died simply because he'd forgotten to keep his medicine handy. But he hadn't, I'd swear to that.' She finished on a choking note. 'He didn't die a natural death. He'd struggled with someone . . . someone had taken his life, a pillow over his face, perhaps . . .' She covered her own face with her hands.

'The doctor didn't notice anything amiss,' Reardon said gently, after a moment. But he knew that suffocation like that was notoriously difficult to prove; it didn't always leave marks.

Her hands dropped to her lap and she looked directly at him. Her eyes were tragic but there were no tears. 'I'm in no way blaming Dr Fairlie for anything. He's a very good doctor, as well as a personal friend to both of us, but I think he saw what he expected to see: a man he'd been treating for a serious heart condition, who he'd examined only two days before and seen to bed the previous night. Noticed that he'd been a little overexcited, perhaps. Besides, he would never have left Pen without being sure his medicine was near at hand. After I found Pen, they fetched Gerald immediately from a house where he was attending a birth – it's May Grimley's fifth and hopefully her last, and as it turns out, a healthy little boy – but he was worried about her and anxious to get back.'

The doctor had been entirely within his rights in signing the death certificate, having attended his patient in a professional capacity so recently. A too hasty examination, perhaps, understandable in the circumstances. An explicable death, with such medical history; with Penrose's heart condition there had been no need to look for a further cause. Except that instinct – and love perhaps – had told this woman who was going to marry Penrose Llewellyn otherwise. She'd been proved right, too. In the light of what she later said, the coroner had called for a post-mortem, which had revealed heavy bruises on both of his upper arms. The conclusion reached was that Penrose Llewellyn had indeed died of myocardial infarction – a heart attack in layman's terms. But if the bruises on his arms were any indication, it could have been brought on by his being forcibly held down, fighting for breath as his fragile heart finally gave up the struggle to pump blood around his body. At any rate, since the dead don't bruise, they were suspicious enough to justify further enquiry.

'There's something else.' She hesitated.

'Yes?'

'I'm sure his room had been searched. Left to himself Pen wasn't,' she explained, the shadow of a smile chasing away the sadness for a brief instant, 'the tidiest of persons, and everything was so precisely in place it looked unnatural. His clothes put away on hangers, even the towels in his bathroom folded.' After a moment she added colourlessly, 'It must have been someone who was sleeping in the house, mustn't it? And they might have got away with it, if I hadn't . . . No wonder they all hate me.'

'Well, we shall certainly need to speak to everyone who was here.'

She was looking unhappily out over the moonscape that was the future garden. 'Somebody will have to decide what's to be done about all this now. It seems rather pointless to go on with the plans we'd made but . . . They're all wanting to leave and go home – the family, I mean.'

'We'll make it as quick as possible. But first, I'd like to take a quick look round the house, get my bearings, have a word with the housekeeper.'

SEVEN

Gilmour, having done his scouting around for digs, had followed Reardon across to Bryn Glas and was now waiting in the hallway. It appeared that Mrs Petty, the widow who ran the little tea shop – 'Just a couple of tables in her front room, really' – was reluctantly prepared to offer accommodation for one, at a pinch. One paying guest she could cope with, but she really didn't have two suitable rooms, and besides, two hungry men would mean shopping in Castle

Wyvering for extra food supplies, and the bus only ran once a week, on market day.

'It would do me,' Gilmour said, 'and you can take up that invitation to stay with Mrs Reardon's friend.'

'There hasn't been any invitation,' Reardon said testily, wishing he hadn't ill-advisedly used Kate Ramsey and Ellen's fanciful idea of staying with her as a conversational gambit to prevent Gilmour from regaling him with yet more fascinating pregnancy details. 'No joy at that pub, then – the Fox?'

'I tried it before I went to Mrs Petty, but it was closed. According to her the landlord never opens up before six, even if it's someone he knows. He's a law unto himself. She did say that if he feels in the mood – *if* being the operative word – there's a couple of bedrooms. Grub not bad – but the beds might be damp.'

'Try again, later, when it's likely to be open. We need somewhere to lay our heads and we're not going to be here long enough to get rheumatics.'

Mrs Knightly had her own private sitting room where she insisted on serving coffee and home-made shortbread. Gilmour, who had a robust appetite, more than made up for Reardon who was still too full of tea to do it justice.

'I'm speaking to you first, Mrs Knightly, because I understand you've worked for Mr Llewellyn for some time and you can give us an overall picture,' Reardon began.

'Yes, indeed.' She was a brisk, white-haired woman with a nice smile and kind eyes, obviously very shocked by her employer's death, but prepared and seemingly relieved to have the chance to talk. 'I came to Bryn Glas when I was thirteen and I've been here ever since, nearly fifty years. I stayed on after I married my John, who managed the farm.'

'It was a farm when you started then?'

'If you could call it that. Sheep, it was. The boys' father, Mr Gwilym – Welsh family, you see, a long way back – had just bought it after old Basset, who owned it, had died. It was in a sad state, his two sons had pushed off to Canada but he'd refused to go with them, thinking he could manage on his own. Of course he couldn't. Neither could Mr Gwilym for that matter.

He thought he could do better, poured a lot of money into it but he was only what you call a gentleman farmer, he didn't really understand, you know?' She looked at Reardon, who nodded as if on familiar terms with the notion that hill-farming was not for the faint-hearted or the inexperienced. 'Oh, he'd roll his sleeves up and get stuck in at first, but he soon saw he was more hindrance than help – he was the sort of fellow more for his books, you see. My John did his best but then he died . . . and after that, everything went downhill, and in the end Mr Gwilym gave up trying to be a farmer. I think he saw he'd soon have nothing left if he went on like that, losing money hand over fist.'

Having finished her tea, she reached out for some knitting that was nearby, a woman whose hands always had to be occupied. 'When Mr Gwilym died, the house came to Penrose as the eldest and he asked me to stay on and look after it. They all used to come back and use it for holidays and weekends and then after Penrose had that heart scare – it was quite a bad one – he retired from business and came to live here permanently.' She knitted on, expertly weaving three colours, dark green, red and white, her fingers moving so fast it seemed to Reardon as though the argyle-patterned sock that descended from the four needles grew inches by the minute. When she spoke again tears were not far away. 'He was the best of the bunch, you know, Pen. He was a good man, always willing to help, and people liked him. He'd have been happy with Anna, with Mrs Douglas – but somebody here has seen to it he didn't have the chance.' She laid the knitting on her knee in order to search for her handkerchief and dab at her eyes. 'I speak my mind, as you'll have gathered, but I don't think I'm far wrong.'

'Who exactly was staying in the house, after the supper party, Mrs Knightly?' Gilmour asked.

'Just the family.'

'No one else?'

'No,' she said, resuming the sock. 'And that was enough, let me tell you. Too much for me and Prue, the girl who helps me. Though I'd arranged for extra help for the birthday party. There was his brother Theo and his wife . . . and his sister, Ida, Mrs Lancaster, and her daughter Verity . . . and Huwie.' Her lips compressed. 'That was a surprise, him turning up like a bad penny after all these years.'

'Another brother? Not a regular visitor?'

'He didn't visit at all. He's very much the baby of the family, a little surprise he was, coming so long after the others, but he was always a trouble to his father, getting expelled from one school after another and goodness knows what. Spoilt by his mother, of course. And then, oh, years ago, I don't know how many, there was a big row between him and Theo. His father never forgave Huwie. Mrs Llewellyn wasn't strong and she took family quarrels badly, especially where Huwie was concerned. She died shortly after that one and Mr Gwilym always blamed Huwie for it, went purple whenever his name was mentioned. He was the sort, Mr Gwilym, that doesn't lose their temper much but when they do! They all have a touch of that, even Penrose. Huwie disappeared and no one's seen hide nor hair of him until he turned up the other day, reckoning he'd been invited to stay for the birthday party. Well, it looks funny, doesn't it?' She held up the plate of biscuits and the coffee pot. 'Sure you won't have another cup?'

'Thanks, but no.' Both of them shook their heads, Gilmour regretfully. 'You didn't hear anything that night?'

'No. But I wouldn't, would I, my bedroom being downstairs, just along the passage? To tell the truth, I was glad when the supper party broke up, there was a lot of clearing up to do before I could get off to bed. I was that tired I slept like a log.'

'The doors would be locked, of course?' Gilmour asked.

'I saw to it myself,' she said quickly. 'And the windows – all of them. There's a stray tomcat seems to think he's entitled to bed-and-breakfast here and I wouldn't put it past him to get in, even through the cloakroom window.'

'All right, we'll push on now with seeing everyone else. Do you think you could provide a written list of everyone who slept in the house that night – names and so on?'

Mrs Knightly was happy to comply, as well as adding a few observations on the way, sharp and to the point. Apart from herself, there was only the family, she repeated. Although she'd known them all from children, there seemed little love lost in that direction for any of them, except when it came to the young woman, Verity, Ida Lancaster's daughter. The housekeeper seemed very fond of her, although it had evidently been Penrose Llewellyn who had engaged her deepest affection.

Gilmour finished writing down the details. 'Thank you, Mrs Knightly. You've been very helpful.'

'Perhaps we could see Mr Penrose's bedroom and the rest of the house before we go any further,' Reardon asked. *Mr Penrose.* It sounded feudal and faintly servile, but there had to be something to distinguish him from the other two other Mr Llewellyns.

'I only hope,' she said, tight-lipped, 'whichever of them's done this thing, they'll think it was worth it when you find which one.'

'I hope so, too.' A bunch of obvious suspects. A locked house. Ten to one they all knew or suspected who'd done it, but unless someone spilt the beans, or one of them decided to come clean and confess – both scenarios equally unlikely – the person who'd taken Penrose Llewellyn's life was quite likely to walk away. It was a depressing thought that, although this wouldn't be a complicated case, it might well prove unsolvable. No wonder the local police had shunted it off. 'Lead on, Mrs Knightly.'

Except for her own bedroom on the ground floor, and two small attic rooms, one empty and the other occupied by Verity Lancaster, Mrs Knightly's guided tour of the house showed the other bedrooms to be on the first floor, all with easy access to Penrose Llewellyn's. Any one of the occupants could have crept into his bedroom in the silence of the night and held him down until he stopped breathing. Theo and his wife had one bedroom. Ida occupied a room further along, and Huwie an adjacent one, and the shared bathroom was at the end of the corridor, opposite the door to Pen's bedroom, near a short flight of stairs that apparently led to Verity's attic room. 'She was his favourite, poor lamb,' the housekeeper said, her eyes filling with sympathetic tears. 'She'll be the one who feels it most.' She hesitated. 'She's in her room now. Do you want to see her?'

'Not just now. If you've somewhere we can use as a temporary office, we'll see everyone downstairs.'

'There's Pen's study, you could use that. You'll be needing a telephone, I expect, and we're the only ones in Hinton with one, apart from the doctor.'

'Seriously?' asked Gilmour.

'No one else has much use for them round here,' she said simply. 'And we always managed without, too, until Pen had it put in.'

Reardon thought perhaps it might have been preferable to have used somewhere else as a base, away from the house, but the likelihood of finding anywhere else in Hinton seemed remote, and the telephone clinched it. 'The office will do nicely, Mrs Knightly.'

He hadn't expected to find anything much in Pen's bedroom, nor did they. The bed had been stripped, except for a white coverlet spread across it, the furniture shone with polish, the medicine cupboard in the small adjoining bathroom had been cleared out. The room had been divested of both its late occupant's possessions and any indication of his personality. Even his clothing had gone from the wardrobe, and all the drawers had been emptied. The need to get rid of painful reminders of the deceased was understandable but Reardon was taken aback at the speed with which it had been accomplished. Mrs Knightly explained that both she and Mrs Douglas had agreed that the longer the task was put off the more distressing it would be. They had done it together, the day after he died. When of course the question of an unnatural death hadn't yet arisen.

Hearing male voices, and Mrs Knightly's, at the bottom of the stairs, Verity held her breath. That would be the police. She waited for the knock that didn't come. They were evidently not ready for her yet. Still, she shivered, the gooseflesh rising on her arms, and she wrapped them tighter around her knees, trying to hold in the warmth. There was no fireplace in this little room and it was very cold, a room used in former times for storage or as a bedroom for a maid, like the other attic room across the landing. But she'd loved it as her own special place ever since she was a child, when she'd spent long holidays here at Bryn Glas. Lately it had come to feel like a refuge, somewhere she could escape to, where she could shut out the rest of the world. She didn't mind that you banged your head on the sloping ceiling if you sat up in bed a bit too quickly, nor did she usually mind the cold too much. Today she'd wrapped herself up in the blue and white Welsh quilt from her bed and huddled on the little cushioned seat under the dormer window. She'd cried so much the source of her tears had dried up, but the awful pain was still there and had formed itself into a hard, indigestible knot somewhere in her chest. She'd tried valiantly not to dwell on what had happened to her uncle – the man who had been more of a father to her than the one who disappeared over the horizon when she was ten. But Uncle Pen's image refused go away. Not the vibrant presence he'd been in life but stiff, cold and dead. And someone had apparently done that to him.

A great surge of self-pity welled up from inside her. They could none of them feel as she did – her Uncle Theo, or the other one, Huwie, whom she'd never met before. Her mother. At the thought of Ida, panic once more made her heart beat faster, like the jackdaw that had got itself trapped in the chimney last week, beating its wings hopelessly in an effort to escape.

She hated her mother, she told herself. Ida probably hated her. At any rate Verity knew with a dreary certainty that Ida was irritated by her, must have been ever since she was born, when Ida was thirty-six and had stopped believing she would ever be saddled with a child. I hate her. Unbidden, a half-formed picture flitted across her unwilling memory: mumps, and Ida sitting up with her all night, putting warm ginger poultices on her swollen glands, feeding her sips of something warm, sweet and soothing to ease the pain of swallowing. She shoved the memory away, angrily. It was so long ago it didn't count. And anyway, Ida had never been the sort of mother in whom you could confide, and now that the unbelievable had happened and Pen, her dear Uncle Pen, had gone, she couldn't turn to him just when she needed him most. Curling herself into an even tighter ball, she hugged her huge misery to her. Why couldn't it have been her, Verity, instead of Pen?

The night he died, feeling wretched and unable to sleep, she'd lain staring at the ceiling, listening to the familiar sounds of the night: the scratch against her little window of the huge pyracantha

which had outgrown an acceptable height in its search for the
light; the occasional small, sharp crack as the old timbers of
the house settled; from somewhere in the fields outside the scream
of a rabbit caught by a fox. The creak of the floorboards as
someone walked on the landing below to visit the bathroom.
Except there had been no water-sound like the rush of Niagara,
no thumping and gurgling of the old water pipes. Instead, footsteps: slithering, cautious footsteps, but the old floorboards
creaking despite that. The soft closing of a door. Her mother's?
Oh, please God, no.

Ida, who was always chronically short of money and who had
no scruples.

'I suppose,' Huwie Llewellyn asked his brother, 'you wouldn't
mind running me to somewhere I could pick up a train?'

'When?'

'Oh, this afternoon. I have some, er, business in town,' Huwie
answered unconvincingly.

Theo gave the short sharp bark that constituted his laugh. 'You
should have gone while you had the chance – you don't suppose
they're going to let you go now, the police?' He fixed Huwie
with his dark, melancholy stare. 'Or any of us, for that matter.
You realize we're all suspects? Although you, I should say,' he
added nastily, 'are probably the chief one.'

'Here now, that's a bit thick!'

'Why did you come back if not to screw something from
Pen? You stay away, nobody hears a dickey-bird from you for
decades and then suddenly – here you are, large as life. You
were actually invited to join the celebrations? Pull the other
one!' Theo's lips twisted. 'Then Pen puts the cat among the
pigeons by announcing he's going to get married again, which
means it's almost certain he'll be changing his will, and the next
morning there he is, dead.'

'You think I believed he would have left anything to me?'
Huwie asked bitterly. 'The outcast, the one who killed his mother
which he's supposed to have done – even though you were not
exactly blameless there, either? Yes, I did come to see him, as a
last resort . . . though I might have thought otherwise if I'd known
he was planning a bloody party, with all of you lot here!' he

went on, goaded. 'I don't mind admitting I'm on my uppers, brother. The sort of people you don't want to know about are after me for money and if they don't get it, I'll probably end up in the Thames wearing cement shoes.'

Theo laughed again but didn't reply.

They were at the bottom of the garden, leaning over the sandstone wall that marked the place where the grassy slope finished and the precipitous cliff began its descent. You couldn't see the river below, but you were always aware of it, the indolent grey snake, sliding under the overhang. A tributary of the Severn and its occasional but unpredictable, dangerous surge. Those boyish exploits about climbing the cliff recalled at the supper table that night had been told for amusement, with no mention of the punishments meted out for disregarding rules created for their safety.

Money, thought Theo. No prizes for thinking that had to be why Huwie had finally returned. In spite of the trouble which had been the cause of his abrupt departure from Bryn Glas, he had been left his fair share when their father had died. There hadn't been much to leave by that time, but Gwilym's moral principles had compelled him to see to it that what there was would be scrupulously divided between his children – and that included Huwie. Ida's husband had spent most of what she'd inherited before leaving her and Verity for another, younger woman. For Theo, his share had been a drop in the ocean as far as keeping up the lifestyle Claudia considered her due. It was only Pen who had used it wisely, starting off small and gradually building a little empire. And Huwie? God only knew what Huwie had done with his.

'Well, unless you did bump Pen off, you'll be all right. He's left nearly everything to us, his family, including Verity,' Theo said, with an unusual air of buoyancy. 'You'll get your cut, though maybe not as much as you'd hoped.'

His brother's shoulders sagged, a burden lifted, but he asked, 'How can you be sure? Oh, I see. You've drawn up his will.'

'It's always been in both our interests for me to give him legal advice over the years. In exchange for being put in the way of certain . . . investments.'

'Feathering your nest as usual,' Huwie sneered.

'If that's so, it hasn't done me much good,' Theo answered, his gloom returning. 'I don't have Pen's Midas touch. I think there might be more of Father in me than I like to admit – hopelessly inept with money.'

'I don't think,' said Huwie, 'that you've ever been inept with anything.'

Theo threw him a glance from under those slanted dark eyebrows that could sometimes look devilish. Then they both fell silent. Their father's shadow lay between them.

Gwilym had on the whole been a tolerant father, something of a dreamer except for that Puritan streak which demanded the utmost probity from his children – the same trait which indeed had prompted him to abandon the family coal-mining and other business interests, and take up a simple, sober and God-fearing life at Bryn Glas. Which had turned out to be, if not disastrous, very nearly so as far as his children's inheritance was concerned.

Theo asked curiously, 'What *have* you been up to, Huwie, all this time?'

Since his arrival, Huwie had been oddly silent, parrying questions to which everyone was dying for answers. 'Oh, this and that,' he answered vaguely. Then his voice sharpened. 'Never mind me, what about this woman Pen was going to marry? Presumably she knew what she was taking on? Prepared to do it because of what she'd get out of it, was she? What do you know of her, apart from the fact that she lives in Hinton and runs her own business?'

'Don't you remember her? Anna Goodridge, lived on the Townway? One of those who used to come up and play with us sometimes? No, you'd be too young. She left Wyvering when she got married and came back here about ten years ago, after her father died. I think her husband died early on. I'll give her this, she seems to have made a success out of that gardening business of hers,' Theo admitted grudgingly. 'As for her getting anything from Pen . . . Well, under the present will she gets nothing, but I spoke to him on the telephone last week and he told me he wanted to make changes. I must admit I hadn't seen that one coming though – getting married again, at his age.' He plucked absently at the velvety moss growing between the cracks of the sandstone wall, his dark face lengthening even more. 'She's deep, that one.' He amended this. 'I mean, she plays her cards pretty close to her chest. She could have brought those accusations merely out of spite because she knows she won't be getting anything now.'

'They're not without substance though, are they? You've said yourself, suspicion's bound to fall on us. All his family in the house when he died, no one else here.' Huwie's voice rose.

Theo's hand shot out. The knuckles as he grasped his brother's arm showed white. Huwie tried to shake it off but the grip was too tight. Theo's flat measured tones didn't change but there was no mistaking the threat. 'You keep your lip buttoned, do you hear? If you didn't have anything to do with it you've nothing to fear, have you? Nor have any of us.'

There was a silence. The wind blew across the valley, through the scrub on the cliff below and eddied up over the wall. It had an icy bite to it.

'That's what they always say, don't they?' Huwie answered bitterly.

EIGHT

The house consisted of a series of small consecutive rooms, some of them knocked through to make larger ones. A corridor ran the length of the house and additional wings jutted out towards the back at either end, providing respectively the kitchen quarters and the room previously used by Penrose as an office.

The latter proved to be a nondescript room, its windows overlooking the side of the house. It was a little bit scruffy compared with the rest of the immaculately kept house, Mrs Knightly or the girl, Prue, evidently not allowed in here often. It wasn't large, and taking up much of its available space was a vast desk, the sort known as a partner's desk, with drawers back and front and two straight chairs facing each other across its top. The desktop was clear, but a small table set to one side was home to a large, heavy-looking typewriter. The office had either been cleared since he died, or Pen Llewellyn had been a tidy worker. Reardon tried each of the multiple drawers in the desk, and found them all locked. If they should be full, going through them was likely to take some time. A job for Gilmour, he decided, keep his mind off Maisie and his coming fatherhood for a while. The only other furniture, a low table and a couple of cracked leather armchairs with the stuffing escaping from the arms, seemed like discards from the rest of the house. Van Gogh's *Sunflowers* on one wall made a startling contribution.

They spent time working out a plan of action and had almost finished when the smiling girl, Prue, who'd been working in the kitchen when Reardon had first arrived, came in with a tray laden with cold beef sandwiches, slices of Dundee cake and a large earthenware pot of tea. Mrs Knightly was going to see they didn't starve while they worked here. 'Draw up to the fire,' Reardon said, when she had closed the door behind her. Bryn Glas, it hadn't taken long to discover, was a draughty house and the room was chilly, despite the small but blazing fire and a well filled log basket to keep it so.

After they'd eaten, while Gilmour went to seek out family members to be interviewed, Reardon wandered around the room, hands in pockets. An avid reader, gravitation towards the bookshelves in the fireplace alcoves was inevitable. He was disappointed to find the slightly dusty shelves were sparsely filled and the selection of reading matter, by his standards, uninspired. True, there was a nod to a few classics but mostly it was a collection of contemporary authors, a mixture of fact and fiction with nothing particularly outstanding. Until his eyes came to rest on one shelf which held promise of something more interesting. Here the books were evidently old, possibly even falling into the antiquarian class. Some of them had obviously seen better days, but others were leather-bound and gleaming, with gilt lettering on their spines. Holding a beautifully made book, its structure and fine bindings paying tribute to the contents within, was to Reardon one of life's greatest pleasures; his fingers itched, his hand went out to pick one up to examine it more closely, but before he could do so the door opened and a woman came into the room. She was tall and striking looking, with heavy chestnut hair coiled in a bun low on her neck, perfectly made-up and seductively perfumed. She looked expensive. Doubtless this was Theo Llewellyn's wife, easily recognizable from the description given by Mrs Knightly.

'Looking for a book to read?' she enquired in a slow drawl. 'I was on the same mission. I'm simply bored to tears, though I doubt there's anything here worth reading.' She looked him up and down.

'I was admiring these old books. Mr Llewellyn must have been something of a connoisseur.'

'Connoisseur? Pen?' She laughed. 'He knew nothing about them, they were bought as an investment on Theo's advice. He's the one who's the collector. Theo is my husband,' she added, sitting down in one of the leather armchairs and crossing elegant legs. 'I am Claudia Llewellyn. And you are the policeman.'

Reardon gave her a steady look, followed by his own name and rank, took the chair at the desk that faced the room and indicated the other. Since she was here, he might as well start with her, and putting her across the desk from him gave him an advantage he felt he might need. But before she could move, the door opened once more and Gilmour stepped inside, another woman beside him. 'Oh, sorry, I didn't realize . . .' he began. 'This is Mrs Lancaster, sir.'

'Come in, both of you. No reason I can think of why we shouldn't see you two ladies together.'

Claudia Llewellyn lifted a graceful shoulder while Ida Lancaster crossed the room to take the other armchair. She immediately lit a black Russian cigarette, a thin, nervy, raddled-looking woman who was obviously not happy without one between her painted lips. The brittle veneer of sophistication made her the antithesis of her brother's elegantly well-dressed, self-possessed wife. Nevertheless, Reardon instinctively felt he would prefer to deal with her, rather than her sister-in-law, who addressed him with a sort of languid amusement, as though he might be a stage policeman. Gilmour she did not address at all.

He dealt with both women quickly. Their versions of the evening before Penrose's death were substantially the same: there had been a pleasant supper party which had, however, broken up fairly early. Pen had seemed in good spirits but had tired rather quickly, and after he had gone to bed they had all dispersed to their various rooms, except for Verity, Mrs Lancaster's daughter, who had not been feeling well and had already gone up. They had neither of them been aware of any noise or disturbance during the night.

A little probing into their finances didn't get him very far with Claudia, although it was pretty obvious that money would be essential to oil the wheels of her lifestyle. As for Ida, she stated rather grandly that she was considering an offer she had just received for her 'millinery establishment', as if it were in great demand, not as though she was itching to grab the offer, which Reardon, reading between the lines, thought was more likely to be the case. Neither of them, he surmised, would be exactly averse to a windfall arising from Pen's death.

He extracted a few more details, but didn't think the time was ripe for questioning them about the startling news of Pen's marriage they had been given at that supper gathering. That would do later. He would need to see them again, speak to them more fully, but at the moment it was the dead man's two brothers he was more concerned with.

First was the younger one, Huw, known as Huwie, lounging in a chair, smoking as much as Ida Lancaster and demanding when he could leave. 'Not yet, I'm afraid,' Reardon told him. For all his Welsh name, Huwie had left any Welshness he might have possessed behind him long ago, and spoke in the cultivated accents of an English public school, but during the course of his career Reardon had put away much less suspicious-looking characters than the man in front of him. It wasn't just his general loucheness and distinctly shifty attitude, which would immediately have alerted any policeman worth his salt. Stronger than that was a gut instinct telling him Huwie Llewellyn was not to be let out of his sight until he was satisfied he had nothing to do with his eldest brother's death.

He began with the usual questions. Huwie's eyes flickered when he was asked for his address but he gave a London one that was respectable enough. When asked if he was married, he replied archly that he had never seen the necessity.

'Hmm. I understand you and Mr Penrose Llewellyn haven't been in touch over the recent past, but you suddenly decided to change the situation and come here?'

'Contrary to what everyone believes, I was invited. I'd remembered it was his sixtieth birthday and I wrote to him, suggesting it was time to let bygones be bygones – not that old Pen and I had ever actually quarrelled. We'd just lost touch, you know how it is.'

'Since you left this house, in fact, after a quarrel with your other brother, Theo.'

His facial muscles twitched with a wry amusement. 'You've informed yourself pretty well already, it would seem.'

'It's our job. What's yours, Mr Llewellyn? How have you been supporting yourself for the last – twenty years, isn't it?' he asked, making a show of checking the notes Gilmour had made while they were talking to Mrs Knightly.

'Twenty-four,' Huwie said shortly. 'I've been around. Done my stint in the army. Travelled, knocked about the world, doing whatever offered. I'm not choosy. It's surprising what unexpected benefits can come with the most menial jobs.'

'I'll bet.'

'What lot were you in?' Gilmour asked. Huwie looked blank. 'In the army. What regiment?'

'The King's,' he replied after a split-second pause.

'Shropshire Light Infantry?' He nodded. 'And currently?'

'Currently I'm unemployed – like a million and a half others. Despite our wonderful Prime Minister Baldwin insisting it's less than that,' he added, revealing an unexpected concern with current social concerns.

'So you came here to see if your rich brother could help you,' Reardon suggested. Huwie chose not to rise to this and merely shrugged. 'And learnt that he was to be married, which put a different complexion on things, a possibility that his will might be changed? Did you kill him before he could do that, Mr Llewellyn?'

A direct question like that was a ploy not always as useful as it was meant to be in catching suspects off their guard, but this time it did get a reaction. Huwie thrust himself forward in his chair and with the flat of his hands on the desk at which Reardon was still sitting, leant across. 'No, I bloody well did not. You think I'm an idiot? As far as I knew then, I was more likely to get something from Pen when he was alive than after he was dead! What obligation did he have to leave me anything? Look closer to home, those who *knew* they were going to get something. They're the ones who wanted him out of the way, which means all of them!' He straightened. 'And if that's it, I'd like to get back to London.'

'We haven't quite finished with you yet. But that's all for the time being, thank you. We shall need to see you again.'

Reardon knew there was every chance that if they once let him go he could slip through their fingers and they might never see him again. He stopped Huwie as he was about to leave the room. 'Actually, stay a moment, there is one thing you can tell me. What was that disagreement with your brother Theo about? The one which made you leave home?'

'What?' He stared, still belligerent, then shrugged. 'Why do brothers squabble? Theo and I have never been soulmates. He's too po-faced for me, always was. Heavy-handed elder brother and all that. There was always something, some spat or other. I've actually forgotten what that particular one was about.'

Reardon let him go, though he didn't believe him for one moment. A rumpus that had caused a family rift of nearly a quarter of a century – and he didn't remember the cause? How credible was that?

The other brother, Theo, older by more than a dozen years, was a different matter altogether. The two men inhabited different worlds, it might almost have been different planets. A suave, well-tailored lawyer, ready with plausible answers at his finger-tips, Theo had his polished wife, a fashionable address and a no doubt affluent lifestyle. Quite the opposite of the down-at-heel brother.

He immediately demonstrated his intentions by choosing attack as the best form of defence. 'You realize we're taking this matter further? The family is going to request another post-mortem.'

Reardon regarded him steadily. 'That's your prerogative, Mr Llewellyn. But I have to tell you, it would be a waste of your time – and your money.' Hiring another pathologist for a second opinion didn't come free. 'The original autopsy was conducted in a perfectly professional manner.'

'I'm not satisfied by the conclusion drawn from those bruises they say they found. They could have been caused by anything . . . the way his body was handled after he died—'

'The pathology shows otherwise,' Reardon interrupted shortly. 'You must do as you see fit, of course. But in the meantime, we need a few details from you.' He nodded to Gilmour to begin the questioning and sat back to watch. Instinct warned him Theo Llewellyn would be an altogether trickier proposition than his brother. Gilmour began with the usual routine questions, including family circumstances, and his occupation. Two sons, a partnership in a general-practice law firm. How often was he in the habit of visiting Bryn Glas? Regularly, in fact every six weeks or so since the heart attack that caused his brother to live here in permanent retirement.

'You were on good terms with him, then?'

'Extremely. We'd been close ever since we were boys.'

'Did you know the terms of his will?'

'Of course I did. I'd looked after his affairs – his private ones, I wasn't his business lawyer – for years.'

'Then you'd be aware of its contents?'

He smiled faintly. 'I drew it up. What he left, apart from a few small bequests, was to be shared between his legal heirs and assigns, those of his family who survived him.'

'And the amount he left is not inconsiderable, I take it?' Theo lifted his shoulders. 'Tell us something about Mr Penrose's business. What exactly was it he did?' He knew, of course, having brought himself up to date on Penrose Llewellyn and his affairs before coming here, but it would be interesting to hear what version of it came from Theo Llewellyn's own lips.

'He was a property developer – you must have heard of Llewellyn Holdings, they're all over the Midlands.' Reardon nodded, and once started, the lawyer didn't seem reluctant to go on. 'He began as a small builder and made a fair success of it, but it was the building boom after the war that really put his name on the map – Lloyd George's homes for heroes and all that. Housing schemes for returning soldiers. Pen was astute enough to gain contracts with local authorities and he also branched out by buying up ancillary firms all over the place – those making fireplaces, bathroom fittings, anything needed for a new house. You had to admire him for his business acumen.'

Reardon noted a flicker of something – jealousy, or resentment? – in his eyes before he added those last words. Theo Llewellyn seemed to be a man entirely without humour, the sort who had a dampening effect on everyone, the spoilsport at the party. Was he as cold as he appeared to be or was he just adept at concealing his emotions? On the surface, despite what he'd said about their closeness, he wasn't grieving at his brother's death. Unless they were genuinely unfeeling, as a family they all seemed adept at hiding what they thought. The housekeeper had seemed more upset than any of them. But although Theo Llewellyn was, like all lawyers, a breed whom Reardon instinctively looked on with suspicion, that didn't make him guilty of taking his brother's life.

'Is Mrs Douglas mentioned in the will?'

'No.' He examined his manicured nails. Long, strong fingers. A gold signet ring and a gold wristwatch. 'As far as I knew, she was just a friend, not someone he would have thought of leaving money to. It came as a surprise to everyone that he was intending to marry her, although he'd already told me he wished to talk about his will. I didn't think anything of it, it was something we did as a regular thing, once a year. Reviewed the situation to see if any changes were necessary, though I have to say he wasn't one to chop and change once he'd made up his mind.'

'As a family, you must have been aware that his marriage might radically affect your expectations.'

'Of course,' he said smoothly. 'But it was his money to do as he liked with. He'd been a widower for a long time and Mrs Douglas is a nice woman. We were all happy for him.'

Reardon managed to hide his scepticism. 'Were you surprised that your brother Huwie turned up for this birthday party?'

'Astonished,' came the dry reply. 'We all of us thought he'd severed all connection with this family.'

'We've been told the reason for that was some altercation he had with you.'

He looked as though he wasn't going to answer this but after a moment he shrugged. 'I suppose it's no secret that we quarrelled. That, and the fact that my father refused to mention his name again preyed on my mother's mind so much she went into a decline from which she never fully recovered. Huwie was always her favourite, very much the baby of the family. It was only because he knew how it would have grieved our mother that my father didn't cut him out of his will altogether.'

What a curiously old-fashioned phrase! Did people, other than in Victorian novels, go into a decline? Under another more scientific name, perhaps they did, perhaps the mind could affect the body in ways we couldn't yet explain. 'He says he wrote to your brother Penrose and was invited to come and stay at Bryn Glas.'

'I shouldn't,' Theo said, 'take too much notice of what Huwie says.' He prepared to stand up. 'If you've finished, I have other things to occupy me.'

'Not so fast, Mr Llewellyn. Sit down a moment longer. You're a lawyer . . . disregarding your reservations about the post-mortem, I don't need to spell it out to you that the circumstances of your brother's death are suspicious to say the least. A locked house with only a few people in it, most of them with a motive for wishing him dead. If you discount the women – though we haven't done so as yet – that leaves you and your brother, Huwie. Did the shock announcement about this marriage make one of you decide to kill him?'

The mask slipped momentarily. Stripped of pretension, his expression was for a brief moment vicious, before he changed it to outraged. 'I have just lost a dear brother and you see fit to make tasteless accusations!'

'That quarrel with your brother, Huwie. What exactly was it about?'

He seemed taken aback by the sudden return to this question, but only momentarily. 'What did we ever *not* quarrel over? To be frank, I thought him a spoilt brat who wheedled his way round our mother. She couldn't see any wrong in him. He was always her darling little boy.'

'You weren't boys when the quarrel happened – you were both grown men.'

'Inspector,' he answered with exaggerated patience, 'let's nip this line of questioning in the bud, shall we? What happened years ago has nothing whatever to do with your enquiry. No one in this house killed Pen. His death was upsetting, but natural.' Reardon stayed silent. 'Look here,' he added suddenly, 'I didn't hate Penrose. None of us did.'

Perhaps that was true, but not all killers hated their victims; there were plenty of other reasons for wanting someone dead. And whether Theo Llewellyn chose to ignore it or not, there had been considerable violence attached to Pen's death, a need to silence him, perhaps born out of desperation, which could easily have overridden other emotions.

'Has it occurred to you, inspector, that those bruises may have been caused by someone helping him to sit up and get his breath? He'd had a nasty cough for weeks.'

Reardon had been wondering when that theory would be brought forward. It no more held water than the claim that no one had been aware of any disturbance, or of hearing any noise in this old house of creaking stairs and floorboards. 'From what I've heard,' he said mildly, 'Mr Llewellyn was quite capable of raising himself to deal with a coughing fit, without needing help to the extent where he ended up black and blue.'

For a moment, Theo looked quite capable of murder. 'You won't get anywhere with this, you know,' he said through his teeth. Reardon didn't stop him from leaving the room this time. He didn't think they were going to hear any more about second post-mortems.

'Well, what do you make of that, Joe?' he asked when the door had closed behind the lawyer.

'Rum lot, aren't they? But I'd say they have to know – or don't want to know – who it was. Or else the lot of them were in it together.'

It was, of course, in the collective interest of the Llewellyn family to keep mum. Because if a charge of murder couldn't be brought, there would be no long-drawn out court case to delay probate and prevent them getting their hands on whatever they were hoping to inherit. But . . . in the quiet of the night . . . a man held down in his bed, fighting for his life . . . he wasn't going to go quietly, was he? Yet not one person, in the adjoining bedrooms, only a few yards away, had heard a thing. Pen Llwellyn couldn't have got where he was without making enemies. But none of them were likely to possess supernatural powers, able to get soundlessly into a locked house, one with floorboards that creaked like pistol shots, and silently kill.

He rubbed a hand across his face. 'If Theo Llewellyn drew the will up, he'll have the original, but Penrose must have had a copy, and I'd like to have a look through it before we talk to Theo about it. It's most likely in one of these locked drawers. What's happened to his keys? Why haven't they been handed over yet?'

Gilmour confessed he didn't know but it was getting late in the afternoon and they were ready to pack up. He promised to locate them when they returned to Bryn Glas in the morning. Outside the house they parted company. Reardon prepared to make the acquaintance of Kate Ramsey by delivering his wife's letter to her, while Gilmour was to try his persuasions on the unwilling landlord of the Fox to make available his two rooms, however small, even with the less than attractive prospect of the beds being damp.

His suspicions as to the nature of the accommodation at the Fox were confirmed when he was shown the two dark, poky rooms available, but the savoury smells issuing from the kitchen and a few words with the smiling, comfortable lady who was the surly publican's wife went a long way towards stifling his doubts. When she told him what was on offer for dinner he took the plunge and booked himself and Reardon in for as many nights as might be necessary. A savoury pie and jam roly-poly to follow couldn't be bad. And the snug, with its fire already blazing, looked inviting. If they had to be away from home, a good dinner was a comfort they couldn't afford to ignore.

Emerging into the darkening afternoon, he began to make his way back to meet Reardon at the place where he'd left the car. He was in no hurry – his arrangement with the publican's wife hadn't taken long. All at once, from somewhere behind him a small young woman being almost dragged along by an energetic Jack Russell attached to a lead swished past him in a colourful whirl of yellow flapping coat, long scarf and a heady waft of scent. The suddenness of it made him nearly lose his balance. She half-turned to call out, 'Sorry!' but he heard her laughing as she and the dog almost fell into the doorway of one of the small shops a few yards further along the road, leaving Gilmour with a glimpse of black shiny hair cut in a fringe and a wicked little heart-shaped face, alight with mischief. He carried on, almost convinced that this glimpse of exotica in the quiet workaday street had been a figment of his imagination.

NINE

Kate Ramsey's husband, like Kate herself, had been a teacher at Uplands House, near Castle Wyvering, a school for the sons of well-heeled parents. When the teaching of German was discontinued at the outbreak of war and she'd lost her post, she'd considered herself lucky, as a married woman, to have been allowed to understudy for the schoolmaster at the nearby Hinton church school, which all the children of Hinton attended until they were old enough to transfer to the bigger school at Castle Wyvering. She'd been forced to give up her live-in accommodation at Uplands House and for the duration of the war had occupied the attached schoolhouse. Having been forced to quit when the schoolmaster returned, she now lived in a rented cottage at the end of the back lane which ended at the junction with the main road that ran along the ridge into Castle Wyvering. Reardon had been directed to take the lane as a shortcut from Bryn Glas and she welcomed him in warmly after he had surprised her by introducing himself as Ellen's husband.

'How nice to meet you, at last. Come in and tell me all the news about Ellen.'

Her front door opened into a room that stretched from front to back. The walls were painted a warm cream colour and it had an untidily comfortable, lived-in look with a big, squashy old sofa, a lot of bookshelves and by the large window at the far end a desk and table littered with papers and a typewriter.

Through the window could be seen a garden with a path down the middle of a grass patch. There was an old gnarled tree set in the grass, with a seat around it, where no doubt it would be very pleasant in summer.

When he was seated, Reardon handed over his wife's letter. She didn't open it immediately. 'Of course, you're a policeman, aren't you? I suppose you're here about poor Pen Llewellyn?'

'That's why we're in Hinton, yes.'

'He was a friend, a good friend,' she said sadly. 'I shall miss him very much, we all will. I was there at Bryn Glas for supper, you know, the night he died.'

'Then I'd like to hear about it, at some point.'

'I can do better than that. I have it all written down.' She smiled at his surprise. 'I keep a journal and that night I wrote it up before bed. You can read it while I read Ellen's letter.' She fetched a hard-backed exercise book with a marbled cover, opened it and leafed through it until she reached the page she wanted. 'You can start there. It's not private from there onwards.'

He read with interest as Kate walked up and down, turning over the pages of Ellen's long letter. She was a great letter-writer, Ellen, witness the hundreds of pages, the thousands of words she'd written to him during the war, before they were married. Mostly in French, he remembered with a smile, because she'd been the teacher, he the pupil. That was how they'd met, at one of the self-improvement classes he was addicted to. Glancing up from his own reading occasionally, he saw Kate smiling as she read. She was tall and fair-haired, a good looking woman with an athletic way of moving and a self-assurance that came, possibly, from making her own way in the world after the death of her husband. What was the work she had referred to at the beginning of this journal extract he was reading? he wondered. Perhaps she had become a writer. The account of the supper party given by Penrose showed she was observant, with a shrewd assessment of the effect the news of his forthcoming marriage had had on the Llewellyns. He found it interesting that she had speculated they might all have been living above their incomes and sponging off Penrose, though she had retracted that. She had mentioned something of the other guests, too – the three he had yet to meet, and would have to follow up: in particular, the good doctor who had later issued Pen Llewellyn's death certificate and who could not be feeling very chipper about the situation, and Anna Douglas's son. He wondered, too, what connection the young woman who had also been invited to share the supper, Carey Brewster, had had with Penrose Llewellyn.

'Poor Gerald – Dr Fairlie,' Kate said, as if picking up his thoughts, folding Ellen's letter. 'All this has hit him very hard. I don't suppose anything like this has ever happened to him before in his career – he'll be seeing it as a slur on his professional integrity. Knowing Gerald, I doubt he'll ever get over it.'

'Very upsetting for him.' No doctor liked to admit a mistake – they were supposed to bury them, weren't they? 'You mentioned Miss Lancaster being taken ill. What do you think was wrong with her? You didn't seem to believe it was something she'd eaten?'

'Verity?' She looked troubled. 'No, I think that was an excuse, she was upset over something else.'

'The fact that her uncle was going to be married again? I've yet to speak to her. She was in her room and according to Mrs Knightly, that's where she's spent nearly all her time since her uncle's death, doesn't want to talk to anybody.'

She looked concerned. 'I didn't know that, perhaps I should go and see if she'll talk to me. She adored Pen, but I can't believe she'd be upset about the marriage. She gets on really well with Anna.' She was sitting on the sofa with her legs drawn up beneath her and leant dangerously forward to pick up the poker to stir the fire. 'The fact is, she's been a bit of a handful to her mother, ever since her divorce. I'm afraid they're not getting on at present. Ida's not . . .' She stopped herself. 'No, I shouldn't.'

'I've met Mrs Lancaster.'

'Oh.' She pulled a face. 'Then you probably know what I mean. I have to say, it sometimes seems she's too concerned with that wretched hat shop and her so-called smart friends to spare time for her daughter. Which is a beastly thing to say, but all the same . . . sorry, I'm too outspoken.'

'I'm used to that. I live with an outspoken woman, remember.'

At that she laughed. 'Still the same, is she? Oh, how I'd love to see Ellen again! It's years, you know, we ought to have kept up better.' Giving him a sideways glance, she added, 'Any chance of her coming to stay while you're working here?'

'No.' The too-casual way she'd said it told him that wasn't her own idea. Ellen wouldn't actually have suggested it outright after their conversation about it, would she? But she had evidently managed to put the notion into Kate's mind. 'Sorry, work and pleasure don't mix.'

'No, of course not, I should have realized.' She looked contrite. 'But you'll be staying here, in Hinton, will you?'

'At the Fox, if my sergeant has managed to persuade the landlord to open up and arrange rooms.'

She laughed. 'Oh, Fred Parslowe! He's a law unto himself, but he's all right, really, and so's his wife, Flo. She'll see you get a good dinner. She fattens geese up for Christmas, and Fred likewise.'

'Which reminds me it's time I went to see how he's fared.' But Reardon was comfortable and disinclined to move. He almost wished he hadn't declined the offer of tea. The fire was warm and he stretched out his legs and steered the conversation away from the enquiry, venturing to ask about that work she'd mentioned in her journal.

'Oh, it's doubtless very boring to anyone who isn't actually concerned. In lieu of the teaching job I was trained for, I devote my energies to obtaining justice for women – married, widowed or unmarried. Or at any rate, trying to. We might have succeeded in getting the vote, but I'm afraid that's only the beginning. We're a long way from equality with men, or being treated fairly, in practically anything.' She stopped abruptly. 'Sorry, you've touched a nerve. I'm afraid I tend to bore people once I start.'

'Someone with such passion is never boring, Mrs Ramsey. In any case, it's a subject not unfamiliar to me.'

'No, it won't be. Knowing Ellen, I'd expect nothing less.' Her warm smile brought home to him how close Ellen had said they'd once been.

'It's been the saving of me, you know.' She waved a hand at the papers strewing the table. 'I used to love teaching, any kind of teaching, so I found it very hard when I was forced to leave. It's a monstrous rule and that's why I'm working for the NCW

– the National Council of Women – to get it revoked, among other things. It's appalling you have to choose between marrying the man you love and having children, or the work you love and a life of spinsterhood.'

'A hard choice and hard work.'

'Yes, it's uphill work, with all the endless letters, meetings. But worth it . . .' There was a certain fervour in her manner, a light in her eyes that reminded him of those women who had fought for women's suffrage before the war. It wouldn't come as a surprise to learn she'd been one of them. But she stopped herself with a small laugh. 'And that's enough of that. If you'd like to step in for a cup of tea any time while you're around here, I promise I won't bend your ear again.'

Regretfully, he stood up, offering his hand. 'When all this business is settled, I'll bring Ellen over to see you, I promise. I'm glad to have met you – no doubt I shall be speaking to you again before we've finished.' He stepped to the door, then turned. 'I didn't mean to be churlish about her visiting, you know, Mrs Ramsey.'

'Don't give it another thought. But if Ellen can persuade you to change your mind, I should be more than pleased.'

'I should think the likelihood of that is remote. For now, let me wish you luck in your work.'

She had a very attractive smile, with something mischievous in it as she said, 'You might be sorry you said that one day, Mr Reardon. The NCW is lobbying for women police and I know what you men think about that.'

Kate waited for the sound of the latch on the garden gate. Tree roots had lifted one of the paving slabs on the path to the front door and the gate needed to be eased up and over to enable it to be closed. Not everyone bothered to do this, and then it swung to and fro and banged in the wind. But her visitor had closed it properly, adding another point in his favour. She liked her friend Ellen's husband, with his honourable scars, and thought it good that a man like him had been sent to find out about Pen's death.

She drew the curtains and lit the lamps, though it wasn't quite dark, and the action reminded her of how she had pulled

her curtains the night Pen had died and watched Jack, his
mother and Carey walk away down the lane after they'd left
her. Under moonlight bright enough to read a newspaper by,
they had all been able to see their way clearly that night along
the stony, rutted lane that lessened the distance from Bryn Glas
by almost a mile. As the other three reached the junction with
the main road, Gerald Fairlie's car had caught up with them.
He'd stopped and offered them a lift, and they'd accepted,
although they were less than ten minutes from home. It was
then, after the car had disappeared, that she had fancied she'd
seen that shadow moving in the darkness. Had it been imagination? Ought I to have mentioned it to Inspector Reardon? she
asked the photograph on her sideboard. Her husband, Captain
Rupert Ramsey, looked silently out at her, as he and all his
dead comrades did in these photographs, spruce in their
uniforms, eyes calm and confident, shoulders back, allowing
no admission to be captured by the camera of the terror that
they might be dead even before the recipient received the
photograph. Tears welled before she turned away, angry with
herself. How long before such habits – talking to a photograph,
seeing imaginary shadows – became eccentricities? She was
no better than a lonely old maid talking to her cat, though at
least a cat could respond, by the simple fact of being alive.

She picked up Ellen's letter and read it again and presently
began to smile.

TEN

Mrs Ramsey hadn't been exaggerating when she said the
food would be good at the Fox. It very nearly, if not
quite, made up for the poky rooms and the beds which,
although they gave the lie to the dark insinuations of dampness
made by Mrs Petty, she of the tea shop, were as lumpy as if rocks
rather than flock filled the mattresses. More than that, the rooms
were dismal, approached by a back staircase and overlooking the
backyard. Breakfast this morning had been an uncommunicative

meal, taken too early because both of them had been wakened at the crack of dawn by the horrible honking of the geese the land-lady was fattening in the backyard, eight Christmas dinners making their presence felt.

'Another night like that and they'll be foie gras before they know it,' Gilmour muttered.

But after being fortified by sausage, egg, bacon and black pudding, the world had taken on a rosier hue. After a last cup of satisfyingly strong tea, alone in the Parslowe's private parlour – which was where their meals were to be taken, as it was the only suitable room, Mrs Parslowe had insisted – its fire already lit, they went through the plans for the day. Gilmour was to return to Bryn Glas, and begin a search through those desk drawers, while Reardon had made an appointment to see Dr Fairlie before he set out on his daily rounds. By then he hoped Verity Lancaster would have recovered sufficiently to allow herself to be inter-viewed. All the supper party guests would then have been accounted for, with the exception of Mrs Douglas's son, Jack, and Miss Carey Brewster.

It was into a murky November morning they emerged from the Fox. Still very cold, no rain, but a clinging dampness in the air, and Hinton already going about its everyday business. Half-day closing on a sunlit yesterday had given a false impres-sion of sleepiness. The place could hardly be classed as humming with purposeful activity today, either, but the shops were open and Hinton was awake. A brewer's drayman rolled beer barrels into the cellar of the Fox; a scant few stalls had been set up as a market in the middle of the main street, the Townway, and were being well patronized by women with shopping baskets. Clanging sounds issued now and again from the smithy and the adjoining wheelwright's premises. A horse harnessed to a pony trap waited patiently, while a small boy on a bicycle too big for him wobbled along the centre of a road otherwise empty of traffic. A dog barked somewhere in the distance. An ordinary, dull little community with nothing special about it.

Reardon had decided against using the motor, now parked with Fred Parslowe's permission in the pub's alleyway alongside the Fox. It was more bother to get it out, he reckoned, to start it up and have to worry about how far away the nearest petrol pump was – not to mention the state of the country roads around here and the probability of punctures – than it was to walk, when nowhere in Hinton Wyvering was more than ten or fifteen minutes away from anywhere else.

Gilmour was to call and speak to Jack Douglas on his way to Bryn Glas. He waved a postcard at Reardon. 'I'll walk a few yards with you, sir. Just want to pop this in the postbox for Maisie.'

'Give it here, I'll do that. But you only wrote one for her last night, didn't you?'

'Yes, but it occurred to me afterwards, she can leave a message at Bryn Glas to let me know if – if she's all right. Or – er – even speak to me,' he added with a grin that didn't quite disguise his hopefulness.

Reardon suppressed a sigh. In the circumstances it seemed churlish to object to something as harmless as that, when Bryn Glas was the only place round here which boasted a telephone, except for Dr Fairlie's. The Gilmours themselves didn't run to such luxuries, and the convenience of a public telephone kiosk, such as Maisie (or someone else on her behalf, if things became urgent) would have to use if it was necessary to contact Gilmour, hadn't yet reached these rural parts.

At that moment, into the quiet street erupted the sudden roar of an approaching motorcycle. As if a tableau had come to life, everyone present on the Townway turned in a concerted move-ment to watch this phenomenon. In a moment it had passed them.

'That was your motorbike, sir!' Gilmour's awed voice seemed to echo in the silence left as the engine noise receded into the distance. His eyes were popping.

'And that was my wife,' Reardon said grimly.

He thrust the postcard back at Gilmour and set off in the opposite direction to where he'd been going, this time towards Bryn Glas and the little lane where Kate Ramsey lived, leaving Gilmour to his call on Jack Douglas, who lived with his mother further along the Townway.

Ellen was no stranger to motorcycling. For the duration of the war, she had taken on a man's job. Wearing breeches, and riding one of the two-stroke motorcycles they called the Baby Triumph, she had delivered mail: parcels, letters from the Front, besides all too many of those tragic telegrams giving news of sons, husbands and brothers who had been wounded, killed in action or were missing, presumed dead.

Reardon's own powerful BSA was a different, more powerful matter. He was looked on as eccentric by those he worked with, using it whenever he could rather than one of the official means of transport. It was his pride and joy. He would have ridden it here had he been on the investigation alone. By the time his rage-propelled stride had got him to the end of Kate Ramsey's lane, he was red-faced, sweat mingling with the atmospheric moisture that beaded his face, hair and clothes. Ellen had dismounted by the side of the road, removed her gloves and goggles and was taking her time about consulting a map. She stood stock still when she saw him and waited for him to reach her.

'Ellen. Well.' He breathed deep, leant across the motorcycle and kissed her.

For a moment they were very still. Her hand as it rested on his arm was still trembling from the vibrations of the engine. Her legs were probably feeling like jelly, too. He hoped her heart was still in her mouth at what she'd done. She'd ridden pillion a hundred times, of course, her hands clutching his waist, but she'd never before, thank God, expressed any desire to take control and ride it alone. This fine drizzle had made the road surfaces, diabolical at the best of times, greasy. They could have been a death-trap. For a split second, watching her speed past him as he stood outside the Fox, a panicking memory had invaded his mind and images of that near-fatal wartime collision of his own as a dispatch rider had ricocheted crazily around: the hail of continuous shellfire and deafening guns; the groans of injured men, the screams of terrified horses, the chaos of wagons, gun-carriages and ambulances on a muddy road made nearly impassable by bomb craters ten-foot deep and more. The column of wounded, limping along, that he'd made a desperate bid to avoid. The next months spent in various military hospitals. Ending up with a medal, a face scarred for life and a woman still waiting to marry him. Ellen.

He might never have ridden a motorbike again if he hadn't got on one as soon as he possibly could after leaving the last hospital. And the thought of such a thing ever happening to her almost stopped his heart.

'That was a stroke of bad luck,' she said softly. 'I'd meant to break it gently to you that I was here.' He didn't reply and she went on in a rush: 'Kate doesn't know, but I'm sure she'll be pleased to see me. I came before I could change my mind and I didn't tell you because I didn't want you to forbid—'

'Forbid?' he stopped her, stung.

They had neither of them been in their first youth when they had met and later married. Ellen had already been a woman leading an independent life, with a career of her own, long before he had his feet on the first rung of the promotion ladder. That teaching career had been cut short, firstly by the war, and then by marriage. But that last had been her choice, and she had never by word or deed shown that she regretted it. He had married a wonderful, freethinking woman whom he didn't want to be any other way. 'Good God, Ellen, I've no right to forbid you to do anything!' And immediately, heard himself, two days ago: *'I can't allow it.'* His official voice, when he'd been too preoccupied to consider the impact of it on Ellen. Provocation, to anyone with any spirit. 'You could have come here to stay for as long as you liked, at any time. But why now – and when it's so damned inconvenient?'

'It needn't be, not at all. I came because it seemed such an opportunity to see Kate again, with you away. Please, just forget I'm here.'

How did she imagine he could do that? With her not half a mile away and always at the back of his mind? He looked at her, grey eyes wide and her chin up in a way he knew so well, and realized with a sinking feeling that this could build up to some sort of confrontation. He couldn't believe it. Himself and Ellen? There'd never been anything much more than an occasional disharmony between them – and in any case, wasn't this something he'd wanted, a kindling of interest after her illness? Somehow, the rage that had taken hold of him now seemed irrelevant, and despite himself, he could feel it beginning to fizzle out like a damp squib, leaving only exasperation. He sighed. 'Look at the size, Ellen. The size of that bike.' The size of it, and Ellen, five foot nothing.

'It was an impulse, and I'm not an impulsive woman, am I?' she said with a small attempt at humour that didn't hide the shake in her voice. He was glad to know she'd not only scared him, she'd frightened herself. Yet it was something more than an untypical act of defiance, something she had to do for reasons he didn't quite understand.

'I really have come just to see Kate, you know. Not to get in your way.'

He felt a smile beginning. 'I'll never get the better of you, woman, will I? All right, put that map away, you've got yourself to the right place. It's just up this lane.' He lifted the kickstand and began to wheel the bike towards the cottage.

She was wearing her wartime breeches and a leather coat with a large fur collar. There were some women who, while they had no fear of riding a motorcycle, still wore a woolly cap rather than run the risk of looking unbecoming in a close-fitting leather helmet. Ellen wasn't one of them. She pulled the helmet off and shook her head to free her hair as she walked beside him. He stopped as they reached Kate's door. 'You understand we shan't be able to see anything of each other, no cosy evenings together, right?'

She nodded. 'Forget I'm here,' she repeated.

As if he could.

'Well. Well, right now I've got work to do – but look here. Don't you go riding home on this bloody machine, do you hear?'

They stood looking at each other. Bloody machine. His beloved motorbike, his treasure. The absurdity of it struck them simultaneously. It seemed a long time since they had laughed together. They were still smiling when Kate Ramsey came round the corner from her back garden. She stopped in her tracks and then gave a delighted cry. In a moment, she and Ellen were embracing.

'Coffee, Mr Reardon?' she asked after a moment, her arm around Ellen, preparing to lead the way indoors.

'Thank you, but I have an appointment with Dr Fairlie,' he said drily. 'If you'd just tell me where my motorbike can be safely put away?'

Anna Douglas's house was small and neat, situated right in the centre of Hinton, its front door opening directly off the Townway.

Rosy pink brick, red tiled roof. Three windows and a door at the front, a long and narrow garden at the back. In the kitchen-living room were shelves, home to dozens of mismatched china plates, some of them cracked, all of them pretty and colourful, plus a battered desk at that end of the room which constituted her office. A gently purring fire warmed the room and from the oven came the smell of a savoury casserole which she'd made and had no desire for. But Jack had to be provided with something to eat, even if he was lately eating the food she put before him as though he had little taste for it.

He'd disappeared upstairs immediately the red-haired police sergeant had left, after taking his statement about the night of the party, as if he wanted to avoid talking with her about it. It wasn't only a mother's perception that told her he had something on his mind. Ever since the night of the supper party at Bryn Glas, he'd been preoccupied – which had nothing to do with the rather scratchy attitude he'd been adopting towards Pen lately, she told herself, resolutely ignoring the plunging feeling this gave her. It had to be Carey's return that was upsetting him, for some reason. She had tried to face the fact that the thing she'd always wanted to happen between Carey and her son wasn't going to. Jack's face was set towards yet another stint for God knows how long somewhere at the end of the world and Carey was preparing to sell her house and make off, possibly to the other end of it. She sometimes wanted to shake him.

She poured another cup of tea.

A hard worker all her life, she could now settle to nothing. Since that moment when she'd seen Pen lying in the midst of those roiled, tangled sheets and had the intimation that he had not simply been taken peacefully and gently in his sleep, but had died a terrible, awful death, the drive to work had deserted her – work which had hitherto supported her through thick and thin. Through times that were sometimes good, but had often been very bad indeed. Yet now . . . a job started, left half done and the two young lads who were working for her at Bryn Glas becoming disorientated at not working under her hitherto clear direction.

'What are you going to do about the garden?' she'd asked Theo, but he'd simply shrugged and said he didn't know, and yesterday, when she'd asked him again, he'd impatiently told her to go home and leave it.

Dismissed like a redundant employee, she'd left the boys to potter about as best they could, come home and attempted work on her own garden, but there wasn't much to be done at this dead end of the year, everything tidied up for winter, little growing but winter vegetables. In previous years this seasonal hiatus had given her space to enlarge on schemes that had been running through her head and which she'd had no time to get down on paper during the busyness of the previous growing season. But this year Pen had had great ideas for what they would do together after they were married: travel, catch up on the cultural life neither of them had previously had time for, and she'd been only too happy to agree. She was nearly sixty herself and the idea of retirement wasn't unwelcome. Now, it had gone, all of it, Pen and with it the happiness that had come just when she had thought she was past all that.

Yesterday's conversation with Theo tumbled over in her mind yet again. Wearing a black tie and a suitably doleful expression which nevertheless was easy for him to assume, since it came naturally. Touched with arrogance when he told her she need no longer bother with the garden. Go home and take a break, Mrs Douglas. Not Anna. *Mrs Douglas* – when she'd known him since he was in short trousers and skinned knees, into mischief with Pen but always, even then, the one to wriggle out of trouble, the clever one. And look where he's ended up, Pen had said with a short laugh. Up to his ears in debt, running to catch up with a wife streets ahead of him, in every way.

When Pen had told them all he was going to marry her, she'd watched them looking at her, smiling but not able to hide their dismay or their thoughts, believing she'd caught him for what she was about to get out of him: his money. How far from the truth this was they couldn't even have begun to guess. Nevertheless, one of them had taken steps.

She scraped back her chair, cradling her teacup in both hands as she stared out of the window down the garden of a working gardener, its utilitarian path leading from the house directly to a large greenhouse and a potting shed at the bottom. There were no flower beds but row after row of plants and shrubs being brought on. She had allowed Jack to build a seat in front of the crumbling, disued privy and planted a Rambling Rector which had lived up to its name by climbing up to twenty feet and smothering the ugly old ruin with its creamy white blossoms. In summer, its intense fragrance took over the garden. It had been in her mind to plant the same rose at Bryn Glas, to mark their marriage.

By the time he died, Pen had become as committed to the project as she was. He'd shared her excitement at the prospect of uncovering a lost, forgotten garden – possibly Tudor – and had enthusiastically suggested a knot garden. Trying his hand at copying complex designs from old books for interlacing box hedges, diamonds, lozenges and lovers' knots, he'd laughed when she warned him that the undulations in the ground which she'd first suspected might be the outlines of a sunken garden might simply be the foundations of an old byre, or a row of pigsties. When Pen wanted to believe something, it was already a fait accompli in his mind.

The main project was doomed now, of course, but however the enquiries into his death turned out – her mind skittered away from what she actually meant by that – it was inevitable that the house would at some point have to be sold. None of the family would ever want to live in it again, that was for sure. And even Theo must appreciate how much more it would fetch if the landscaping should be finished, Tudor garden or not.

She was not, she thought, suddenly energized, going leave it in the desolate condition it was now, no matter what. She reached for her coat and a woolly scarf, pushed her feet into her working boots that stood on a folded newspaper by the back door, determined not to be intimidated by merciless Theo, and not to mind Ida's barbed comments, or Claudia's studied indifference. And to ignore Huwie, for whom she was finding it too easy to be sorry, when after all he – perhaps more than any of the others, come to that – might be the one who had ruthlessly killed Pen.

In any case, there was something else tugging at her conscience, another problem. Not mine, if we're being honest, she told herself as she began the brisk walk to Bryn Glas, but if Ida Lancaster either isn't capable or doesn't care, someone has to do something about the one person who was grieving over Pen as much as she herself was: that poor child, Verity.

ELEVEN

Since Dr Fairlie lived at the other end of Hinton, Reardon now had to retrace his steps, lengthening his stride to make up for lost time. The early morning drizzle had turned into a slanting, ill-natured rain, but it might at least, hopefully, clear the air. It was a stiff climb towards his destination, for perhaps half a mile, along yet another awkwardly twisting road known as Upper Bank, with only a few houses scattered along its length, until it eventually levelled out at a cluster of ancient cottages and other buildings that seemed to mark the extremities of Hinton like a full stop.

At one side of the road stood the small school and its schoolhouse, where Mrs Ramsey had once lived and taught, its playground presently deserted. From inside the school came the faint sound of a piano and infant voices raised in the ragged singing of a hymn. Morning assembly, of course. Regardless of all that had happened, it still wasn't much after nine. On the opposite side of the road was a small green, on which ancient stocks stood. Nearby was a churchyard with massive, dark yews, a lych gate and a path leading to the church. No house that looked like a vicarage, but Reardon guessed the parish wouldn't be large enough to warrant a resident incumbent, and would share a vicar with Castle Wyvering. There was Fairlie House however, facing the church, a square Georgian brick-built house with a shallow roof and many windows. The juxtaposition of the big house, church and school, and the few cottages nearby suggested this might once have constituted the centre of the original Hinton village which over the centuries had gradually crept, as villages were apt to do, nearer to a more convenient and accessible spot; in Hinton's case around the junction where steep Nether Bank emerged to join the Townway.

He made for the only building to mar this peaceful, harmonious little enclave: a squat, uncompromisingly utilitarian affair which had to be the doctor's surgery, separated from Fairlie House only

by a gravel drive on which stood a motor car. Ellen's escapade
on his BSA earlier that morning now gave him reason to scru-
tinize the chocolate-brown, bull-nosed Morris parked in front of
him. Reputedly reliable, suitable for a woman to drive. A little
two-seater like this wouldn't be beyond his means, would it?
Making for the surgery, he could see that any garden Fairlie
House possessed must lie to the rear; at the front there was only
a short drive and a gravelled forecourt. A large group of elms
stood behind it, at present bare, with rooks' nests high in the
branches; when they were in full leaf, the trees would form a
softening backdrop to the not-very-attractive house. A big place
for an unmarried man living on his own, thought Reardon,
reminded of what Kate Ramsey had written in her diary about
Gerald Fairlie's devotion to the young woman, Carey Brewster.

That a humble country doctor should occupy such a house
didn't surprise him as much as it might have done if Flo Parslowe,
the Fox's large and cushiony landlady (a tribute to her own
cooking) hadn't enjoyed a bit of gossip as much as she enjoyed
her own renowned fidget pie. Last night, the half-dozen regulars
to the pub had been happy to find a new source of entertainment
in visitors willing to listen to chapter and verse about the area,
its traditions, shortcomings and its characters. After they'd all
departed homewards, he and Gilmour had sat with Fred Parslowe
and his wife around the dying fire, nursing a last drink, and been
regaled with the further history of most of those who lived in
Hinton.

The Fairlies, it seemed, had been around this part of the world
since the first of them had come over with William the Conqueror,
or very soon after. At any rate, the name in one form or another
– Ferrelys, de Ferelye, Faireleigh, among other variations –
appearing in memorials and brasses in the church and on the
churchyard tombstones, went back to Norman times. Yet the last
of them, Gerald, chose not to live as unofficial lord of the manor,
but earned his living working as the local doctor.

'You munna think worse on him for that,' Fred Parslowe had
suddenly commented, a man of few words who had hitherto left
the conversational ball to be kept rolling by his wife, which she
was more than capable of doing. 'Even though he be a Fairlie.'

'Now, Fred.' Flo turned to the others. 'He means they weren't

all they should have been, some of them Fairlies.' But it was late
by then and she hadn't been willing to expand on that. She had
begun gathering up glasses and casting glances at the clock.
Reardon would have been interested to hear more, but he wasn't
averse to taking the hint. It had been a long day, with no prospect
of a shorter one to follow.

He had made an appointment to see the doctor before his
morning rounds and was greeted immediately he entered the
premises by an untidy, middle-aged woman wearing a white
overall and a bothered expression, who popped her head around
a door marked 'Dispensary' as he entered the waiting room.
'Doctor's ready to see you,' she announced, and took it on herself
to add, 'but you'll have to be quick, he's a busy man.'

Reardon was no stripling himself, but Fairlie matched him for
weight and height. Perhaps only a little over forty, but looking
older. Light-haired, with a not particularly handsome face, a
strong nose, a long upper lip. The last scion of the Fairlies looked
as though he'd be more at home riding in a point-to-point, or on
the back of a hunter, but he came with all the country doctor
accoutrements: tweeds, pipe clenched between his teeth and a
firm handshake. He was unsmiling but his eyes were quick and
intelligent.

He spoke with slight impatience, a busy, practical man with
no time to waste, a little guarded and stiff. After the first moments
he became more willing to talk, though whatever he was feeling
about the gaffe he'd made over Penrose Llewellyn's death he
wasn't showing it. 'The night before, I'd become rather concerned
about him. He sounded chesty and looked flushed, which I put
down to all the drama and so forth following the announcement
he'd just made to his family . . . You know about him and
Mrs Douglas, I take it?' he asked abruptly.

'That they were to be married? Yes.'

'Would have been a very good thing, for both of them. She's
a brick, Anna.' He paused to knock out the ash from his cold
pipe. 'Well, anyway, I went upstairs with him and gave him the
once-over and there seemed nothing a good night's rest wouldn't
put right. He was fine when I left him, advising him to get straight
to bed. One can never be a hundred per cent certain, of course
. . . It could have happened at any time, yet he could have gone

on for years, if he'd been careful to avoid stress, excitement, overexertion. But it seemed as though the previous evening had been too much for him, after all.'

'Did you happen to notice if he had his medication by his bedside before you left that night?'

'The amyl nitrate?' He gave Reardon a sharp look. 'No, I can't swear to that. But I can tell you it definitely wasn't there when I returned in the morning, which made it fairly evident that was why he'd died. Perhaps I should have questioned why it wasn't there – Anna's quite right about Pen being careful always to have it by him – but people tend to be forgetful, especially if their minds are full of other things, which no doubt his was. I was also rushed at the time, anxious to get back to a very difficult birth I'd left when I was summoned to Bryn Glas, where there was a very real danger to the mother.' He paused. 'In fact, I made a few rather short remarks about Pen's carelessness with his medication, which I'm exceedingly sorry for now.' Reardon liked him for having the guts to admit that. The call for a post-mortem must have shaken him. 'I should have known him better,' he finished abruptly.

'How well did you know him?'

'Known him all my life. Him, and all the Llewellyns. The older ones weren't my generation, of course, but age differences don't matter so much as you get older. Since Pen came back here to live permanently and I became his doctor, we'd become very good friends.' His face looked drawn. 'Perhaps the best friend I've ever had,' he added quietly.

'What sort of man was he? Unbiased opinion?'

He thought about it for a moment, tapping the stem of his now empty pipe against his teeth. 'They say he'd been a bit wild when he was a lad, but that's not so unusual, is it? He was generally a good sort, good company, generous, very hospitable – and good-hearted, too. He sat with one of my patients, old Mrs Brewster, many a time so that her daughter, Carey, could have a break, and there's not many would have done that, believe me. Off the record, Muriel Brewster could be a malicious old trout when she wanted to be, I'm afraid.' His eyes had softened at the mention of Carey's name. 'But Pen? Well, for all that, he was a human being like the rest of us, he had his faults. And his share of the Llewellyn temper. He was inclined to manipulate people, too. By that I mean if things – and people – were not going the way he thought they should, he arranged it so that they were.'

'People including his family?'

'Too true, I'm afraid. As far as I'm aware, he never directly referred to what they stood to gain on his death, but they must have known. Hence their deference to him. That isn't to say they kowtowed exactly, but they usually managed to find it convenient to fall in with his wishes.' He stopped abruptly. 'I've said too much.'

'Do you believe any of them capable of killing him, Dr Fairlie?'

He suddenly stood up and walked to the window. The room seemed all at once smaller. Yet for such a big man he moved easily, quietly even, as he marshalled his thoughts. He would be a good man to have about the place in a time of illness – a quietly dependable, reassuring presence. Practical, unimaginative maybe, but the sort who got on with a sometimes difficult job without fuss. He sighed as he resumed his chair. 'We both know, in our professions, don't we, that you can never know what anyone is capable of, until it comes to the sticking point? Yes, of course, I've come across cases like this before. You, too, I dare say. We know what can happen when a wife or a husband just can't take it any more – a moment when someone decides to put an end to the suffering caused by an agonizing, terminal illness. A baby born not as it should be, an old person who's lived too long and is in the way. Thankfully it's rare enough.'

How often had he turned a blind eye in those cases? Was he saying he'd done so this time? Professing to have seen nothing that would prevent him signing the death certificate with a clear conscience? But he'd known that Penrose Llewellyn hadn't been a burden – to himself or anyone.

'Are they what you'd call a close family?' Reardon's opinions about that were his own, and best kept to himself, considering what they were, but he wanted to hear what Fairlie would have to say about the Llewellyns.

Again the doctor took his time in answering. 'They were most of them grown up before I got around to noticing such things, but from what I gathered from my father, Pen and Theo used to be very close.'

'Used to be?'

'It's all water under the bridge now, of course, but . . . I believe Cora, Pen's wife, was originally engaged to Theo. She chose to marry Pen, however, instead. I suppose he was always a charismatic character and Theo . . . well, you've seen Theo. Cora was probably swept off her feet.'

'It didn't cause a rift?'

'Not permanently. In fact, it was Pen who baled Theo out later when he got himself into a spot of trouble.'

'That usually means money trouble.'

'So it was, I believe. Expensive wife. Living beyond their means. The usual story. Thought he was marrying into money when he married Claudia, baronet's daughter and so on. It turned out when the baronet died he'd been in a worse case than Theo was. When Theo needed help, Pen seems to have been generous enough to forget their estrangement. Blood's thicker than water, after all.'

'And nothing so hard to swallow as gratitude?'

'Maybe. But don't forget, I only heard about all that second-hand, years later, from my father, who might, if we're being honest, have harboured certain prejudices against the family.'

'Why was that?'

Fairlie laughed shortly. 'He once had hopes himself of marrying Penrose's sister, Ida. He was a widower and more than twenty years older, so it wasn't reciprocated, more's the pity for her, because the one she eventually chose turned out to be an absolute rotter. She apparently had quite a following in her day, could have had her pick . . .' Catching Reardon's glance, he smiled slightly and added, 'She wasn't always like she is now. I don't think she was ever a beauty but that isn't always what counts, is it? And they've had a pretty rough time, she and Verity.'

'We haven't spoken to Verity yet. She doesn't appear to have recovered from being taken ill at that supper party.'

'Still? That's odd. When she ran out of the room she looked as though she was going to be sick, white as a sheet, which I put down to one glass too many.' He frowned. 'She should have recovered from a hangover by now.'

'I dare say she just doesn't want to talk to us. We have that effect on people,' Reardon said drily. 'We'll see her sooner or later. So, they seem to have been a quarrelsome lot at one time, the Llewellyns . . . what can you tell me about that row between Theo and the younger brother, Huwie?'

'The prodigal son? Yes, there was some sort of bother, I believe, while I was away at medical school. Can't help you there.' He shrugged. 'Huwie appears to have knocked them all sideways with his sudden reappearance. Especially since he hasn't evidenced anything in the way of money, a settled life, or family of his own.'

'He told us he was unmarried.'

The doctor lifted an eyebrow. 'So he says. I always had the impression he was . . . not the marrying kind.'

Reardon tried to recall whether this had occurred to him but all Huwie had left behind had been an impression of general unsavouriness.

As police, they weren't allowed to own up to that thing known as intuition, even when it was called sixth sense. But they could have gut feelings, that told them when something didn't smell right and Reardon was getting it right now. Something that he'd failed to grasp, and now was gone. Some dark thought that wasn't going to rest until it was caught and pinned down. Unable to say what he really felt, he stood up. His time with the busy doctor had run out. Fairlie's level-headed opinions on the other party guests might be useful to have, but that would have to wait.

'I've taken up enough of your time, doctor, but there's just one more thing before I go. You would be the last of the guests to leave that night?'

'Yes, they'd all – apart from the family, of course – set off for home by the time I came downstairs, but I wasn't long in following and in actual fact caught them up. Mrs Knightly couldn't wait to lock up after me. Dead on her feet, I suppose, poor old duck.'

'Thank you for being so frank with me.' Reardon stood up and they shook hands before he left.

TWELVE

The look on the gaffer's face as he'd gazed after that disappearing motorbike didn't bode well, and as Gilmour made his way down to Bryn Glas after speaking briefly with Jack Douglas, he was still thinking about it, knowing Reardon's wife was on the receiving end. He thought a lot of Ellen Reardon. He thought even more of Reardon, though, enough to fight with him on the barricades: it had been Gilmour's ambition to be made up to detective ever since he entered the Force, and it was Reardon who'd had faith in him, made that possible and been his mentor ever since. He was a decent bloke, if he had a fault it was that he kept his cards too close to his chest. He wasn't always easy to read and . . . there was no denying he could be, well, intimidating, on rare occasions. Not furiously angry, but a bit deadly all the same. Never to his wife, though, Gilmour was sure. He would have said they were the best-adjusted couple he knew. All the same . . . his motorbike! It was a brave woman who'd dare to do what she'd done.

Putting these thoughts aside as he reached the house, he went along to the office that was now their base, bracing himself to search the contents of that enormous double-sided desk. It wasn't a task he was looking forward to, but when he enquired for the keys, he discovered they couldn't be located. Nor could any of Pen's other keys be found, for that matter. It didn't seem to have occurred to anyone before that they were missing. Mrs Knightly, when consulted, was very much concerned that when she and Anna Douglas had undertaken the miserable task of sorting out his clothes, the key ring may have been left in a suit pocket. If so, they'd been dispatched to the church jumble sale, along with all the rest of his belongings. She was mortified. She could have sworn they had gone through the pockets very carefully before parcelling everything up and, intent on proving to herself that she hadn't made a mistake, she announced she'd be off directly to see the churchwarden's wife, who stored jumble donations until the next sale, which fortunately wasn't due for several weeks.

'Isn't there a spare key?' Gilmour asked, but no, it seemed not. Or if there was, no one knew where it was kept. He eyed the desk speculatively. He'd already tried several of the keys on the extensive bunch he routinely carried, but had found none that fitted. He had his pocket knife and wasn't above picking a lock, but he decided that in this case the action wouldn't be well received.

'Miss Bannerman will probably know,' Theo, who had appeared during the search, announced belatedly.

'Miss Bannerman, who's she?'

'She was Pen's secretary. There hasn't been any need for her to come in, of course, not since he died, but she's probably still in Hinton.'

'Does she have a telephone?' he asked, before remembering the dearth of them in Hinton.

Mrs Knightly looked slightly scandalized. 'She does not.'

'Right. Give me her address, then, and I'll go and see her.' There was nothing else he could do until those drawers were open.

'Prue will go,' Mrs Knightly stated. 'She knows her way and she'll be there and back in a jiffy.'

'No need to take her from her duties,' Theo offered surprisingly. 'I'll take a walk up there myself.' He didn't at all look the sort to take walks, but his saturnine face gave no indication that it would be a penance on such a lousy morning. Perhaps he was glad of any pretext to get out of Bryn Glas for a while.

The rain, however, had now eased off and Gilmour, left cooling his heels, decided he needed a smoke and maybe a look-see around the outside of the property, for which so far there'd been no opportunity.

Bryn Glas sat on a wide natural plateau, a parcel of land scooped out of the side of the hill, at a point high above the river. Behind the hill the land rose even higher to the moors, the great windy spaces of heathland, where the undulating countryside became wilder, rockier and even dangerous at times, littered with disused quarry workings, they'd been told by those old codgers in the Fox last night. A great outcrop to the east was a place of cliffs, caves and precipitous drops down to the river. Reardon had pricked his ears up when told the area was great for walking, if you were careful, and Gilmour himself might have found some appeal in that, yesterday, with the sun out, giving a warm glow to the dying heather and bracken in the distance. Today, the aspect against the cold, colourless sky was bleak. He finished his cigarette and turned his back on it. It made you almost homesick for Dudley.

Not wanting to think too much about home and start himself worrying about Maisie, so near her time, he walked round the side of the house towards the back, where the view was less grim. Given the hilly terrain, Bryn Glas's sheep-farming history wasn't any surprise, and although it hadn't been a farm for decades now, various long-disused buildings in a poor state of repair still stood about on the periphery, presumably waiting for demolition in this new garden scheme there was so much talk about.

The kitchen was situated in the opposite wing to the office, and as he turned the corner of the house, through the open door on to the flagstones gushed the contents of a bucketful of soapy water. He stepped back hastily, though not in time to avoid a copious dousing of his beautifully polished shoes.

'Oh, rats, I didn't know anyone was there!' It was Prue, drying her wet hands on the sacking apron she wore over her white one. 'I'm ever so sorry, your shoes are wet through. Come inside and I'll dry them for you.'

He could see she'd spread newspapers over the red, quarry-tiled floor she'd just finished washing. 'Just bring me a rag or something out here, that'll do. Don't want to spoil your clean floors.'

'No, come in,' she insisted, 'there's nobody here but me. Let me give you a cup of tea to make up.'

He stepped inside, careful to tread only on the newspapers. She produced a piece of old towelling and would have dried his shoes off herself if he hadn't stopped her. Luckily, the water hadn't reached his socks. 'No harm done,' he said with a grin when he'd finished with his shoes, 'that's why I keep 'em well polished. Helps to waterproof them, see?'

She smiled, moving efficiently about the kitchen and quickly

producing tea which she poured into two blue-ringed white mugs.
'Like a biscuit to go with it?'

'Er, no thanks. I've not long had breakfast.'

'Oh, right. You're staying at the Fox, aren't you? You won't
be hungry then.' She glanced at the big, loudly ticking clock,
hesitated, then joined him at the table, pushing the sugar bowl
across.

'Don't let me stop you from your work.'

'That's all right. I reckon I'm due a sit down,' she said collect-
edly. 'All these folk in the house, everything upside down, it's
keeping us on the go.'

'Have you worked here long, Prue?'

'Three years, since I left school.' She stirred her tea. 'It's not
much of a job, I know. Our Elsie's left home and works in an
office in Birmingham, has her own flat and all, but my mother's
not all that strong and she needs help with the little 'uns. My
dad was gassed in the war and can't work much, and my brother
– well, he's clever and he'll be off soon, so they need my bit of
money—' She broke off, flushing. 'Well, that's how it is.'

He wondered what Maisie, and Ellen Reardon, both of them
ardent on the subject of women's emancipation, would have had
to say about the future for a bright, intelligent girl such as she
seemed to be. She was a nice looking lass of about seventeen
who got on with her work and didn't say much and he guessed
it was rare for her to confide in anyone as she had just done.
The flush of embarrassment had deepened. She was annoyed
with herself, surprised at what had come over her.

He helped her out. 'It must be a difficult time altogether,
here in the house. Everyone seems to have been very fond of
Mr Penrose.'

'He was a lovely man. I can't bear to think of him dying . . .
especially like they say he did. It's awful. He was really looking
forward to his birthday, you know – and then he never got to
enjoy it. The last time I spoke to him was that afternoon. He was
asking after my dad. I was busy, what with the supper party that
night, but he made me sit down and tell me how he was. And
. . . and he gave me *three pounds* – made me take it.' Her eyes
filled with tears.

'It's a nice memory to have of him,' he said gently. 'And from what I can gather, he did enjoy the first part of his celebrations, that supper. I'm sure he appreciated how hard you'd all worked over it.'

'You're right, it was hard work, rushed off our feet we were, without—'

'Without what?'

'Oh,' she said, blushing again, 'oh, nothing. It was all such a palaver, that's all. I didn't get to go home till after eleven.' She lived in one of the little streets off the Townway and would have had to walk.

'Alone? That's a long way to walk, in the dark.'

She shrugged. 'Never measured it. Any road, I used the back lane, and it cuts a big corner off.'

That dark, tree-lined lane. A seventeen-year-old girl. A possible murderer hanging about! 'Weren't you scared?'

'No. Why should I be?' She laughed at his townie sensibilities, making him feel a right softie.

'Well,' she said, 'this isn't getting the baby bathed, so if you've finished your tea . . .' He had, and she picked the mugs up, took them to the sink and turned on the tap to rinse them.

'Thank you for the tea, Prue. I'd better get back to my work, too. I think I've just heard the inspector.'

As he left the kitchen, he wondered what it was she was keeping back.

There was no sign yet of either Theo or Mrs Knightly with the keys, but Reardon had arrived, acting as if events in his personal life had never intervened.

'His secretary probably knows where the desk key is,' Gilmour told him. 'She hasn't been in since Pen died but she only lives a few minutes away and Theo's gone for her.'

'Secretary? What did he want with a secretary if he was retired from business?'

'Nominally retired, from what everyone says. Seems he was the sort that doesn't know when to pack it in.'

Ten minutes later, the secretary arrived. Gilmour, who for some reason had expected a staid person of mature years, was somewhat taken aback to see the laughing girl who had nearly fallen into the shop doorway with the dog the day before. The yellow coat had been exchanged for a more sober-coloured one of olive green, but her hat was a flame-coloured cloche, decorated with ruched velvet, fashioned on one side into a huge, double rosette. Her vivid face, framed with tendrils of dark hair, peeped out between the coat's huge fur collar. She wore a matching lipstick that accentuated a pale skin, echoed by the vibrant red of her nails. 'Miss Bannerman?' he asked, still not quite believing in her as a secretary.

'Sadie Bannerman. Yes, that's me.'

'Detective Sergeant Gilmour. And this is Detective Inspector Reardon.'

Reardon indicated the chair that stood on the opposite side of the desk. Shrugging off her coat, she arranged herself on the seat, crossing legs clad in flesh-coloured silk. The would-be sober coat concealed a wool dress of the same colour, worn with two long strings of large, coloured beads, a matching, chunky bracelet and a scarf of many colours draped fashionably, if precariously, from one shoulder. Tossing it back, she gave Gilmour a curious glance. 'I've seen you somewhere before, haven't I?'

'When you passed me yesterday afternoon with your Jack Russell.'

'Oh, Lord, yes, sorry about that – I nearly knocked you over, didn't I? But Tolly's not mine. He belongs to the shop owner. I walk him for Adrian, though it's a moot point as to who's exercising who.' She smiled, brilliantly. 'That dog, you won't be surprised to learn, is a real handful.'

'I noticed that.'

Gilmour had also noticed the sign over the shop: Adrian Murfitt, bookseller. Presumably people in Hinton read just as much as people elsewhere but given the size of the place, a bookshop, standing out like a sore thumb amid the town's few utilitarian shops, was surprising, to say the least. Trade could hardly have been brisk.

'How long have you worked for Mr Llewellyn, Miss Bannerman?' Reardon began when they were all seated and Gilmour had his notebook out.

'Only a few months . . . well, nearly four, actually.' She was well spoken, confident enough to take out a lacquered cigarette case and a lighter, though she left the case on the desktop, unopened. 'And I would have been leaving by Christmas, anyway, even if . . . if this hadn't happened. It was never meant as a long-term appointment, you know.'

'Why was that?'

'He was getting rid of most of the business interests he still had, which actually meant quite a lot of work, though I'm quite sure he could have coped himself with what there was to do. He'd probably have preferred it, as a matter of fact,' she said with a little laugh. 'But he'd been persuaded to employ me because he was supposed to be taking life more easily. To be truthful, I suspect he was finding that much harder than working.'

'Oh yes, these work obsessives,' agreed Reardon, the corners of his mouth turning down.

Rich, thought Gilmour, hiding a grin, considering Reardon's own tendencies when he had his teeth into something.

'Well, yes, I suppose you could say he was one of those – but he didn't expect everyone else to be. It's all too awful, all this, isn't it? I'd known him such a short time but I liked him terrific-ally, you know, liked working for him, which you can't say for every boss! He was kind to me. I was in need of somewhere to live when I started here and would you believe, he let me rent a dear little house, one of several he owned in Hinton. It was in a frightfully bad state, but he had it repainted and no end of other things done as well, before I moved in.'

An almost unreadable expression crossed her face. If he'd been pressed to name it, Reardon would have said it was guilt, though it was puzzling why Sadie Bannerman should feel guilty because her new employer had been kind to her.

'Well. Now I'm here, how can I help?' she asked, impatiently adjusting the wayward scarf that would insist on detaching itself from its uncertain position on her shoulder. 'I haven't known what to do since he died, but Mr Llewellyn – Mr Theo – thinks I should try to carry on where we'd left off.'

'Well, for a start, we need to see what's in the safe, and in this desk here, but we haven't been able to locate a key.'

'It was kept on his key ring.'

'Which nobody seems to know the whereabouts of at the moment.'

'Oh? Oh, well, that's no problem. There's a spare one here,

just in case . . .' She jumped up and danced over to the book-shelves, fished about in a tobacco jar that had appeared to contain nothing more than paper clips and elastic bands, and produced a small key from the bottom. 'Voilà!'

She handed it to Gilmour, wafting a breath of whatever sweet-sharp perfume it was she wore. 'This opens the top drawer on each side of the desk, which releases all the others. Business things this side – personal details the other.'

'What about the safe? Is there a spare for that as well?'

'Not much point in locking a safe if you have another hanging around, is there?' she remarked astutely. 'The desk's different. There's nothing all that private kept in there. He was the only one who ever used the safe, anyway, so I expect that's on his ring as well.'

Gilmour pushed the key she'd produced into the lock of the top desk drawer. It slid open sweetly, as did the others when he tried them one by one.

'Are you going to go through everything?' Yes, they were. Looking for what? They wouldn't know until they found it. 'You'll have your work cut out, I warn you, sorting it all out. There's simply masses.'

'In that case, Miss Bannerman,' said Reardon, 'it would be helpful if you could arrange to be here with Sergeant Gilmour when he begins.'

'I thought you might say that.' She laughed, dimpling at Gilmour, wasting it on the devoted father-to-be had she known. He was in fact wondering why this laugh was so different to the one he'd noticed before – that one of pure fun at the absurdity of being dragged along by such a small but exuberant dog, this one with something . . . well, almost calculated about it.

'Then I suggest you make a start now, if it's convenient,' Reardon said drily, watching her and wondering whether Pen Llewellyn hadn't, perhaps, been a dark horse, whether he'd hired this exotic bird of paradise – and what a flutter among the drab little sparrows she must have caused when she alighted here, in humdrum Hinton! – entirely for her secretarial skills. 'All right, sergeant?'

'Yes, sir.' Gilmour wasn't too successful at hiding his gloom. It wasn't the expected dullness of it he minded. Dullness was part and parcel of the job, the boring duties, the drudgery of being the junior officer on the case, the one whose fate it always was to get the mucky end of the stick. 'We've all been through it, lad,' was what he'd have been told if he'd complained. But as far as he was concerned, paper-sorting wasn't being a detective, or not the side of it he enjoyed. All right, it had to be done, but out of all the chores it fell to his lot to do, this was the one he hated more than most. Looking for needles in haystacks. Papers that usually meant nothing, except to the deceased, which in itself could be heart-rending: precious photographs, old theatre programmes that had marked some treasured memory, invitations, birthday cards, love letters. Anna Douglas and Mrs Knightly had rightly been anxious to get rid of painful reminders: it was no fun, weeks, perhaps months later, coming unexpectedly across some poignant reminder of the dead person you had loved, though more were probably here, in this desk.

'Then I'll leave you to it,' Reardon said. 'But first, Miss Bannerman, tell me about this supper party the night Mr Llewellyn died. Were you there?'

'Me? Lord, no! It was just family and a few friends.'

'Then you wouldn't have known what it was set up for, that he intended to make an announcement to his family?'

'That he was going to marry Anna Douglas? No.'

Reardon threw her a sharp look. 'But you're aware that they were?'

'Hinton Wyvering is a very small place, inspector, as well as being extremely dull, I'm afraid. It didn't take me long to learn you can't blow your nose at one end of the town without the other half knowing. They call it being friendly.' She didn't sound as if that sort of friendship made her happy.

'You're a newcomer to Hinton, then? Not local?' he asked, voicing what he had suspected.

'I'm a Londoner. I like the bright lights.' Of course, she was one of those young flappers who'd dance the night away in jazz clubs. Fast cars and young men. A good time girl. Cocktails – and maybe more. Excitement, and maybe a little danger, would be the spice of life to her.

'So what brought you to this extremely dull little place?'

'Well, a girl has to live, you know. And the salary Mr Llewellyn was offering for a few months' work . . . why not?' She smiled again.

'I'll leave you to it, then.'

Reardon crossed the room and opened the door, not knowing who was the more surprised when he found himself face to face with Anna Douglas, with her hand raised at that identical moment to knock on the door. They both stepped back a pace, but she recovered quickly. 'Oh, I'm so glad you're here, Mr Reardon! Please come quickly, we're all in the back sitting room. Theo thinks you should know . . .' She was obviously agitated. 'It's Verity. She seems to have disappeared.'

A long passage ran the length of the house, windowed on one side. The plaster infill between the oak beams on the opposite side had been removed, which gave a little more light to the dark rooms behind, if less privacy. Strains of melancholy, Russian sounding piano music drifted along as they approached the room used as a sitting room. He was surprised to see it was Theo who was seated at a piano that took up too much space in such a small room, but he ceased playing and swung round on the stool as Reardon came in. Why hadn't anyone stopped him before? It was the sort of music guaranteed to get on nerves which were on edge to begin with. All of them except Ida were lounging in various poses around the room, the air thick with smoke. She was standing in front of the window, gazing out, left arm crossed tightly across her chest, supporting her other elbow. From her fingers descended one of her black cigarettes, smoked almost to the gold filter tip.

'There was no need to have brought you into this, inspector,' she announced sharply, turning round as Reardon entered. 'Verity hasn't *disappeared*. All this fuss over nothing – it's just being paranoid.' She cast a venomous glance at Theo. 'She's just taken her car and gone off for a spin without letting anyone know, that's all. Thoughtless, as usual.'

'And taken all her things with her, clothes, everything, including Mr Fred?' asked Claudia, raising her eyebrows.

'Mr Fred?' For a second, the stout, unlikely figure of Fred Parslowe flashed before Reardon's eyes.

'He's a frog,' said Ida.

A Frog? A Frenchman?

'A stuffed animal, Mr Reardon,' Claudia supplied, rolling her eyes.

'She's had him since she was three,' Ida said. 'She calls him her mascot and he's scarcely out of her sight. She takes him to bed and puts him on the dashboard of her car every time she goes out, so it's only to be expected he's with her now.' With an impatient gesture, she stubbed out her cigarette. She seemed determined to play down her daughter's disappearance, but a strained look in her eyes belied it, and her hand shook a little as she fumbled to light yet another Sobranie. 'She is so thoughtless,' she snapped, tightness masking the attitude of a very worried mother.

'Why do you insist on thinking she's only doing this to annoy you?' Theo demanded, his eyes narrowed. 'Anyone would think you didn't know full well the tiresome child's taken herself off rather than being kept cooped up here, like the rest of us.'

'Good for her if she has.' Huwie was lolling in an armchair, one leg draped over the arm. 'If I had a motor I dare say I'd have done the same before now,' he added flippantly. Today he looked almost presentable. He'd exchanged his cheap suit-jacket for a sweater, and someone, Mrs Knightly no doubt, had washed and neatly ironed his shirt, and while they were at it sewed on a missing button.

Like all the other rooms in the house, this was comfortable, normally tidy and well kept, with its deep armchairs and soft rugs covering most of the stone floor. Smelling of burning apple wood, and the dry scent of old timbers. Now, used coffee cups still stood around and the ashtrays were full. The level of the bottles on the silver tray on the side table had gone down considerably. The room was in a mess that must be irritating Mrs Knightly no end, Reardon thought, glancing at the half-read books, an open cribbage board and decks of cards that were being used to pass the time and contributing to the general clutter. Scattered over chairs and parts of the floor were newspapers, one of them the local weekly, open at a half-page obituary for Mr Penrose Llewellyn, with a picture of him cutting a ribbon at the opening of the new housing estate he'd been instrumental in getting built. It wasn't going to take long for it to become known that his death had been due to something more sinister than a mere heart attack, when it would become front page news – and not only on this paper. And he, Reardon, would be expected to conduct an orderly investigation, with half the press at his heels everywhere he went.

He eased a finger round his collar. He was finding the atmosphere in here unpleasant, claustrophobic. The linenfold panelling on the fireplace wall, though finely carved and no doubt highly regarded, was of dark oak that absorbed the light. With all the cigarette smoke, it was unbearably stuffy. As if reading his thoughts, Claudia rose in a movement graceful in such a big woman, sailed majestically across the room and with a sweeping gesture threw open one of the windows. Ida shivered theatrically and moved away as the cold air rushed in, but she didn't object.

'So when did you last see your daughter, Mrs Lancaster?'

'Last night, at supper. She didn't come down for breakfast but that's nothing. Since Pen . . . she's taken to her room and only comes down for meals and then goes straight back again – not that she eats anything to speak of, mind.'

'And now she's taken her precious little Baby Austin—' Huwie began.

Ida turned on him savagely. 'Naturally she's taken her car. But . . . oh, God, the way she's been driving lately!' Suddenly, she choked.

There was a deep, uncomfortable silence. It lasted until Claudia said, 'What about Carey?'

'Carey Brewster?' Theo looked at his wife as if the marble bust of Queen Victoria, which had stood on top of a high shelf near the fireplace for as long as any of them could remember, had suddenly given voice. 'What has she to do with it?'

'They've always seemed pretty thick to me. Isn't that so, Ida?'

'I don't think they've seen each other since Carey came home, apart from the supper party.'

Claudia explained. 'We're talking of a little friend of Pen's, Mr Reardon. She's been living in France since her mother died, wise child – it's put some polish on her. She looked positively chic at the party. We could ring up and find out whether Verity is with her.' Her face fell. 'Oh. Oh, well, of course not. Why *are* people so reluctant to have the telephone installed?'

Although she seemed today to have plumped for sounding cooperative, perhaps to relieve the boredom, Claudia was beginning to make Reardon feel tired. Couldn't she see that a telephone was a needless, unaffordable luxury to ninety per cent of the population? When would most of them have any use for such a newfangled, suspect instrument anyway – apart from the remote possibility of needing the doctor in a dire emergency? But she had at least put the excuse to leave right into his hands, plus the opportunity to kill two birds with one stone. 'Tell me where Miss Brewster lives and I'll go along and see what I can find out. But first, I'd like to take a look at Verity's room, Mrs Lancaster.'

'You won't find anything. I've told you, she's cleared everything out.' She seemed unaware of her own contradictions – the insistence that her daughter had simply gone out for a day's jaunt while in the same breath stressing that she had taken all her belongings with her.

'It won't take long. Standard procedure, I assure you.'

Ida shrugged and it was Anna Douglas who eventually led the way. 'You'll see she really has gone, Mr Reardon,' she said when they were out of the room. 'She was so fond of Pen and no one seems to have thought how upset she must be. I include myself in that. I did come here today intending to have a word with her, but I'm afraid I was too late. Poor Verity, she hasn't been very happy lately.'

'It's easy to blame ourselves after the event, Mrs Douglas. I shouldn't worry, she's sure to turn up or let you know where she is.'

'I hope so.'

Verity's room was tiny, created from a space between roof-beams that sloped right down to the floor at one point. Its redeeming feature was a pretty little dormer alcove with a cushioned seat under the window, just big enough to curl up on. The entire room and its contents could be taken in at a glance and it seemed evident that Verity had indeed deserted it – except that, when he lifted aside the curtain across the corner that served as a wardrobe, a couple of summer dresses still hung there, and a pair of sandals stood on the floor. Had she left them behind simply because they weren't the sort of clothing suitable for this time of year, or as an intent of her return?

He took a last glance around. Apple green walls, a blue and white Welsh quilt, crisp white muslin skirt around a tiny dressing table. She'd taken her stuffed frog but she'd left a teddy bear and half a dozen other stuffed animals, plus children's storybooks on the little bookshelf. And on the dormer windowsill, where they caught the light, dozens of small, oddly shaped pieces of sea-washed glass in magic colours, probably collected from long ago seaside holidays. It was a child's room. He left, wondering why Verity Lancaster, age twenty-two, did not want to grow up.

THIRTEEN

Shanks's pony again. Reardon had to admit as he walked once more uphill towards the town centre that he'd definitely underestimated the time and energy that could be wasted by to-ing and fro-ing between one house and another, even in this small place. Where you couldn't just hop on a passing bus or a tram, and where the only bicycle he'd seen – understandably, given the terrain – had been the boy wobbling along the Townway this morning. The grey, inhospitable day was getting seriously cold now that the afternoon was drawing in, and he thought he felt a touch of sleet on his face. He pulled the collar of his coat higher, lengthened his stride and reached the road called Lessings Lane in seven minutes.

It straggled off in a hairpin bend at a midway point on Nether Bank and wound its way in an equally twisting fashion up the hillside to emerge further along the Townway. Sporadic building had occurred along its length over the years, wherever there was a suitable stretch of level land. About halfway along stood a short row of modest Victorian dwellings, with no gardens, but with a view to the river valley glimpsed over the barely visible top of a retaining wall on the other side of the road. Due to the furtive nature of Verity Lancaster's disappearance, he hadn't expected to see a little Baby Austin standing parked outside Carey Brewster's door, so he wasn't disappointed to find the road empty. A baby carriage with its hood up and a sleeping baby tucked under blankets outside the first house was the only form of transport in sight. These terraced houses stood in two blocks of three with a passageway to the back between the blocks, and they weren't the sort to have garages. Small and unpretentious, respectable houses, each with a narrow window on one side of the front door, a wider one on the other. Most of them had lace curtains and paintwork that was varnished in durable if unattractive dark brown. The notable exception was the third door along, painted in a bright scarlet. What was the betting on that being one of those owned by Penrose Llewellyn, presently occupied by Sadie Bannerman?

His knock at Number Six was answered by a large, rumpled young man with untidy dark hair and enough family resemblance to Anna Douglas to proclaim him her son. 'Jack Douglas,' he said, confirming this after Reardon had introduced himself and asked for Miss Brewster. 'Carey's in here.' He had lively brown eyes and a humorous mouth. Despite his rangy and athletic build, it was noticeable that he walked with a very slight limp as he went towards a door on the right of a small hallway, where stairs rose at the end.

The young lady herself was kneeling on the floor in front of a large tin trunk from which rose a powerful smell of mothballs. She was a small, fair-haired person wrapped in an overall several sizes too big for her. She had a smut on her nose, and was nothing like the chic young woman conjured up by Claudia Llewellyn's condescending remarks, or for that matter the description of her in Kate Ramsey's journal.

Scrambling to her feet as introductions were made, she cleared a chair of a tottering pile of old framed photographs by placing them on the floor and gracefully inviting him to take a seat. 'Please excuse the muddle.' And indeed this room, evidently the parlour, was in its own way as much of a mess as the one he'd just left, with miscellaneous objects occupying every available surface, obscuring any impression of what the room might be like when it was tidy – except for the feeling that it would always be cold and inhospitable. 'Jack's helping me sort things out. I feel I ought to keep more than I want to throw away, but I can't take it all with me,' she said rather helplessly.

'You're going away?'

'Yes. My mother died recently, you see, and I've been living in France for the last three months. But I shan't be staying. I'm leaving Hinton.'

'We're both leaving,' said Jack, who had perched himself rather elegantly on the edge of the central table. 'Me, as soon as this pesky leg of mine lets me, and Carey when she's sold the house. I'm off to wherever I'm sent and Carey to parts unknown.'

This somewhat cryptic remark was received in silence. Carey picked out what looked like a pair of very old curtains from the trunk and began to unfold them. Suddenly, with a look of distaste, she crammed them back, shut the lid and rubbed her fingers together. 'None of this stuff needs keeping. I'm tempted to just leave it, and everything else, close the door and walk away. In actual fact,' she went on, addressing Reardon and not looking at Jack, 'my destination isn't unknown. I'm going back to stay with my friends in Paris until I find some sort of job. Which might take some time, considering I'm not trained for anything.'

'I've told her it's too soon to be making decisions, but the lady's too stubborn to listen.'

'And I've told him,' she answered rather coolly, 'there's nothing for a dreary old spinster like me here in Hinton.' She smiled very slightly, but there was a subtext going on here beneath the presumably friendly sparring passing between these two. Despite the smut on her nose, she was really very pretty, quick and active in her movements, and couldn't possibly have been the wrong side of thirty. A gently spoken young woman with soft fair hair that fell in a bell around her face. The dark, smoky-blue eyes that Kate had mentioned were indeed beautiful. 'Look, Mr Reardon, we were just going to stop for a cup of tea,' she said. 'Will you join us?' He said he'd like that very much. 'Or coffee? I've got rather good at coffee lately.'

'Coffee it is then.'

She went out and across the passage, leaving the door open. Still perched on the table, Jack's eyes followed her.

'You have an interesting career, Mr Douglas, I'm told.'

'I suppose I do. No – correction – I know I do, and a lot of people out there who might envy me. Lots of travel, doing what I most want to do and getting paid for it. That can't be bad.'

He smiled, showing very white teeth. 'But at the moment I've mucked things up a bit. Fell off a mountain ledge in China, being too impetuous. Reaching out too far for a specimen before I thought about the risk. Stupid. Meanwhile, I've been helping my mother a bit, and writing up my notes, plus a few articles, but to tell the truth I'm getting restless. Trouble is, this damned leg is taking too long. The medics tell me I'm too impatient, but to hell with all that.'

Reardon made sympathetic noises. He'd been through it himself, with the difference that Jack Douglas's problems appeared to be merely physical. But when you're an active young man, the time taken for recuperation after any sort of accident isn't easy, especially when you blame yourself for it.

Carey put a head round the door and announced the coffee was ready. 'Let's have it in the living room – it's a bit tidier, and certainly warmer.'

Warmth and tidiness were surely its only attributes. Small and cramped, it was indelibly stamped with the decorating tastes of thirty years ago, probably furnished when Mrs Brewster had come here as a bride. Although a cheerful fire was going in the black iron range, the place was depressingly dark, the narrow window facing the street being the only source of light. The impression of dinginess wasn't helped by a wallpaper that had faded into an overall muddy yellow, and doors and cupboards painted the same serviceable dark brown as the outside of the house. It struck Reardon that Carey Brewster was to be congratulated for wanting to shut the door on all this and start a new life. She showed spirit beneath that soft, pliant exterior. Not many a modern young miss would have put up with it for a minute, never mind for as long as she apparently had, he thought, recalling Dr Fairlie's remarks about the regular tyrant Muriel Brewster had been.

When they were seated at a central table covered with dreary maroon chenille, she poured coffee. 'Have a macaroon, they're home-made.' She pushed the sugar across to Jack. 'You want to ask us about that night at Bryn Glas, don't you?'

'I know from Sergeant Bridgstock over at Castle Wyvering that you've already given preliminary statements and it's tedious to go over them, but I'm afraid it can't be helped and since you were both among the last to see Mr Llewellyn before he died, it would be useful to have your impressions. I believe my sergeant's already spoken to you, Mr Douglas?' Jack nodded.

'Were you surprised at the announcement Mr Llewellyn made?'

'That Anna and he were to be married?' Carey answered. 'In a way, yes – but everyone was.'

'Except me,' Jack remarked. 'My mother had already told me. Naturally, she didn't want to spring that sort of news on me with all his family present.'

'That's understandable. How did you view the prospect?'

'Did it matter what I thought? It was right for them and that was the only thing that counted. The only surprise was that it had taken so long.' He met Reardon's glance. 'All right then, might as well say it as think it,' he said, rather less cool. 'She was nervous about that evening, which should have been a very happy affair but . . . That family – two-faced, every one of them, pretending to be pleased when anyone could see they were anything but. Terrified my mother would persuade him to change his will in her favour. I wouldn't put anything past any of them.'

'Including Pen?'

'Pen was—'

'Pen wasn't like that,' interrupted Carey, whose colour had risen.

'What they haven't the wit to see is that she's supported herself – and me – for many years, and if she'd been that way inclined, she could have found herself a husband before now willing to keep her. Or even relied on me if necessary.'

He drained his coffee in one gulp, then shoved his hands deep in his pockets and thrust out his legs, though he winced a little.

'The thing is, Mr Reardon, Jack's right. They weren't pleased at the news. To be honest, I felt we were in two camps that night – Pen's friends, and his family. I don't include Verity. She didn't join in or say anything, not a word. But that's because she wasn't well that night.'

'Yes, I've been told about that. She was attached to Mr Llewellyn, I believe?'

'We all were,' she said, with a slight hesitation. 'Of course, we saw the best of him . . . they say he was tough in his business, and he wasn't always easy, I have to admit. He liked to rule the roost a bit, you know?'

'In the nicest possible way, of course,' Jack added. She looked at him reproachfully, but he was smiling.

'He could be very kind, as well, you know.'

Reardon came back to the breaking-up of that supper party. It added nothing new to the statements already made but he heard them out. 'All right, that seems satisfactory.' Shutting his notebook, he remarked casually, 'By the way, you don't happen to have seen Miss Lancaster today, do you, Miss Brewster?'

'Verity? No, why? Is anything wrong?'

'Only that no one seems to have seen her since yesterday evening. She didn't put in an appearance at breakfast and they're a bit worried. They seemed to think since you were good friends you might know where she is.'

'Well, she hasn't been here,' Carey said. 'Yes, we are good friends – whenever she comes to stay in Hinton, that is. But I haven't seen her since that supper, and for ages before that, me being away. I hope she hasn't been taken ill somewhere – I must say she did look pretty rotten that night. She really was pale as anything, and on edge, and she had to leave the table, though Mrs Ramsey made sure she was all right.' She was beginning to look worried herself. 'Perhaps I ought to have left all this sorting out here and gone up to Bryn Glas to see her, but I would have thought visitors were the last thing they wanted at the moment.'

'I think it's unlikely she's ill. She's taken her motor car.'

'Oh, goodness, you don't think she could have had an accident?' But straight away she shook her head. 'No, it's silly to think that, she's a good driver.'

Reardon didn't want to alarm her further by reminding her that it took two to make an accident, but Jack remarked laconically, 'Not recently, she isn't. She careered past me the other day going like a bat out of hell.'

Carey suddenly looked not just worried, but scared.

'Let's not start thinking that way,' Reardon said quickly. 'Since she took most of her clothes as well, it seems the intention to leave was deliberate. She's over twenty-one and if that's what she wants . . . it was a pity she didn't leave a note, but if she should get in touch with you, Miss Brewster, perhaps you'll let me know.'

'Of course I will, but it's awfully odd, you'll have to admit.'

'I don't think you've any need to worry.'

Jack said abruptly, 'Have you tried Adrian Murfitt?' Reardon looked mystified until he added, 'at the bookshop.' Then he remembered where he'd heard the name before, when Gilmour had recounted his first encounter with Sadie Bannerman.

'He and Verity have been seeing quite a bit of each other lately while you've been away, Carey,' Jack said.

'Have they?' Carey frowned. 'Are you sure? He's hardly her type – so much older for one thing.'

He raised an eyebrow. 'Well, she's certainly been useful to him. He hasn't got a decent car of his own and she's been driving him around to book sales and so on. Probably chauffeuring him somewhere even now.'

'I don't suppose anyone else would want to,' Carey replied, rather oddly.

'No.'

There was a small silence. 'May one ask why that should be?' Reardon asked.

'Poor man,' Carey said, 'it isn't really fair, after all these years.'

'True. But he was a conchie during the war, Mr Reardon, and unfortunately people don't seem to be able to forget that.'

'Won't, you mean,' said Carey.

Every town, every village in England had their share of men and boys who had given their lives for their country, and feeling had run high against conscientious objectors, known as conchies, those who had refused to take any part in the war, on religious, moral or political grounds. In a small community like Hinton, where sons had probably been lost, it was easy to see the reluctance to embrace anyone bearing that stigma.

There was a knock on the door. 'That might be Verity!' With some relief Carey hurried to answer it. But it wasn't Verity. Through the window could be seen a small boy standing outside, red-faced and sweaty, wearing a pair of trousers that had once belonged to someone much larger, the legs cut short but the crotch hanging so low it was surprising he could walk, never mind run. They heard him say, 'Miss said to bring this straight away, miss.' He had on a green woollen jersey and a knitted woollen tie, and wore a Wolf Cub cap, a sign of his trustworthiness as a letter carrier.

'Thank you, Ronnie.' Carey asked him to wait, came back to fetch him a few coppers, and then brought the letter indoors. 'It seems the wanderer's been found,' she exclaimed with relief after she'd slit the envelope open and read the short note inside. 'She's with Mrs Ramsey. Kate sent word to Bryn Glas and they told her you'd be here, inspector. She asks that you go there. Kate, I mean, not Verity.'

'Well,' Reardon said, 'I don't suppose Miss Lancaster will welcome the interference, but since I've been charged with finding her . . .'

'I'd like to see her myself,' Carey put in tentatively.

'Then if you come with me we'll pick my motor up at the Fox and I'll drive you there.' It had been a long day and he was getting fed up with hoofing it everywhere by now and he had no intention of letting slip this opportunity to talk to the uncommunicative Verity Lancaster. Perhaps she would be amenable to reason with a friend of her own age. He shrugged himself into his overcoat. 'Your stay in France wasn't wasted, Miss Brewster. The coffee was excellent. And so were the macaroons.'

'She made them herself – and that's not due to French influence. She's a dabster at baking. And she paints, too. Beautifully.'

Evidently needled, Carey retorted, 'Then no doubt *she* could always hire herself out as a cook! Or maybe a pavement artist.'

'Ouch!' Instantly, he looked contrite and put a hand on her arm. 'Sorry, Carey, dear. Bad manners, sorry. Flippancy not appropriate at the moment.'

'All right, I'm sorry too. My sense of humour seems to have gone missing, these days.'

He bent his head and planted a light, brotherly kiss on her cheek. They watched her run lightly up the stairs for her coat.

While they were waiting, Jack suddenly remarked, as if nothing had been said between the first moments of their conversation and now, 'I keep telling her not to rush her fences – Carey, I mean, but she won't listen . . . She doesn't really want to leave Hinton. She's running away, you know.'

'From what?'

'From that stuffed shirt, Doc Fairlie. And that,' he added with a mock-rueful smile, 'is something I'd no right to say. Forget I said anything, please.'

Interesting. Fairlie House in exchange for Lessings Lane? It might not be such a bad bargain at that for this young woman. Nothing further was said on the subject before Carey joined them, but while she locked the door and they all they walked along the lane, until Jack left them for his mother's house along the Townway, Reardon reflected that when women like Kate Ramsey – and his own Ellen, on occasions – accused men of being obtuse and imperceptive, they often had a point. Even an intelligent man like Jack Douglas. Perhaps he was obtuse where Carey was concerned, and maybe jealous, but he seemed to have something on his mind other than that. He was a likeable young man, but also impetuous on his own admission, and with a hearty dislike of anyone called Llewellyn, Pen perhaps not excluded.

FOURTEEN

K ate's cottage at the junction of the road to Castle Wyvering was one of only three along the lane, once tied cottages for workers at Bryn Glas when it had been a farm. The other two, she'd told Reardon, had been sold to a wealthy manufacturer from West Bromwich, who had knocked them together to form one house, and then used it only occasionally as a weekend retreat.

When they arrived, despite the fading light, she was in the garden raking leaves into a pile, a Herculean task at any time given the number of large, deciduous trees growing along the lane, and doubly so now that the leaves still littering her tiny patch of lawn were a wet, half-rotted blanket. She threw down the rake with evident relief when Reardon drew the car up.

'Don't let us interrupt, Mrs Ramsey.'

'On the contrary, you've rescued me – I'm no gardener. I was only doing this so I could catch you before you go in. Young Ronnie's earning a shilling to do it and he can finish when he comes back tomorrow. Hello, Carey. I'm so glad you've come as well.'

'Is Verity still here?' asked Carey.

'I'm afraid she is, and that's the problem. She's insisting she won't go home, and I'm so sorry, but I'm afraid it's impossible for her to stay here. Never mind whether I ought to send her straight back home anyway, in the circumstances. I've only the two small bedrooms, after all.' She had a high colour, either from her efforts with the leaves or because she was flustered, although Reardon doubted the latter; he'd had her down as the least unflappable of women. 'And of course,' she added, looking at Reardon, 'Ellen's insisting she should be the one to leave, which I really, really, can't have, and Verity saying she doesn't care if she has to sleep on the sofa.'

'Where is Ellen?'

'She's gone for a walk. She wanted to blow the cobwebs.'

'It'll do that all right, today.' He managed not to ask if his wife was warmly wrapped up and if she was wearing a scarf. He guessed she'd gone out because she was trying not to embarrass him with her presence, which was what they'd tacitly agreed on, but he'd have given a lot to have seen her, all the same.

'Go in and see if you can make the child see sense, Carey,' Kate said, 'while I have a word with Mr Reardon.'

Carey hesitated. 'I'm not sure she'll listen to me.'

'You can always try.'

'All right,' she agreed after a moment, and disappeared into the house.

Kate looked slightly distracted. 'I don't know how to deal with Verity in the mood she's in, and that's the truth. Running off like this is only making whatever it is that's bothering her much worse, though I can't get her to say what it is.'

'I've no authority to make her go back.'

'I realize that, of course, but I thought you should know she was here.' She paused. 'It was Ellen who volunteered to go down to Bryn Glas to let them know that. She spoke only to your sergeant, and instructed him *not* to tell them she has run away.'

So much for Ellen keeping her nose out of the case, however helpful it might be in this instance. 'I'm not sure that's going to fool them, especially her mother.'

'I'm not sure, either, but it'll give Verity time to think again. She'll have to go home, you know.' She frowned. 'She's dreadfully upset and I can only think it must be something that happened the night Pen died, so I thought if you can get her to talk, away from all the rest of the family . . .'

Years of experience in interviewing people who were determined not to open their mouths had given Reardon a jaundiced view of that sort of situation. Not having seen Verity yet he wasn't in a position to judge how easy or otherwise it would be in her case.

'I'm very fond of her, you know. I've known her since she was a child and . . . her attitude lately has made everyone impatient with her, but it's only an act. I think she's very unhappy, and something will have to be done about it, really it will. Be careful with her, won't you?'

He smiled at the idea that he had any choice, or indeed wish, to be anything else.

She paused to take off her gumboots before they went into the house, and he followed her as she padded into her sitting room in stockinged feet. A person he assumed was Verity, dressed entirely in shapeless dark garments, was standing at the far end, her back to the room, in the same position as her mother had stood earlier, worrying about her. She didn't turn round when they came in. Carey spread her hands in a helpless gesture that said she'd been unsuccessful in persuading Verity to see reason.

Kate said, 'Verity, this is Mrs Reardon's husband, the detective inspector. I think he'd like a word with you.'

The girl spun round. 'I won't go back!'

'Well,' Reardon answered mildly, 'the choice is yours. I haven't come to clap you in irons and force you back.'

He could discern no traces of her mother in Verity Lancaster's face. It was a rather striking one, pale but with large, hazel-green eyes, and she might have been almost beautiful, if she hadn't looked as though she was determined never to smile again. Her gaze was very clear. She immediately gained a plus point, as far as he was concerned, when she looked him directly in the face, not embarrassed or avoiding looking at his scars. The sombre clothes, he guessed, had been the nearest she could get to mourning, which was something the other women in the family hadn't been able – or maybe hadn't wanted – to achieve. 'A few words with you is all I need, Miss Lancaster.'

'Kate had no right to send for you,' she said, ungraciously in view of the fact that she was trying to persuade Kate to be her hostess. 'Because I don't have anything to tell you, despite what she says.'

'In that case, perhaps we can confine our conversation to you answering a few questions?'

'If it's about my uncle, I can't help you.' Her glance went to the other two women and she looked mulish.

'If you'd rather we weren't here,' Kate said, 'Carey can come and help me with the leaves in the garden.'

Carey looked taken aback but after a moment she said, 'Oh, yes, rather.'

As far as Reardon could estimate, there was nowhere else the two of them could go, if he and Verity were to be left alone. Apart from this living room, there was only the tiny scullery-kitchen downstairs, the extent of which could be glimpsed through its open door, too small to house even one chair. Upstairs would be the two bedrooms Kate had mentioned, both icy, he imagined, given today's temperatures.

'I don't think that will be necessary, Mrs Ramsey. I suggest you slip a coat on, Miss Lancaster, and we can take a turn outside, in the lane. We can talk as we go.' It wasn't satisfactory but he couldn't turn the other two women out.

Verity looked as though she was about to refuse. Carey went up to her and put an arm around her shoulders. 'If you don't want to go home you can come and stay with me, love. If you don't mind the mess, that is . . . I'm in a frightful muddle, sorting out all my mother's old things, that's why I haven't been to see you. But do talk to Mr Reardon first. They're going to find out the truth about your uncle, you know.'

Considering the clearing-up chaos Carey was so embroiled in, Reardon thought this was a heroic offer. And, despite herself, Verity clutched at the offer like a drowning person at a straw. 'Do you really mean that?'

'I wouldn't have said it if I didn't.'

'All right – and thanks, Carey.'

A few moments later, she had donned an old-fashioned

musquash coat that must surely have once belonged to her mother, thrust her hands into woollen gloves, and pulled a felt cloche well down on her head as extra protection. So bundled up was she that her eyes were practically all that was visible. Cold as it was, this seemed excessive; he couldn't help thinking of a furry animal trying to hide.

Once outside, she declined to take a walk and insisted they sit in her motor, a vehicle once smartly painted but now much in need of a touch up. He hesitated and suggested the police Wolseley, where there was more room, but she shook her head stubbornly. He was beginning to understand why people found it so difficult to cope with her. After a moment, he agreed, unorthodox and unsuitable as the Baby Austin was for the purpose. It wasn't known as that for nothing. Its dimensions meant being squashed too close together for comfort, or at any rate too close to be able to study her face as he attempted to draw her out. They'd have been better walking up the lane.

'What about these few questions you want to ask, then?' she asked, staring at the stuffed frog – Mr Fred presumably – which sagged on the dashboard, a small, somewhat pathetic creature after all his years of being loved. His bright green plush was worn bare in parts, one of his glass pop-eyes was missing and the stuffing seemed to have leaked from one leg. But his great wide smile had been re-embroidered in scarlet wool. She had asked the question quietly, the childish petulance abandoned now that she was faced with the inevitable. 'Why me?'

'Well, we've asked everyone else if they heard anything during the night, the night your uncle was killed. But none of them did.'

'I slept very heavily.'

'And you heard nothing? Your room isn't far from your uncle's, and it's an old house. The floorboards creak.'

'I'd taken a pill.'

'A pill? Yes, of course, you weren't well. They said you were feeling sick that night.'

'Well, they were wrong,' she answered quickly. 'I wasn't sick, I just had a splitting headache.'

This was a different version to that recorded in Kate's journal; she'd told Kate it was something she'd eaten. A headache wasn't what Dr Fairlie had thought either. 'I see. So you didn't hear anything.'

She hesitated and though he couldn't see her face the silence told him she might be calculating how to answer. In the end she said, 'Well, I went to bed and fell asleep. Then I woke up very suddenly – why, I don't know. Noises, perhaps. It flashed through my mind that something might be wrong with Uncle Pen but then I heard Dr Fairlie leaving, saying goodnight, telling him to sleep well and he'd be right as rain in the morning. After that . . . I suppose I must have fallen asleep again.'

'But you woke later and heard something again?' he hazarded.

'Yes,' she admitted at last. 'I did think I heard someone go along to the bathroom at one point. That's probably what woke me.'

'I don't suppose you noticed the time?'

'Well, after a bit I heard the clock downstairs strike three. So it must've been about then.'

'And that's all?'

She nodded without saying anything, then took her gloves off, reached out for Mr Fred and held him in both hands. Caressing the top of his almost bald head with her thumb, staring out of the windscreen, she said at last, 'I meant it when I said I'm not going back, you know. I left because I couldn't stand the atmosphere, everyone pretending to be sad about Uncle Pen, when all the time, they're rubbing their hands. I just had to get out.'

'Pack up your troubles in your old kit bag, eh?' he asked her invisible profile.

She half turned her head then, giving him a swift glance, a gleam of understanding, and a quick response: 'Well, they'll have to stay packed up, won't they, since I've nowhere to unpack them? Nobody wants to have me to stay, not even Carey, really.'

He wondered if playing the tragedy queen was part of her natural personality, or if it was just due to the present circumstances. She knew more than she was saying, that was obvious, and something was evidently troubling her deeply – more, he was inclined to think, than her unfeeling relatives. Yet, despite what she thought of them, the fact that they were all under suspicion for killing her uncle must hang heavily on her. One of them, after all, was her mother.

'Are you sure you've nothing else to tell me?'

She shook her head and stared mournfully through the windscreen. He was beginning to get cramp and there wasn't the space to stretch his long legs. 'Look, I know how you must feel about going home but,' he ventured to suggest, 'it might really be time to have another think about it.' He felt her stiffen, and added, 'It would put your mother's mind at rest, she's really quite worried about you.' She still said nothing and he wondered if he'd got through to her. 'You know, I talk to a lot of people in my job and I'm not slow when it comes to seeing people finding reasons for avoiding something they don't want to admit.'

He expected her to jump out and slam the door behind her, but she only mumbled, 'I can't go back.'

'You don't have to listen to them, your family.' She was facing him now, not turning away. Framed by the close-fitting hat, her face was sad, really sad, not the drama queen act she'd been putting on before. 'Take your time, Verity. Never make a decision in a hurry.'

He sensed, before she spoke, that she was about to give in. 'I know, really. I suppose I've got to face up to it and go back some time. But I can't do it now . . . when I said I can't, I meant it.'

'Why do you feel that?'

'It's not what I feel – I mean I can't anyway. Literally.' The corners of her mouth turned down. 'Oh, lordy, I can't even do this right, can I? The great escape foiled by . . . I should look such a fool!'

'No one ever said it was foolish to admit you're wrong.'

'I'm not saying I'm wrong – I'm saying I've run out of petrol.'

He knew he must not laugh. Humour didn't appear to be one of Verity's strong points, at any rate not at this moment. Clearly it had become more important to her that she shouldn't look ridiculous than give in. But after a minute she did begin to smile, and he saw he'd been right in what he'd thought when he first saw her. Here indeed was beauty in the making.

'I don't see any problem with that,' he said. 'I have transport here, and I'm on my way to Bryn Glas to collect my sergeant. We can bring some petrol up here later.'

'There's nothing else I can do, is there, but go back with my tail between my legs?'

'It takes courage to admit you're wrong.'

She gave another sad, tentative smile. But in those beautiful eyes he thought he still saw a shadow. She still hadn't told him the whole truth.

He went back into the cottage to report and explain the situation. 'She'll go home with me. Give her a few minutes and she'll come in to see you.'

'Before she does,' Kate said, 'there something I ought to tell you.' Carey tactfully left them, saying she would help Verity transfer her belongings from her car to Reardon's.

Kate began as soon as the door closed behind her 'This doesn't really reflect well on me as a sane, rational being, but well . . . you see, I sometimes have these . . . I imagine I see . . . someone,' she said in a rush.

Someone. He had no difficulty in understanding who she meant. Missing, presumed dead, he remembered Ellen saying. The cruellest of all outcomes, he had often thought, that allowed hope, however fragile, to persist, that a loved one might somewhere, somehow, against all odds, still be alive.

'I know worry can make the mind play tricks, and I've had a lot to think about recently . . . debating whether or not to leave here and take the position the NCW have offered me in London. But,' she went on, her voice gathering strength, 'on the night of the party, just as I was going to bed, I thought I saw this . . . person, walking along the lane. It wasn't much more than a shadow, but thinking about it, I'm sure it was someone real, not a . . . not a hallucination.'

'Could you put a name to who it was you saw?'

'I didn't see clearly enough. I wouldn't even like to say whether it was a man, or a woman. But the thing is, this lane doesn't come from anywhere except Bryn Glas . . . not unless you've walked from Wyvering, five miles away.'

Within half an hour, Carey had been deposited back at home, and Verity returned to Bryn Glas. Her mother, admirably controlled in the circumstances, was seemingly prepared to subscribe to the fiction that nothing untoward had happened, and was ignoring the suitcases which had stayed in the Wolseley until they could be carried discreetly upstairs.

Reardon left them to it and in the study found Gilmour and
Sadie Bannerman who, at last divested of the tiresome scarf, had
donned a pair of horn-rimmed, secretarial glasses, and was
demonstrating undoubted efficiency. Looking slightly punch
drunk, Gilmour exchanged who-would-have-thought-it glances
with Reardon over the neatly stacked piles of papers covering
the surface of the desk and the earnestly bent head of Miss
Bannerman.

She raised her eyes when he came in, consulted her watch and
then removed her glasses. 'Well, we've made a start, anyway,'
she said, scraping back her chair. 'So if it's all the same with
you, I'll love you and leave you, for now. But I can come back
tomorrow, if you like.'

'Thank you. I think Sergeant Gilmour would be happy for
you to do that, eh, Gilmour? We'll let you know if we need you,
Miss Bannerman.'

She had kept on her enchanting little hat while working, and
in a moment or two re-donned the olive green coat, fastening its
big fur collar high around her neck and with another ravishing
smile, turned to go. Then paused with her hand on the doorknob.
'By the way,' she said, pointing to the sunflower painting on the
wall, 'that's mine.'

'You mean Mr Llewellyn was going to leave it you in his
will?'

'No, I mean it belongs to me already. There used to be a
picture of his wife hanging there but it's away being cleaned, so
I offered to lend him this. The place needed brightening up. I'm
a Pisces, and miserable surroundings depress me. It's only a
print,' she added, as if it might have been in their minds that it
was a Van Gogh original. 'I only mentioned it, just so's it doesn't
accidentally go to anyone else. Bye!' She wiggled her fingers
and left.

Gilmour wiped imaginary sweat from his brow. 'Jiminy!' he
said feelingly.

Reardon grinned. 'Been giving you a hard time, has she?'

Gilmour ran a hand through his coppery hair, his face red.
He was tenacious and didn't like having to admit defeat but . . .
the undoubted truth was, he'd been upstaged by a young woman
who had at first seemed nothing more than a decorative office

girl who had then knocked him into a cocked hat with her expertise. Miss Bannerman – or Sadie, as she would have it – had been more than willing to help him understand, but as the piles of papers – copies of contracts, copies of agreements and details of mergers, takeovers, goodness knows what else – grew in height on the desk, Gilmour had felt himself to be a ship foundering in uncharted seas. He'd never precisely shone at school though he'd never considered himself slow on the uptake either. But she was too quick for him, expecting him to absorb and remember complicated explanations without needing them to be repeated.

'Not my territory, sir, all this,' he admitted, knowing the explanation didn't even begin to describe his inadequacy.

'Well, it's not mine, either, if it comes to that.'

'No, sir. The thing is, though, we might be missing something crucial. We're going to need someone else on this job. Someone who knows what it's all about,' he finished hopefully.

'Isn't that what she was supposed to be doing?' Gilmour shrugged helplessly and Reardon gave him an appraising glance. 'She couldn't be pulling the wool over our eyes, could she, our Miss Bannerman? Is that what you mean?'

'She could be pulling it over mine, that's for sure! But why should she? I'm not sure I can take another day of her, though.'

'Soldier on, Joe, soldier on. Meanwhile, what about a copy of the will?'

'I've left that bit till last, sir. There isn't one.'

'Are you sure?'

'Every drawer's been emptied. All his personal papers are here, in this stack – everything on that side is business. It's funny . . . he was a bit of a stickler for keeping things in order, I'd have said he'd be sure to have a copy. If so, most likely it's in the safe.'

'And the safe key's with the others which have miraculously disappeared. Wonderful. Well, never mind that for now. It seems I've been having a more interesting afternoon than you. Let me enlighten you.'

Half an hour later, he had filled Gilmour in with what had happened during his meeting with Carey Brewster and Jack Douglas, and afterwards with Verity Lancaster, and what Kate

Ramsey thought she'd seen. He'd just finished when Mrs Knightly came in, triumphantly dangling a bunch of keys.

'So they were in one of his suits, after all?'

'No, they weren't. I got Mrs Harris to get everything out of the shed where she stores the jumble, and it was all still in the same boxes we'd packed it into. I went through every pocket again. Not so much as a bit of fluff left in any of them. But still . . . it's been bothering me all afternoon and just now I went upstairs to have another look. Just in case, somehow, you know . . . And there they were, right at the back of the wardrobe, behind the shoe rack! You know what a monster that piece is, but I still can't see how I could have missed them.' An indignant flush mantled her face. 'I dusted everything out after we'd finished, everything!'

Reardon recalled the wardrobe, a massive affair with a central bank of drawers surmounted by a cupboard, with two hanging sections, one either side, the whole mounted on a sturdy plinth. Mrs Knightly, flustered and indeed highly affronted at the implication of any oversight she had made, wouldn't thank him for the suggestion that the bunch of keys could easily have slipped back into the dark recesses of one of the hanging sections and not been seen. 'Thanks for your efforts, Mrs Knightly. How they got there doesn't matter so much as the fact that they've been found.'

'If you say so.' She didn't look convinced, but he left it at that, having no wish to plant in her mind the suggestion that the keys could have been appropriated before Pen's body was discovered – and later replaced.

When the door had shut behind her, Reardon held up the keys and waved a hand towards the pile of Pen's personal papers. 'You're thinking what I'm thinking.'

'Somebody pinched them, to get a dekko at the will copy. To see if he'd changed it in favour of Mrs Douglas? And killed him afterwards when they found he hadn't, before he could get round to it?'

'Which rules out Theo. If he drew up the will, he'd have no need to look. But I'd rather see the copy than ask him for details of it, as yet. Let's get that safe open.'

There was no key to the safe on the ring with the others.

FIFTEEN

Reardon slept uneasily that night. Tossing and turning on the lumpy mattress, he couldn't rid himself of the nagging suspicion that something about this enquiry was escaping him. The time they'd spent here, though short, hadn't exactly been wasted, and on the face of it everything he'd learnt had confirmed his original gut feeling that they were on a hiding to nothing: he was going to have to prepare Cherry, his detective superintendent, for the fact that it was by no means beyond the bounds of possibility that they might never find the identity of Penrose Llewellyn's killer.

Yesterday, when he'd telephoned in a report of what had transpired so far, the extension line in the office had been infuriatingly scratchy, resulting in an altogether less than satisfactory conversation and, as he dressed the next morning, Reardon decided he owed the super a face-to-face explanation. Cherry, with whom Reardon had worked for a long time, was a reasonable man, not the sort of superior who demanded instant results regardless, but he liked to feel he had had his finger on the pulse of every case, and he always wanted everything cut and dried – and the ultimate responsibility for this investigation did rest with him, after all.

He watched the sergeant's face light up as he told Gilmour of his decision to drive over and see Cherry, which would allow Gilmour to pop in and see how Maisie was doing. 'Then we'll tootle over to Brum to see this lawyer chap, this Mr Harper. He's the man to make sense of all this paper he seems so fond of.' Harper, Kingdom and Harper were the Birmingham solicitors who had taken care of the business affairs of Llewellyn Holdings for years, where all these documents had originated. 'I dare say Cherry will want most of it packed up anyway and sent over to HQ. Which should give the legal eagles something to do.'

Gilmour beamed at the load being lifted from his shoulders, but he felt bound to add, 'In fairness, sir, not everything in the desk was generated by the lawyers. The household accounts are in there, too. Deeds, insurances, things such as plans and sketches for that new garden and such . . . And there's bills and receipts for everything he's ever bought, I should think – you wouldn't credit the amount he spent on those old books! They must be worth a pretty penny on their own. Most of them bought locally, too, from that bookshop across the way. Adrian Murfitt, the chap with the Jack Russell.'

The books Pen had never intended to read. Bought as an investment, Claudia Llewellyn had said. A concept Reardon found it hard to sympathize with, though it was probably no worse than buying anything else to sell for profit at a later date. And difficult as it was to comprehend, her husband Theo was, according to Claudia, a knowledgeable collector. 'We'll go across and have a word with him, as soon as we've finished breakfast,' he decided.

It was a very small shop, situated almost directly opposite the Fox, a mere slice of a building not much wider than the narrow passage which separated it from the corn chandler's next door.

The bell clanged as Gilmour pushed the door open, and the little dog he'd previously encountered leapt from his basket in the corner and began a series of short, staccato barks. 'No,' said the man seated at a paper-strewn table, without looking up. 'No,' he repeated more sternly, and this time the perky, bright-eyed little Jack Russell terrier, white with black and tan markings, went obediently back to his basket, where he sat up with an expectant air, tensed to spring out again at any sign of encouragement.

'Mr Murfitt?'

'Yes.' Murfitt looked up and blinked, then frowned, as if an actual customer was a disturbance rather than a welcome event. Nor did he get up from where he was sitting. 'Were you looking for anything in particular, or do you just want to browse? Take your time, don't mind me.' He wafted a hand towards the shelves and went back to the writing he'd been occupied with when they entered.

The educated accent was at odds with his appearance: a man of forty-odd, with thick dark hair touched with grey, wearing a collarless shirt with the sleeves rolled up, and over it a knitted Fair Isle slipover. His scruffy corduroys had the pile worn off at the knees.

'We're not here to buy, Mr Murfitt,' Gilmour said.

'Like most of those who come in here then,' he replied indifferently. This wasn't hard to believe. The wonder was that anyone would want to step beyond the threshold, once they'd glimpsed the interior. The whole place was an affront to anyone who loved books. Bookshops should, in Reardon's opinion, be veritable Aladdin's caves, whereas here was an uninviting collection of what appeared to be mostly shabby second-hand books ranged haphazardly on the shelves, with a few new ones in brightly coloured dust jackets between, almost as a concession. There had been no attempt to display the stock to advantage – or what stock there was. More than that – owing to the cramped dimensions of the interior, the shelves were few, and yet so sparsely filled that many of the volumes, having no others to support them, leant drunkenly to one side.

Gilmour bent to fondle the dog. 'Nice little dog you have. What's his name?'

'Tolly.'

'Dolly?'

'No, Tolly. Short for Autolycus – a snapper-up of unconsidered trifles.' Obviously accustomed to the blank looks this received, he explained in a bored voice, 'He'll eat anything – Jack Russells are famous for it, he'll even scavenge from dustbins, given the chance. Give him a biscuit and you're his friend for life.'

People did give their pets weird and wonderful names, for all sorts of reasons, but this was a new one on Gilmour, on Reardon too, he suspected. But Reardon merely remarked drily that unfortunately they didn't have any biscuits.

'So, what can I do for you then? I don't buy, unless you have something in the antiquarian line.' His tone as he looked them up and down didn't suggest he thought that likely.

'We're not here to sell, either.'

'Then may I ask why are you here?' But something in his manner changed. He had realized who they must be. It wasn't easy for a policeman to remain incognito, somehow it always showed, even if you weren't unfortunate enough to have red hair like Gilmour, but in any case, even Murfitt, for some reason reminding Reardon irresistibly of a spider hidden in its dusty web, must surely have heard something about the enquiry going on at Bryn Glas, and the possibility that Penrose Llewellyn had died of something other than a mere heart attack.

'We're making enquiries into the death of Mr Penrose Llewellyn,' Gilmour said. 'I believe you knew him?'

'Yes, I was sorry to hear he'd died. But I didn't know him well.' He threw them a sharp look. 'I don't see why I—'

Reardon held up a pacific hand. 'We're talking to everyone who had any connection with him. And it seems he bought most of his books from you, the antiquarian ones, at any rate.'

'He was a good client.'

'I can see he might have been – don't suppose you have many local customers, do you?'

'That's true, as it happens, but my business doesn't depend on local custom, which is just as well. Natives not friendly, you know,' he added with a sarcastic smile. 'I sell mostly old books – rare ones, first editions, collectables . . . usually by catalogue. Don't be misled by this,' he said, flapping a hand to take in most of the shelves, 'my real stock is too valuable to be left lying around. I keep it locked up.' He jerked his head in the direction of a door on his left.

'Interesting. So what brought you to Hinton, Mr Murfitt? It's not very accessible for your line of business, surely?'

'Doesn't make much difference, actually. Let's just say I was sick of life in London. It's cheaper to live here, for one thing – and quieter, what's more, so I can work here.' Perhaps sensing they found this a less than adequate explanation, he added, though his hand automatically covered the page he'd been writing on, 'I'm a poet, or try to be. As many of us were, we who refused to join in the Great Fight. Which without doubt you know applies to me . . . the old tabbies' tittle-tattle round the village pump having been passed on to you.' His mouth twisted, his dark, almond-shaped eyes sparked a challenge. He was actually very good-looking in a sulky-mouthed way, thick brown hair, high cheekbones and a determined chin.

He was not to know that the information about him had not been conveyed as a piece of idle chat, but received incidentally in regard to Verity's disappearance. However much the landlady at the Fox enjoyed a gossip and was a mine of information on all things Hinton, she wasn't malicious, and whatever she thought about the young man who owned the bookshop across the street hadn't been voiced.

Murfitt saw neither policeman rising to his challenge, and went on more moderately. 'But I also know about books, and I care about them – though I've no time for most of the modern stuff,' he added dismissively. 'I worked for a long time for an antiquarian bookseller down the Charing Cross Road before coming here. And that, in case you're wondering, is how I met Pen Llewellyn and came to Hinton. He used to come into the shop, we talked, he learnt of my ambitions to run my own business and when he heard this place was empty he let me know.'

'Your sort of books seem an odd thing for Mr Llewellyn to buy. Not a bookish fellow, from what we've gathered.'

'Collectors come in many guises, I've found. He began through his brother, who is a serious buyer.'

'Mr Theo Llewellyn, you mean? How serious?' Theo's wife hadn't been exaggerating then, inferring her husband was knowledgeable on the subject, when she'd poured scorn on his brother's reasons for trying to emulate him.

It seemed Adrian Murfitt might actually share this view. 'I'm sorry to say Pen Llewellyn bought books for the wrong reasons, hoping to make money out of reselling. If that was how he looked on it, he was going to be sadly disappointed, as I warned him. It doesn't work like that. One thing Theo Llewellyn and I have in common – he has nothing but contempt for anyone who looks on beautiful old books merely as saleable commodities.'

'And that "anyone" included his brother?'

'Possibly. But who was I to quibble? I'm a dealer, with my bread and butter to earn. I would much rather see books going to those who appreciate them for what they are, but, well . . .' His gaze sharpened. 'Actually, I should like the opportunity to buy back those I sold to Penrose. Most of what he has is run-of-the-mill stuff, but he did buy a few interesting items.'

'If you speak to his brother, I'm sure something can be arranged,' Reardon told him. 'He may want to keep them, of course, as he's a collector himself.'

Murfitt smiled. 'I doubt it. Like every other wise collector, Theo Llewellyn specializes. He's passionately interested in music and music history, and he's a genuine bibliophile, he loves his books for their own sake. Books on composers and their work, rare and out of print, mostly early German composers – Bach, Handel and so on. He goes for anything to do with music history – old letters, correspondence even – and it can take years to find anything, and at the right price, but it's the only way to gather a respectable collection. One makes the odd mistake but that's all part of the game . . . and Theo has a good eye.'

'He buys old manuscripts? They can be worth a mint, I've heard?'

'And therefore bought by millionaires or great libraries and universities, sergeant.'

Gilmour reddened. Reardon didn't like the patronizing tone either. But all this was throwing a new light on Lawyer Llewellyn. Music, books. He seemed to know his stuff. It seemed that Murfitt did, too. He'd lost some of his belligerence and grown quite loquacious, seeming glad to get off the subject of Pen and on to one more in tune with his interests. Which begged the question of how – and more importantly why – he had set himself up here. Did he have money? It would have been needed – to rent, if not to buy the premises, for one thing. To purchase stock. Money to live on. How many books did he sell, and how much profit did he make? How many customers would come to this place searching him out?

This last question was answered by Murfitt himself saying shortly that if they'd finished with him, he had to get a parcel to the post office in Wyvering. 'My business depends on mail order. Can't let the customers down.'

'Wyvering? Presumably you have a motor car.'

'What? Well, yes, if you can dignify it by that name. She's an old Tin Lizzie, getting on in years, but the old girl's managed to get me around . . . until recently.' He flashed a quick smile that gave a whole new aspect to his countenance. It was possible to see there might be quite another side to him. 'She's been playing me up lately and it looks as though she might have to go.'

Gilmour kept his face averted from Reardon. Nothing was guaranteed to annoy the boss more than men who called their cars 'she'. Unless they called them Gertrude, or Florence . . .

Reardon didn't seem to have noticed, or wasn't showing it,

and Murfitt was saying, 'However, getting a new motor – or the money for it . . . doesn't grow on trees, does it?'

'If it does, I've never noticed. But Miss Lancaster's very obliging in helping you out with driving, isn't she?'

He stiffened. 'Occasionally, yes. I haven't seen her recently.'

'All right, Mr Murfitt, we won't keep you any longer. We're staying just across the road at the Fox, so if you think of anything else that might be useful, you know where we are. Hope you get your parcel to the post office in time.'

As the doorbell clanged behind them, and they began to cross the road, Gilmour, still stung by Murfitt's patronizing attitude, muttered, 'Conchie or not, can you wonder he's not liked. Autolycus, would you credit?'

It was a comment Reardon had every sympathy with but he said, 'It took guts to do what he did, Joe.'

Gilmour grunted a reluctant acknowledgement. By the time the war had reached its bloody conclusion, a lot of people had been forced to accord a certain amount of respect to those objectors who had stood so staunchly for their beliefs, even to imprisonment and the threat of being shot for cowardice. If Murfitt had gone through all that, he was no coward. 'All the same – it's a bloody silly name for a dog.'

When the two big men who had used up too much of the space in his shop for the last half hour had finally left, Adrian Murfitt felt able to breathe. Flopping back in his chair, he watched them out of his dusty window as they crossed the Townway. His arm hung over the chair and his hand scratched the head of Tolly, who'd come to sit beside him. His eyes closed. The parcel destined for the post office in Wyvering sat disregarded on the corner of the table. It would have to wait – he wasn't up to coping with the vagaries of his temperamental old motor, not at this moment, and he certainly wasn't going to try and get round Verity, obliging as she'd always been, in every way, until lately.

'Time to depart, Tolly?' he muttered, 'Time to depart?'

It had probably been time to go a few weeks after he'd arrived in this benighted spot. He would never be admitted here. He'd been a fool, too, not to take into account that in those of limited country mentality, the hatred for conscientious objectors who refused to fight in the war hadn't yet gone away. Yet he'd only come here, after all, to seek what was his by rights.

He'd been a serious, clever and thoughtful boy, an only child who was the centre of his mother's world until he was sent away for an expensive education, where it was very soon made clear to him that his cleverness was suspect, that his lacklustre participation in rough team games set him apart from his fellow pupils, and where his refusal to learn boxing branded him a coward. His schooldays were not happy, and it wasn't until he went up to Oxford and found like-minded souls that his views began to crystallize and take form. There he embraced socialist politics and became a peace activist. An anti-militarist who believed that war and aggression was for the benefit of capitalist elites, and that the working classes were being conned by governments into supporting it. He joined in anti-war demonstrations, but when it did break out he registered as an absolutist, refusing in any way to be part of the war machine. He would not put on a uniform, pick up a rifle or take orders. When compulsory conscription arrived in 1916, he had ultimately been imprisoned, had suffered solitary confinement and at times lived on bread and water.

What he himself had gone through physically was less than millions of men had experienced in trench warfare, yet it had left its mark. His experiences as a pacifist in a jingoistic world had changed him, instilled in him a bitter cynicism. Was it that which had, in some twisted way, turned him into a *non*-pacifist? Or more correctly, into a selective pacifist, one who only wanted to hit back at those who were wronging him. Who couldn't now turn the other cheek. Pacifism as a general idea, but not when it came to personal issues.

Gnawing his lip, he thought of the Llewellyns and what had just passed between him and the police. That inspector, Reardon, that scar on his face . . . he'd seen too many disfigurements like that not to know the man had almost certainly been a casualty of the war. Undoubtedly one of the ones who wouldn't forget, or forgive, too ready to apportion blame.

Sometimes, in the depth of a sleepless night, he wasn't altogether sure that the accusations of cowardice that had once been flung at him – the hissed insults, the white feathers given him by self-righteous women, the cold contempt – hadn't been deserved . . .

and more recently, the indifference of these smug folk here in Hinton when they'd discovered – how? – his history. Well, he'd learnt the hard way that something like that wasn't ever going to remain hidden.

Yes, it was time to depart. He shoved aside the papers and the poem he'd been writing, and picked up another sheet of paper and his fountain pen. He unscrewed the cap, wrote the salutation, began and then stopped, tapping his teeth with the pen.

Five minutes later, and no further on, he screwed the paper up and aimed it in the direction of the cardboard box that served as a waste paper basket. He began again.

SIXTEEN

Reardon, after his meeting with Cherry, was unusually silent as they drove into Birmingham city centre, but Gilmour, at the wheel, was happy with his own thoughts. He was feeling quite chipper, after spending an hour with Maisie while Reardon had been talking with the superintendent. He'd found her looking well, blooming in fact, sitting beside a warm fireside, knitting baby garments and gossiping with her sister, Ruby, who was staying with her for as long as Gilmour might have to be away. She'd hardly seemed to be missing him, in fact, until Ruby had tactfully slipped out to the shops and left them alone for a while to talk.

He found a place to park near the green oasis surrounding the cathedral. The paths that crossed it were busy with people going about their business, feeding the pigeons or simply sitting on the park benches, taking advantage of the weak sun which the vagaries of the weather had brought out on this wintry day. After leaving the car, the two of them made their way down Bennett's Hill, a prosperous commercial street of banks, insurance and other office buildings. The solicitors' office they sought, unlike some of the newer, larger and more dignified buildings, was squeezed between two others, with a narrow frontage and a heavy door, though a brass plaque indicated this was indeed the offices of Harper, Kingdom and Harper. Outward appearances were deceptive. The premises evidently went a long way back and, inside, the front office was a hive of bustling activity with an overall impression that red tape and the stacks of paper on every conceivable surface might one day take over what little space was left. From behind frosted glass doors men, and sometimes women, emerged and disappeared through other doors on mysterious errands. An elderly clerk peered from behind an overloaded desk and asked in an offhand way what their business was, and when they'd shown their badges, spoke into an internal telephone. 'You can go up,' he told them. 'Mr Robert's office. Top of the stairs. He's busy but he'll see you for a few minutes.'

'Thank you,' Reardon answered, with no little irony.

Robert Harper was also surrounded by papers. The mountains they'd left behind at Bryn Glas, which had so overwhelmed Gilmour, were beginning to look like mere molehills beside these Himalayas. Could anyone ever find time to actually read them all? Presumably Mr Robert did; in the next few minutes he proved himself admirably au fait with the affairs of Llewellyn Holdings.

'I was very sorry to hear of Mr Llewellyn's passing,' he said, swinging his spectacles by the earpiece. Removing them had the effect of making him look much younger than he had at first appeared. He was probably in his early forties, despite a receding hairline and a somewhat corpulent frame. Was he conscious of a lack of gravitas so that he chose to wear pinstriped trousers and black jacket, plus an old fashioned 'come to Jesus' wing collar? 'And even sorrier,' he added, resuming the glasses, 'to hear there are distressing circumstances connected with it. How could such a thing have happened?'

'We'll come to that, but at the moment we're here to learn what you can tell us of his business affairs.'

This caused a certain amount of eyebrow raising, a pursing of his lips. 'Everything in order, I can assure you of that. Mr Llewellyn was a stickler for such things – he came here only last week for a discussion. Always very keen to keep his finger on the pulse, Mr Llewellyn.'

'Well, as we understand it, there's likely to be a fair amount of money involved, and it would appear his affairs were fairly complicated, so in the circumstances of his death, you'll understand we

need to have our own people look at them.' Good grief, it was
infectious, Reardon thought, hearing himself. 'We'd appreciate
your cooperation.'

Mr Harper agreed readily enough with that. 'That goes without
saying. You will find everything strictly in order, I assure you,'
he repeated.

'It would be useful to know the contents of his will, but so
far, we've haven't been able to find a copy.'

Mr Harper maintained a silence, during which his scrutiny
became sharper. Reardon, watching him, said carefully, 'Have
you recently drawn up a new will for him, Mr Harper?'

Gilmour shot him a look of surprise but Harper answered,
equally carefully, 'That was why he came in last week. He wished
to write one which would revoke his previous will.'

'It would be useful if you could help by giving us an idea of
its contents.'

He appeared to consider. 'The beneficiaries will be informed
in due course. It's impossible to say how much will be inherited by
any legatee until all the business of the estate has been settled.
As we speak, everything is being prepared for probate. Until it's
been granted, as I'm quite sure you know, inspector, I cannot
possibly breach my client's confidentiality.'

'Your client is dead, Mr Harper – in suspicious circumstances.'

'Therefore you will understand my caution.'

And that, it transpired during the next half an hour, was as far
as he was prepared to go.

'No point in forcing the issue, all lawyers are born cautious,'
Reardon said as they set off for Hinton once more. 'It was what
I suspected – no copy left around for anyone to get their hands
on. I wonder if Theo knew about the new will – or suspected?'

They drove in silence for a while, until Reardon remembered
he ought to give Gilmour an account of what had passed between
him and the superintendent while he'd been with Maisie. He
appreciated, Cherry had said, that they'd hardly been two minutes
on the job but unless Reardon came up with something more
tangible to convince him otherwise, he didn't feel justified keeping
two of his best officers there much longer. He was sympathetic
but his own hands were tied . . . directives from above . . . a big

flap on because of a series of arson attempts at one of the big steel works, a moneylender murdered . . . And some possible new information had come in on the illegal dogfighting ring Reardon and Gilmour had been chasing up for months. None of it, especially the last, had Reardon any stomach for. But Cherry needed them both back.

It wouldn't be a matter of case closed, of course, Cherry said, but rather a temporary suspension. Unless or until some new evidence turned up that warranted reopening it . . .

PART THREE

SEVENTEEN

'**D**ang-blast, I'll strangle 'un, soon as I get the chance!'
growled Fred Parslowe, pummelling his pillows to find
a place where he could bury his head.

'Wha-at?' Flo struggled upwards from the depths of sleep,
pulling from her ears the cotton wool she'd stuffed into them in
an attempt to blot out Fred's snores. 'What you on about now,
Fred?'

'That bloody Jack Russell from across. Kept me awake half
the night with his barking, he has. Hark at him now!'

Flo sat up, now fully awake, and listened. 'That's not barking,
Fred Parslowe, that's howling. Summat's up.'

First Reardon, and then Gilmour, was dragged from sleep by the
agitated landlady, still wearing her metal curlers, knocking on
their doors. The distant sound of a howling dog, the reluctant
clomping of Fred Parslowe's boots down the stairs and the geese
honking below did nothing to lessen what soon became a general
pandemonium. Their rooms being at the back, neither Reardon
nor Gilmour had been aware of the noise the dog was making
during the night. By the time they threw on a few clothes and
crossed the Townway to the bookshop, Fred was hammering on
the door, only there because he'd been chivvied by his wife into
seeing what was going on. Several interested spectators hung
around and the blacksmith was offering advice and a crowbar if
necessary. Parslowe had already tried the door and found it locked,
and the only effect of his knocking had been to turn Tolly's
piteous howls into frantic barking.

An alley ran behind the shop. Gilmour sprinted along it, past
Murfitt's old car and into the yard. It didn't take him long to
shoulder the locked back door open and then to free the dog
from the tiny storeroom where he'd been shut in, and hand him
over to Parslowe. Not without furious protest on both sides, he
was manhandled across the road to the Fox and finally chained

up in a disused kennel. Inside the shop there was no sign of
his owner, upstairs or downstairs. His bed had been slept in, a
lamp on the bedside table still burned, but of Adrian Murfitt there
was no sign.

Eventually, they found him. Beyond a door which opened
directly off the shop on to a yawning black hole which was the
cellar. He lay at the foot of the perilously steep stone steps, slipperless but wearing socks and pyjamas that revealed a natty taste
in menswear. His limbs and his head lay at awkward angles. He
was not quite stiff, but cold and unmistakably dead.

Claudia Llewellyn might have had a point, after all, Reardon was
now ready to admit, when she'd raised her eyebrows at the lack
of telephones in Hinton. Communicating the news of this death to
all those concerned was urgent. 'Get your skates on and down
to Bryn Glas straight away, Joe,' he said. 'There's some tele-
phoning needs to be done.'

'Soon as I've made myself decent, sir. Bit parky, going like
this.'

'Don't take too long about it.' It was too early in the morning
for humour. Too early for a lot of things, especially what they'd
already found. Reardon needed to get dressed properly himself.
Like Gilmour, he only wore the jacket and trousers he'd thrown
on over his pyjamas, and the body in the cellar wasn't going
anywhere. All the same . . .

Before he left he took the opportunity to take a quick look
around the premises and mentally note what he found. It didn't
take long. At the top of the narrow, creaky old stairs was just
the one small bedroom. Beside the lamp was a pair of spectacles
and an opened book – the newest Sayers detective story, one of
Murfitt's disparaged modern authors, he noted with a touch
of grim amusement. The clothes he'd worn the day before lay
tossed in a heap on the floor, others hung on various pegs, and
an open suitcase on the floor held underclothes. Underneath the
bed was a chamber pot and in the corner stood a marble wash-
stand, complete with jug and basin, a mirror and a grubby towel
on a hook beside it.

Downstairs, behind the shop and the small adjacent storeroom
was the kitchen. Compared to the generally scruffy state existing

everywhere else, it was fairly tidy – mainly because there was so little there to be untidy with. It smelled damp. Condensation ran down the windows. The fire had gone out but there was still a breath of warmth issuing from it, and a heap of ash in the grate, so it had presumably been banked up the night before. The shop itself appeared to be undisturbed. The papers and writing materials Murfitt had been occupied with when he and Gilmour had visited still sat on the table, as did the parcel which he'd said he so urgently needed to put in the post. Two keys on a ring lay beside it.

Reardon left everything as it was and went back to his room at the Fox, dressed fully and then hastily breakfasted on the man-sized bacon sandwich Mrs Parslowe insisted on preparing for him. He took the opportunity to speak to her and Fred while he was eating it. She was dressed and now divested of her curlers, her hair in its usual tight waves and curls, and was full of the events that had so abruptly started the morning, agog for details he wasn't prepared to give.

'Well, that poor dog!' she exclaimed. 'The wonder is he didn't stifle to death, locked up like that.'

'He was in the storeroom, and there's ventilation, Mrs Parslowe.' A small grille six feet up, a device possibly there to keep those valuable books stored at an even temperature, it was the reason Tolly's howling had been audible enough to disturb Fred Parslowe's beauty sleep.

'Not that he ever sleeps very deep,' Flo commented with a sideways look at Fred. 'Wakes himself up with his snoring, he does. Or I wake him up if it gets too bad.'

'When did the dog start howling, Mr Parslowe?'

'Been at it all night, I shunna wonder! But it was from two o'clock sure, when I looked out the window to see what was up and saw somebody walking from the door.'

'You saw someone leaving the shop?' All this going on, and it hadn't occurred to him to say a word about something as suspicious as that. Sometimes Reardon didn't believe in people like Parslowe.

'Leaving, or mebbe just passing, I wunna swear to either.'

Just passing, at two in the morning? 'What sort of man? Can you describe him?'

'Never said it were a man. Mighta been a woman. But if so, she were powerful big.'

'Tall, you mean?'

'Both ways. Not so ample a wench as Mrs Parslowe, mind, but a fair armful.' Having delivered himself of this bon mot he went back to polishing pewter pots with an energy he didn't expend on much else.

Unoffended, Mrs Parslowe excused him placidly. 'He didn't sleep much last night.'

Reardon couldn't by any stretch credit Fred with enough imagination to conjure up what he'd seen. Any doubts he might have had that Murfitt's death was anything other than suspicious disappeared. He thought of the women he'd met in Hinton, only one of whom, apart from present company, could fairly be described as big. But Fred Parslowe was highly unlikely to have met, not to say recognized, Claudia Llewellyn. He rarely stirred from his pub and she would certainly never have put a toe inside it. The other woman, Ida Lancaster, was also fairly tall, but thin as a beanpole. As for either of them being capable of what he'd just seen . . . Reardon had virtually discounted them for Pen's murder – Claudia too indolent and Ida, for all her apparent brittleness, he didn't seriously believe capable of killing her brother. He gave up on the idea of either being involved in this latest killing and also on the attempt to get any more out of Fred, and concentrated on his more sensible wife.

'What do you know of Adrian Murfitt?' he asked.

'Not much, always kept hisself to hisself, you know, hardly stirred out of the shop. When he did he was lately wrapped up in that big green coat and his cap pulled down right over his eyes, and never a word to nobody!' She began clearing Reardon's used breakfast things. 'Your sergeant will be wanting something hot when he gets back.'

He sensed evasion and recalled what Jack Douglas had said of Murfitt, and what Murfitt himself had said about the situation and the feeling against him in Hinton. Perhaps it had been stronger than anyone realized. Even so, it was difficult to believe that might have extended to death at the foot of his cellar steps.

'Apart from customers, were you aware of any other visitors he might have had?'

Mrs Parslowe shrugged her comfortable shoulders. 'Well, being a shop, folks came and went, didn't they? Not many, but some.' She clattered crockery together, looking quite upset. 'Look, if you want to hear some sense and not just mischievous gossip about that poor soul, you talk to Phyllis Knightly.'

'Mrs Knightly, housekeeper at Bryn Glas?'

'That's right. Now, if you've finished your breakfast . . .?' He knew by now that when Mrs Parslowe looked like that, he'd get no more from her.

'Yes, thanks, I've finished. That was a great butty.'

She smiled. 'Could you fancy another?'

'Enough is as good as a feast, Mrs Parslowe.' He was beginning to feel sorry for the geese.

When he crossed the Townway again, a smart maroon-coloured Morris Roadster was parked outside the bookshop, and standing by the door was a uniformed policeman, whom he recognized as the sergeant from Castle Wyvering.

'Sergeant Bridgstock, good morning. You got here in good time.'

'Came over with the doctor, in his car here, me and PC Kitchin, soon as we got the telephone message from your sergeant. I thought it best not to do anything until you came back, like.'

'Not a great deal any of us can do, I fancy. We'll have to wait for the back-up now.'

Which meant the arrival of the photographer, the fingerprint man, the ambulance and all the accompanying paraphernalia increasingly associated with the discovery of a suspicious death, much as Reardon would have preferred to be left alone for longer to digest the implications of this second one. Nowadays forensic evidence was playing an ever more important part in the detection of crime and it was useless, not to say backward-thinking, to deny the forward march of progress. Not when so much could now be scientifically proved – although he would be the last to wish to disregard the old, tried and tested methods of observation, the patient questioning of suspects, the application of ordinary common sense and even the much despised gut feeling that as policemen they weren't supposed to rely on.

'They should be here at any time now. And Sergeant Gilmour

will be with us shortly.' Having returned from Bryn Glas, Gilmour was now occupied with his own bacon butty.

'The doctor's with the body in the cellar, sir.'

The low door in the corner of the shop opened in a highly dangerous manner, without any sort of landing, on to the precipitous flight of stone steps that led to the cellar. Reardon trod gingerly down, stepping carefully aside when he reached the bottom to avoid the splayed body which the doctor was busy examining, by the light of candles that had been begged, borrowed or stolen. In a ghastly parody of some Danse Macabre, the eerie light they generated threw huge, leaping shadows on to the whitewashed walls every time the doctor and the constable standing in attendance nearby moved.

This time it wasn't Fairlie who was doing the honours, but another doctor, an elderly, grey-haired man with a small tooth-brush moustache, wearing gold-rimmed glasses and rubber gloves. He barely glanced up from his kneeling position by the body. 'John Emerson,' he introduced himself briefly. Reardon immediately recognized the name as being that of the pathologist who had carried out the autopsy on Penrose Llewellyn.

'DI Reardon.'

The doctor raised his head from what he was doing and gave him a quick look. 'Good to meet you – you're the man here on the Llewellyn case?'

'That's right. Dr Fairlie not around?'

'They tried to get him, but he's not back from a call out.' Levering himself upright, he remarked drily, 'We're about to make history – two cases like this within a week in a place the size of Hinton. Queer sort of coincidence. This'll set the tongues wagging.'

'Cases like what, doctor?'

Emerson said, after a pause, 'I can't properly see what the devil I'm doing in this light, but frankly, from what I can see, I don't like it. His injuries aren't consistent with simply falling down those steps, damned dangerous though they are. His neck's broken all right, but there's also this nasty wound on his temple, yet there's not much blood anywhere around . . . not enough anyway – head wounds like this bleed a lot, as you must know. Did he fall or was he pushed? I won't state unequivocally until

I've examined him properly, but I'd say you're going to have to start looking for someone who had it in for this poor devil.'

The possibility of accident hadn't even occurred to Reardon. He couldn't imagine any reason compelling enough for anyone to leave his bed and go down the cellar steps – especially these steps, a deathtrap if ever he'd seen one – in the middle of a freezing cold night. And where was the candle or matches he'd have needed if he *had* started to come down here and then just tripped? And if he had fallen, why had the door at the top been closed? A more likely scenario was that someone with nefarious intent had managed to pick the lock of the shop door at some time during the night, forgetting, or not knowing, that the shop doorbell was spring-activated to ring when the door was pushed open; Murfitt coming downstairs to investigate, pausing only to thrust his feet into a pair of socks, and meeting the person who had turned out to be his killer: the man – or woman – Parslowe had seen. The snag to that was that there didn't appear to be any signs of forced entry. And what about the dog, Tolly? His basket was in the shop and presumably he slept there. At what point had the killer imprisoned him in the storeroom? And possibly how? Reardon asked himself, thinking of the strength of that high energy, muscular little body.

Emerson stood up and snapped off his rubber gloves. 'He hasn't been dead long. I'd go so far as to say only a few hours, can't make it more specific.' He was being cautious, as they all were, these doctors, about the notorious difficulty of establishing a time of death. 'And I suppose you want to know what weapon? You could make a start by looking for the traditional blunt instrument – or perhaps not so blunt, something with a flat round top, but heavy. And used with considerable force.'

He indicated the wound on Murfitt's right temple – deep, with several strands of the victim's hair plastered across it. Splinters of bone showed through the exposed flesh and other matter, and the weapon had caught and torn the cartilage at the top of his ear. Dried blood covered his face and had soaked into the neck and shoulders of his pyjamas, but as Emerson had noted, there appeared to be little on the steps or the flagstones where he lay. Had he been killed and then thrown down the cellar steps, or thrown down first and afterwards dealt the blow that had killed him? In any case, why the cellar at all? The idea of it as a hiding place was daft. In a small property like this, there was no possibility that a body could remain hidden for long.

Whatever the weapon that had caused such a wound, it hadn't been left lying around, either here or upstairs. The viciously cold cellar was singularly bare, and very small. Nothing at all had been kept here, not even the miscellaneous junk that often accumulated in cellars. A couple of mousetraps, last resting places for their long deceased and mummified occupants, sat on a stone slab primarily designed for helping to keep meat, milk and the like cool, though no meat-safe or anything similar had stood there for a long time. The slab was covered in a layer of coal dust.

'A coal hammer?' Reardon suggested.

'Distinct possibility.'

He walked to the door at the end of the cellar and peered in. It seemed there had been a recent coal delivery, but it was almost impossible to see anything properly. A heavy hammer, the sort often used for breaking up lumps too big to go on the fire as they were – or any other weapon, for that matter – might well have been tossed in there, or even buried under the coal to hide it. 'Nice job for someone, sifting through that lot,' he remarked.

Constable Kitchin, to whom the remark was addressed, managed a grin. 'Yessir.' As long as it's not me, his tone managed to convey.

But this didn't have the hallmarks of a planned murder where the killer came prepared with a means of dispatch, more like a rage-induced attack, the snatching up of whatever was nearest to hand as a weapon. A coal hammer might fit the bill, but it was hard to imagine why Murfitt and his killer would have gone down into the cellar before such a confrontation.

The main question was, however, why? Why, indeed, had Murfitt been murdered at all? A chance intruder, intent on burgling the shop, was hardly on the cards. What was there to burgle? Second-hand books, and little, if anything, in the till? Unless the thief had some prior knowledge of something kept in the store-room where Murfitt had said he kept his more valuable stock.

'Well, the best of luck,' Emerson said as he prepared to go. 'I'll let you have my report as soon as possible, but don't expect any surprises.'

Reardon followed him up the steps. Bridgstock left with the doctor, after promising the extra manpower that would now be needed from Wyvering. A couple of constables would do, one at a pinch. Reardon walked to the desk where Murfitt had been working and sat down in the chair to wait for Gilmour. His hand went out to the 'till' – nothing more than an old, square Oxo tin, a locked box evidently having been thought unnecessary, since all it contained was a ten-shilling note, three half-crowns, a sixpence and a few pennies.

Two murders, within as many days. Coincidence, the doctor had said. If he believed that, Reardon did not. Nor was it inconceivable that the two victims – Pen Llewellyn and Adrian Murfitt – had met their deaths at the hands of the same person. Whoever Pen's killer was, had he been afraid that Murfitt knew his identity and had therefore dispatched him, too? Although it was unworthy, he felt a jolt of adrenalin that this second murder might, just possibly, be the break they needed, the lucky chance that could lead to the solving of the deadlocked first. At any rate, Cherry would have to do without his two officers for a bit longer.

And yet, if there was a connection between the two victims, so far nothing more than the buying and selling of old books had emerged. He groaned inwardly at the implications. The rarefied world of specialist book collecting was as mysterious to him as the workings of the universe. But one thing he'd bet his pension on: if Murfitt had had anything in that storeroom valuable enough to provide a motive for murdering him, it wouldn't be there now. Could he possibly have left behind anything so useful as an inventory? Looking around at the disorganized state of the shop, he decided he wouldn't hold his breath about that. The storeroom, where Murfitt had said the books of any consequence had been kept, might give some indication for such a motive, but it would need someone more expert than he was to assess their worth.

He shuffled though the papers on the desk, about a dozen loose sheets held down by a brass paperweight and an expensive, gold-plated fountain pen. Poetry, as Murfitt had said. Being forced to learn reams of it by heart at school had stifled any desire in Reardon to read it for pleasure in later years, though Ellen had from time to time tried to interest him. Mostly it didn't do anything for him, except for some of the war poets, and that had to be because the sentiments tallied much with his own experiences. Although they had moved him in a way other poetry signally failed to do, he knew himself still unqualified to judge the good from the bad. Ellen might understand this stuff of Murfitt's; he didn't.

He didn't bother to read it all, but folded the pages together and slipped them into his inside pocket, then went across to look through the shelves. Murfitt had given no indication of whether he was published or not, but his search for a slim volume among the other books produced no result. Perhaps he would in time have come to realize he had a better future as a book dealer – had any sort of future not been denied him.

EIGHTEEN

Carey, with the restlessness that had consumed her ever since her homecoming, and finding it unbearable to be indoors, had taken herself out for a long walk. Not choosy about direction, she had let her footsteps eventually lead her down Nether Bank towards the river. At the bottom she stopped and leant against the stone parapet of the ancient bridge, looking down into the capricious though today quiescent river, grey and oily as it slid on its way to join the Severn. Her mind was confusingly full of the hateful thing that had been discovered in Hinton that morning, an inexplicable kind of dread, all mixed up with worries about things she must do before she left, people she must face.

As if on cue, her thoughts were interrupted by the sound of Gerald Fairlie's motor car on the other side of the bridge. He stopped and drew into the side when he saw her, then came to stand beside her. 'Carey. What are you doing here?'

'I needed some fresh air to clear my head. Things seem to be so . . . oh, I don't know . . . that awful thing that's happened at the bookshop . . . I suppose they sent for you?'

'They did but they couldn't reach me. Emerson from Wyvering has seen to it.'

They spoke for a while about the news which, from the time early that morning when Adrian Murfitt's dead body was discovered, had spread like a bush fire through Hinton. 'Exaggerated, no doubt,' he said with a wry smile. As usual, talking to sane and sensible Gerald brought a sense of proportion to the events, the feeling that things would be taken care of. 'But I'm afraid,' he said cautiously in answer to her questioning, 'the police are treating it as a suspicious death.'

'Suspicious? Oh, heavens! What's happening, Gerald? What's happening in peaceful Hinton? First Pen, and now this?'

He stiffened at the mention of Pen and she bit her lip. That had been tactless. She knew that Gerald regarded the enquiry into his death as a slur on his professional integrity, all the worse because Pen had stood so high in his regard. But he merely said, 'It's nasty – but thank goodness it's nothing that need concern you, Carey my dear.'

She shivered a little. 'Only in so far as it concerns everyone who lives here.' Now wasn't perhaps the best time, but she couldn't put off any longer telling him of her plans to leave Hinton. 'As a matter of fact, I shan't be here much longer, anyway. I've made up my mind . . . I'm leaving Hinton for good, Gerald.'

She guessed he had been half expecting it but, Gerald-like, his face had taken on that set, closed expression that hid his feelings. He was a good person but too nice and polite ever to show what he really felt; it must be hard for him to tell his patients what they must sometimes know. The knuckles of his hands were white now where they rested on the rough stone parapet. 'You don't need to leave at all, you know that,' he said at last, gruffly, as if the words had been dragged from somewhere deep. 'I'll risk saying it again . . . I can't offer you much as the wife of a country doctor, but—'

'Please, Gerald.' These were deep waters, deep enough to engulf her if she let them. 'Please, don't.'

In the days before her mother's last illness had made it impossible, she had worked for Gerald, as his receptionist. He dispensed his own medicines for the everyday ailments that afflicted the people of Hinton and the surrounding district, and he'd taught her how to roll pills or measure out and make up medicines, how to dress and bandage minor wounds, all of which she'd been more than happy to do, conscious that it took a weight off his shoulders. She was sorry for him, alone in that great house he could no longer afford the upkeep for, and struggling with managing his practice. He had come to depend on her, but when it began to be more than that, she'd known it was time to leave. Her mother's growing dependence on her had provided the excuse.

The cancer, however, had come unexpectedly, and finally finished Muriel off. Pen had begged Carey to let him find a nurse but the sense of obligation she always felt towards Muriel had made her refuse. Pen had helped so much, coming to sit by her bedside, and he'd been with her at the end, which had come while Carey, exhausted, had been persuaded to snatch some rest. She'd been wakened by a gentle hand on her shoulder. Gerald had popped in to administer the morphine Muriel needed but he had been too late. She had died five minutes earlier.

Since then she had felt a sense of obligation to both of them, to Pen and to Gerald for what they had done. But not an obligation to sacrifice her life . . .

'I'm sorry, Gerald, but it would never do, you know. But I shall always be very fond of you,' she said softly.

'Fond.'

How crass that sounded, when she would really like to say she did love him very much – in every way except the way he wanted. But that would only hurt him more. 'I'll keep in touch, Gerald, I can never forget everything you've done for me – and for what you did for my mother.'

'I would do more than that, for you, much more. You know that,' he said, his face bleak.

A horse-drawn wagon, heavily laden with what looked like sacks of grain began to cross the narrow bridge and they were forced to draw into the side, into one of the passing places. When the cart had gone, he was once more the same earnest, kind Gerald. 'Let me give you a lift home. I wouldn't be surprised if we had some snow before long.'

NINETEEN

Gilmour, now fed and primed for action, presently joined Reardon in the bookshop. He listened intently while Reardon brought him up to date with what Emerson had said, and what he'd thought so far. 'Before the circus arrives, I'd like us to go through the place more thoroughly. Have a look in the cellar first and then upstairs. It's not going to take long and I'd appreciate another opinion. Watch how you go down those cellar steps. We don't want you at the bottom as well.'

Gilmour grinned to himself, imagining the forensic team's reaction to being regarded as circus performers, and at the warning. But he took the advice and went cautiously down the steps and, with the aid of his flashlight, looked at the face of the man he had last met trying to take him down a peg when he'd only been attempting to make sense of the information about those old books Theo Llewellyn was so interested in. The beam of light revealed a face now devoid of superciliousness – or anything else, except the marks of his death. Despite the instant dislike he'd taken to the man, his gut wrenched. Nobody deserved this.

After he'd taken in what he could see of the cellar, and feeling surprisingly shaken by what he'd encountered, he next went up to Murfitt's bedroom to gather what little there was to be gained, before clattering back down the carpetless stairs.

Reardon was leaning against the wall, arms crossed, thinking. The kitchen, far too small to have served as a living room as well, was as comfortless a place as the spartan bedroom. There was a red, quarry-tiled floor with only a thin, cheap, Turkey-patterned mat. A straight-backed wooden chair drawn up to a card table covered with oilcloth, a sink in the corner with a cupboard above. One sagging armchair covered in greasy green plush, with its stuffing escaping and an untidy pile of left-wing weeklies on the floor beside it. Thin cotton curtains with a design that had long since faded into nothing but blurs. Maybe Murfitt had grown accustomed to such privations during his years as a conscientious objector . . . or was it a denial of an upbringing he'd come to despise? An obviously educated man with a public school accent, the few clothes he had possessed were of superior quality, if somewhat the worse for wear. Shirts from Jermyn Street, Lobb handmade shoes. Those fancy pyjamas. The suitcase holding his underclothes had been real leather, not cheap cardboard. His only other possessions appeared to have been his stock of books, the paper on which to write his poems, and the expensive, gold-plated fountain pen.

Gilmour let his glance roam around. 'Not exactly the Ritz, is it?'

'You could say that. But maybe it didn't matter. Do you have the same impression as me, Joe, that he didn't intend being here for long? No photographs, personal papers, letters, anything like that. As if he was only a bird of passage?'

'That is how it looks,' Gilmour agreed. 'Do we know just how long he's been living here?'

'Not yet, we don't.' Reardon looked thoughtful. 'Was he lying, I wonder – all that guff about why he'd set up a business here?'

'Why would he have done that – unless to cover up for something else? Seems a bloomin' funny place to choose, otherwise.'

Mooching around, Gilmour opened the door of the cupboard over the sink. It held nothing more than mismatched crockery and some essentials of food: tea, sugar in a blue bag, a crusted, half-used can of condensed milk, a few other tins. He peered at the two mugs sitting there and pulled a face. 'What kind of slob puts used mugs back in the cupboard? Teapot as well,' he added, using his handkerchief on the handles to lift them all down one by one and set them on the wooden draining board.

The mugs did indeed contain dregs of what seemed to be tea and there were used tea leaves at the bottom of the brown teapot. Murfitt had lived carelessly, scruffily even – his clothes thrown on to the floor, the untidy pile of newspapers, the overflowing ash pan under the grate, the brass fire irons not cleaned for many a day, if ever. The mat that should have lain in front of the fender sat ruckled up and shoved anyhow towards the sink. It was highly unlikely the window would sparkle even when it was clear of condensation.

Still, putting away used mugs – *two*, plus an unemptied teapot – back into a cupboard seemed over the top, even for him. And even odder, the hearth had been swept clean. Reardon's glance sharpened. The white Belfast sink, too, was spotless, and so was the quarry-tiled floor. Automatically he bent to straighten the ruckles in the mat before someone tripped over it. Did he imagine a slight dampness as he lifted it? He left it positioned where it was.

'So he was killed here,' Gilmour said, when he'd explained what he was thinking.

'Looks very much like it. I think it's possible that's why he was shoved into the cellar. To get him out of the way while whoever it was cleaned up in here . . . They'd need a bit of elbow room and there's not much of that. Likewise the mugs and the teapot . . . lifted out of the way into the cupboard, and forgotten. There must have been a heck of a lot of blood. But look how clean the sink is, the whole floor.'

'Right. But why bother cleaning up at all? It's not as though Murfitt was likely to stay undiscovered for long.'

'If it hadn't been for the dog, it could have been days, given the few customers or visitors he had.'

'He was thrown down the cellar steps, hoping it would be taken for an accident? Then why not silence the dog as well?'

'Maybe he hoped it would look as though Murfitt himself had put him in there before going down those dangerous steps into the cellar . . . Unless whoever it was knew about the ventilation grid, he probably thought the barking wouldn't be heard – and anyway, if the room was airless, the dog would eventually shut up of his own accord.'

The thought was nasty enough to silence them both for some time.

Reardon was still puzzled. 'What the hell was he doing here, this Murfitt, and who was he anyway, Joe?'

'We'll find out.' But how? By his fingerprints? Only if he had a police record. Dental records? Only if you'd established his identity. 'Well, I suppose if he was a conchie, there'll be official records. Theo might give some help,' he added hopefully, 'or Sadie

Bannerman, if she knew him well enough to exercise his dog. And he was friendly with Verity Lancaster, wasn't he?'

Reardon thought about it, but another question, with an equally uncomfortable conclusion, intruded. Not only who Murfitt was, or why he'd been killed, but more specifically, why just at this time? Was it possible that the visit he and Gilmour had paid on the book-seller had indicated a dangerous interest, and somehow sparked off the attack? Unwelcome as the idea, was, it remained a possibility.

While he'd been thinking, he'd noticed a check tweed cap hanging forlornly alone from a hook fixed to the door leading into the shop and suddenly his gaze sharpened as he recollected something Flo Parslowe had said. Where was that big coat she said he wrapped himself up in when he went out? He imagined Murfitt coming downstairs in answer to the bell, wearing only his pyjamas and socks. Opening the door to someone he knew. The kitchen cold, the fire almost out. What more natural than to don the coat, conveniently hanging on the back of the door, while he made a pot of hot tea? Two mugs. For himself and the visitor he must have known and admitted. The visitor who had turned out to be his killer. Who had taken the coat away because it was blood-soaked? Or maybe . . . if Murfitt *hadn't* worn it, to cover up his own bloodstained clothing?

'It's a possible theory,' agreed Gilmour. But of course that was all it was, just a theory, unless the coat should turn up somewhere.

The kitchen having revealed all it could at the moment, they went back into the shop. Nothing new there, either. Except that Reardon found he'd been doing Murfitt an injustice. In the store-room, he found a stock list and an untidy notebook recording acquisitions and a few sales. They were, however, unaccompanied by any names and addresses, still less by a note of any monetary transactions.

Gilmour had turned his attention to a cardboard box, half full of waste paper. Tipping it on to the floor, he began to sort out discarded bits of brown wrapping paper and several sheets containing unfinished lines of poetry. Nothing appeared to have any significance until he smoothed out the last crumpled ball of paper. 'Hello, what have we here, then?'

*   *   *

Reardon decided the business he had at Bryn Glas could wait until the crime scene had been photographed, fingerprinted and otherwise minutely examined, and the body taken away to the mortuary. He wanted to talk to the technician in charge.

Meanwhile, what was to happen to the dog?

There wouldn't be any question of him staying at the Fox, not if Fred Parslowe had anything to do with it. The howling had stopped but Tolly was refusing to eat, not even a morsel from the tempting bowl of scraps provided by Flo. She'd put a blanket in the old kennel and kept talking to him, patting his head as she passed. But all her attempts resulted in nothing more than a sad, soulful look from wounded eyes, as his head rested dolefully on his paws. The only time he roused himself was to snap at the geese when they became too curious, who hissed back but waddled away. He was a miserable dog indeed, not used to being chained up and obviously confused and possibly grieving at what had happened to his best friend.

It looked like the nearest police pound for poor Tolly, until Gilmour reminded Reardon that he did have another friend.

TWENTY

Half an hour later, Gilmour had left Murfitt's shop behind and was striding off with Tolly on a lead.

Once away from the environs of the shop the little dog trotted more or less obediently by his side, after one or two attempts to repeat the circus act he'd performed with Sadie Bannerman. 'Stop that,' Gilmour told him sternly, and was gratified when Tolly obeyed, evidently still somewhat subdued and perhaps remembering what they'd left behind. Poor little devil. He still looked down in the mouth and his ears appeared to droop more than was normal, but the further they went from the scene of the crime, the more he perked up. He was a dandy little feller, really, very smart in his white, black and tan fur and Gilmour liked his spirit and the random markings of his coat which had resulted in a sooty patch over one eye, giving him a jaunty, piratical air. He wondered if the dog had witnessed the murder. If so, whoever had done it would have been lucky to get away without being bitten or at the very least, a piece taken out of his trousers.

They were on their way to Sadie's house. 'And a right jolly time she's going to have with you,' Gilmour murmured as they reached the terraced row on Lessings Lane. He knocked on the cheerful, pillar-box red front door and braced himself to deliver the tidings of what had happened to Murfitt, plus a request for boarding the dog that might not be too popular. Bringing news of a death to anyone, and even more especially when it had been murder, was something every policeman might have to face at some point in their career; it was part of the job, but one every man dreaded. In this case, he'd no idea what the relations between Murfitt and Sadie Bannerman had been – whether she'd been simply a friend or acquaintance who'd obliged him by exercising his dog, or whether there'd been more to it. He was also charged with finding out what information she could give on Murfitt's background. On the face of it their association seemed unlikely, the fetching Miss Bannerman and the unprepossessing and much older Murfitt, but you never knew.

After he'd knocked several times and received no answer, he tentatively tried the knob, but the door didn't give and was evidently locked. He was contemplating going round to the back of the house when the next-door neighbour came out with a shopping basket over her arm. 'If you're looking for Miss Bannerman, she's gone.'

'Do you know when she might be back?'

The woman was middle-aged, sharp-featured and with a nosy expression. 'Looks like she's left for good, to me. A motor car came for her and off she went in it with all her baggage. I couldn't help but see, I'd just stepped out to shake my duster.'

'Right.' Gilmour wished he had a pound for every time a duster happened to be shaken by a neighbour when something interesting was going on next door. She no doubt spent all her time at the window, twitching the curtains and on the lookout, and he had no illusions that she didn't know who he was. Word of the arrival of the police in this small place, and why they were there, would hardly be a secret. With a neighbour like this, he could understand why Sadie had said you couldn't blow your nose in Hinton without everyone knowing.

He didn't feel inclined to discuss anything with her, but he'd be daft not to take advantage of her nosiness. 'She left in a taxi?'

'No. There's only Swayne's taxis from Wyvering round here, and it wasn't his. The driver was wearing a uniform, though, very smart.'

Gilmour kept his expression neutral and added a smile. 'Right, thank you, Mrs . . .?'

'Tansley. Martha Tansley.'

'Thank you, Mrs Tansley. I'll just – er – give Tolly here a run around, at the back, then.' He nodded and she laughed as he went through the passage separating the two blocks of houses, but she had no option but to be on her way. He understood the amusement when he rounded the corner and saw the alley behind, with the hillside rising steeply at one side and a series of wooden gates on the other, leading into nothing more than the backyards of the houses. Tolly would get no run around here.

The gate to Sadie's house was on a latch and opened easily on to the flagged backyard, but the back door was as firmly locked as the front. He stood chewing his lip and debating what to do. Sadie had told them her job with Penrose Llewellyn had been only a temporary arrangement. Perhaps she'd felt no need to fulfil her obligations now that he was dead, even though she'd offered her further services to help him with those papers, without any indication that she might be leaving today. He was beginning to get an uneasy feeling. The day hadn't begun well with the discovery of Adrian Murfitt's body. He baulked at the idea of Sadie Bannerman wielding a coal hammer, or anything of the sort, on the man and then making a run for it, but reminded himself again that anything was possible, perhaps especially where she was concerned.

She'd been seen to leave the house, and if what the neighbour had said was true, with all or most of her belongings – and there was no hope now of finding a home here, if only a temporary one, for Tolly. So all he could reasonably be expected to do was to abandon the situation. But he was intrigued, and when Gilmour was intrigued, he took action.

There was an outhouse built against the wall and just above it a small window that had been left open. Either Sadie had left in such a hurry that she'd forgotten it, or she didn't think securing the premises was important enough to bother about. He attached Tolly firmly to the fall pipe by his lead and then dragged the dustbin across and clambered on to it. Thinking this was a game, the dog enthusiastically tried to join in. 'Shut up, Tolly, you'll wake the neighbourhood.' He didn't want another Mrs Tansley poking her nose in. Tolly took no notice; his barking rose and the fall pipe shook. It was odds on which would give way first, the pipe or the dog, but he wouldn't have put his shirt on the pipe. Short of gagging the dog, he would just have to hope there were no more neighbours at home.

It was only a small window and Gilmour was a big lad, but he got through without breaking it and found himself in an empty bedroom. As soon as he disappeared, Tolly ceased barking, probably lapsing into suicidal despair at being deserted yet again, this time by his new friend. Hoping he wouldn't start the horrible howling again, Gilmour thanked the Lord for present mercies all the same and began to look through the rest of the house. It was furnished, though minimally, and with only the bare essentials, pretty obviously second or even fourth or fifth hand. Any trace that Sadie Bannerman had ever been there (with the possible exception of the new-looking poppy-strewn curtains) had been removed. Apart, that was, from the bed, unmade and left just as she had risen from it that morning. And also a quantity of pink face powder spilled on the scratched, oak-veneered surface of the chest of drawers which served as a dressing table, full ashtrays, the remains of breakfast on the kitchen table, unwashed dishes in the sink, two extremely dirty tea towels and the grease-spattered kitchen range on which she'd cooked her meals. It would have given his Maisie a heart attack. The colourful and scented Miss Bannerman, that thoroughly modern miss, had been a slob.

'So what are we going to do with you?' he asked Tolly, who greeted him when they met again as though he'd been away six months rather than fifteen minutes, tearing round him and entangling his legs in the lead as he tried to untie it from the fall pipe, and making gymnastic leaps to reach his face for a loving lick. 'Get down, that'll get you nowhere, mate, if that's what you're hoping. You wouldn't like Dudley, and a new baby in the house.'

*   *   *

The technical squad had arrived at the shop and done their job. The photographic paraphernalia was set up and Murfitt's body photographed in situ, then manoeuvred up from the cellar and through the shop into the waiting ambulance and driven away. While the photographer was flashing away in the kitchen, Reardon had a few words with the technician, Detective Sergeant Ledgerwood. 'Traces of blood in the grouting between the kitchen tiles under that mat you said was damp and more between the floorboards in the shop,' Ledgerwood said. 'There's no doubt somebody did make a fair attempt at cleaning up, though why he bothered . . . you'd think they'd know by now, we always find something.'

But the public weren't as savvy as the sergeant made out. Nor everybody in the Force, either, for that matter. Ledgerwood, on the other hand, was meticulous, a big man with a domed bald head, thick neck and narrow shoulders, the bottle-bottomed specs he wore adding to the impression of a fat, juicy caterpillar. Dedicated to his job, he had fingerprinted everything in sight and bagged up the mugs and the teapot.

'Obviously, he meant it to look like an accident.'

Ledgerwood was unimpressed. 'Not very successfully, then. Bit of an amateur job all round. I suppose he very likely didn't have much time but he took enough to burn something in the fire.' Reardon looked hopeful. 'Hold your horses – it's not going to help. Only ash, not enough left to be useful. Just thought you ought to know.

'Something, you said. Like towels, perhaps?' Reardon asked, having noticed the lack of them in the kitchen.

'*Towels*? Good grief no, nothing like that, it was just paper. Quite a bit of it, I should estimate – but there's no chance of saving anything from it. Whoever burnt it made sure there was nothing identifiable left in the ashes.'

That, then, would account for the absence of anything in the way of documents which would have been useful in identifying Murfitt.

On this cold day the kitchen at Bryn Glas was cosily inviting: a glowing fire, reflected in the shining, blackleaded iron range; the housekeeper lifting risen bread dough from an enormous, brown earthenware mixing bowl on to the table and its yeasty smell permeating the room. She waved him to a seat and apologized for not being able to leave the dough. 'That's all right, Mrs Knightly. You carry on. We can talk as you work.'

'Just as you like – doing two things at once is what we're here for anyway, us women.' She scraped the last of the sticky mixture from the bowl's yellow-glazed interior, floured her hands from a stone jar and began to knead the heavy, doughy mass on the table, pummelling and stretching, knuckling it back into shape, a job she'd done a thousand times and more.

'Tell you what, though, I could do with a cup of tea,' Reardon said. There wasn't really time to waste, in the middle of a new murder investigation, but the universal panacea had its uses. He sensed there might be an unwillingness to talk and sharing a cuppa could invite confidences. 'If you don't object to me making it.'

'Help yourself, do.' She went on with her work, telling him where to find tea, milk and sugar, and what teapot to use. He swivelled the trivet round on to the hot fire for the kettle to boil. Outside the window, the couple of lads who were working with Mrs Douglas on the garden could be seen still beavering away.

Following his gaze, Mrs Knightly remarked, 'Bit of a waste of time, all that, isn't it? I doubt whether any of them will be wanting a fancy garden now . . . but ten to one they'll be selling the house, so I suppose it'll have to be left decent. Put another spoonful in the pot, I like it strong. You'll find a kettle-holder on that hook there.'

The water boiled and when the tea was made, he looked for mugs, found them on the dresser and brought everything to the table. Sitting himself down, he watched her while he waited for the tea to brew and she chattered on about the garden and her late master's enthusiasm for his latest project. But it wasn't the garden he wanted to talk about.

'You'll have heard what's happened at the bookshop, Mrs Knightly?' he asked as soon as he found the right moment.

'I've heard, yes.' Slap, slap went the dough. 'Terrible accident.'

'Yes. It's a sorry business, a young chap like that. I was wondering if you might be able to help.'

'Me? What sort of help?' She paused to give him a sharp glance. 'Why in the world should you think of me?'

'Well, we don't know much about Mr Murfitt but I've been talking to the landlady at the Fox, and—'

'Flo Parslowe? Oh, well then, you'll know all there is to know,' she said tartly, with a final thunk of the dough on to the table.

'On the contrary,' he said pacifically. 'She didn't have anything to tell me, but she did seem to think you might. Since I had the same idea, that's why I'm here.'

She moved a stray strand of hair back from her forehead with her forearm. It struck him how tired she was looking, pale with worry. Keeping house in the aftermath of death, having so many unwilling, and for the most part uncooperative, guests in the house to provide meals for and generally look after was telling on a woman of her age and she was showing the strain. He wondered if she was also worried about her position in the household, now that Pen had gone.

Without having answered him, she had picked up a bread knife and began to divide the now elastic dough into pieces, and then to shape them into loaves for the waiting loaf tins. The loquacious housekeeper who had so freely given them all that information when they had first met her, wasn't so anxious now to talk, seemingly. He let her get on with what she was doing while he poured the tea, now dark and strong, added milk and asked if she took sugar. She shook her head and put the loaf tins in a row on the hearth before the range fire to prove, covering them with a tea towel and then opening the damper to increase the heat for the oven. She had a wicker chair near the fire for an occasional sit-down, but a large black cat going grey round the mouth and ears was curled up on its cushion and didn't look inclined to move. Mrs Knightly didn't try. After she'd washed her hands at the sink she joined Reardon at the kitchen table, sinking on to the chair opposite, and began to sip her tea.

'Why?' she said at last. 'Why should you think I would know anything about Adrian Murfitt?' He took a cautious sip from his own cup and hoped it would leave some enamel on his teeth. It was strong enough to strip paint.

'Look at it this way – how many people do you knit argyle socks for, Mrs Knightly? Or Fair Isle pullovers?'

'Oh.' She was taken aback, but after a moment or two she gave a rueful smile. 'Oh, well, no use trying to fool a detective, is there?'

He spread his hands. After all, that was what detection really amounted to – an association of ideas; in this case, argyle socks on slipperless feet at the bottom of Murfitt's stone steps and the brightly patterned knitting on Mrs Knightly's busy needles, the home-knitted jumper Murfitt had been wearing at their only meeting.

'Poor Adrian, he needed someone to look after him. You know what it is, men on their own. He'd only let me do so much, but somebody had to do something. Doing a bit of knitting for him and a meal now and then wasn't much.' She paused and stirred her tea unnecessarily. 'I reckon you already know he was my nephew, don't you? Everybody else in Hinton does.'

'No, Mrs Knightly, I didn't know, but I thought it must be something like that.' In actual fact he'd speculated on the relationship being closer. 'I'm sorry. It's the worst kind of shock when something like this happens to someone you're fond of.'

She took a moment to answer. 'I suppose I was fond of him, in a way.' Seeing his surprise she explained, 'I didn't rightly know him all that well, you see, not until he came to live in Hinton. And even then, we didn't get close. He wasn't an easy person to know, or to talk to. But I was sorry for him, like.'

'We've heard stories . . .'

'I'm sure you have,' she said drily. 'They'll have told you . . . he wasn't popular. Folks don't forget easy.'

'Not when it comes to being a conscientious objector, I agree.'

'There was that, of course. There was seven lads, see – *seven,* just from Hinton – went away to fight and never came home, so can you blame them? I couldn't altogether bring myself to forgive Adrian for that, either, but it wasn't exactly a bed of roses for him, you know. Tribunals when he fought against conscription . . . arrested and sent to prison when he wouldn't even agree to drive an ambulance or anything. He was made to work as a road mender at one time, and much worse. You can't imagine.' Reardon had no need to imagine. He knew, but there was no point in increasing her evident distress by saying so. 'But there was more than all that to it, besides. It goes back a long way . . . and it's complicated.'

'These sort of explanations usually are. But take your time, I'm in no hurry.' He was, but a long explanation would at least enable him to avoid giving offence by getting down this cup of lethal brew in front of him in small sips.

It took her a minute or two, but once begun, the explanations poured forth. Adrian was her sister's child, she said, her youngest sister, Pattie – 'Patience, she was christened, and never did a name suit anyone less!' It was a familiar story. Pattie had left home to go into service with a wealthy family and had got herself into trouble with some gentleman who was visiting the big house in Shrewsbury where she worked. 'Poor little Pattie. No better than she should be, all the old busybodies said, but they were wrong. She was a lovely girl, high-spirited and maybe a bit spoilt, being the baby in our family, but she wasn't *bad*. A bit flighty, maybe, and I have to admit she wasn't all that bright . . . what I mean is, she just believed everything he promised, that fellow. When you've been poor – there was eight of us children and my father only a farm labourer on the Fairlie estate—'

'The Fairlie estate?'

'Well, it's not an estate now, of course, it's all gone, the home farm, shooting rights, the lot, since Mr Henry, Mr Gerald's father, died,' she said, looking a little put out at the interruption. 'What does a busy doctor want with an estate and lands, even supposing he had the time, or even if he was cut out for it?'

'Of course. I'm sorry, carry on.'

'What was I saying? Oh, yes, just that you learn to take your chances where you can get them if you were like us. It was different for me, I was luckier than most, marrying a good man like my John. Though I'll give him one thing, he did look after Pattie – that one who was Adrian's father, I mean. He bought her a nice little cottage over to Bridgnorth and kept in touch with her, and left money to make sure she was never in need – right up until she died last year. And although he never even saw Adrian, he made sure he had a good education. Had him sent away to school, though I reckon that's where it all went wrong. Uplands House it was, that posh school t'other side of Wyvering. He turned out to be clever, though, and he got some sort of scholarship to Oxford . . . and that was where he learnt to mix with the wrong sort. Politics and what they call socialism and all that. He was against the war and when it came, he wouldn't fight.' She looked troubled. 'I reckon you have to do what you believe is right, but it didn't turn out wonderful for him, as I've said.'

'Was it his father who left him money to buy the bookshop?'

'What? Bless you, no!' Her kindly face, which had creased with distress during the recital of this old, painful story, suddenly grew wary. She opened her mouth to speak, shut it and then changed her mind and said quickly, 'The shop didn't belong to Adrian, see.' Another pause. 'It was Mr Penrose who owned it.'

Reardon digested this as the silence lengthened, broken only by the sounds of the fire drawing up the chimney. It had grown very hot in the kitchen. Mrs Knightly topped up her teacup with what was now a distinctly evil-looking brew, and he only just managed to stop her from doing the same to his. He said slowly, 'Are you telling me *he* was Adrian Murfitt's father?'

'Good gracious no, inspector, that I'm not! And what's more you don't need to know who he was,' she added with a new firmness. 'That one's long gone, and you wouldn't know him, anyway. Mr Penrose bought that shop from the goodness of his heart. And now, if you'll excuse me, I have to see to my bread.' She rose and he watched as she slid the loaf tins one by one into the oven. It gave out a blast of heat as she opened the door and when she'd finally put them all in, closed it and turned round, she was mopping her face with a corner of her apron. But he didn't think it was perspiration she was wiping away. After a moment she said quietly, 'They're saying he fell down them cellar steps, Adrian. Is it true?'

'He was found at the bottom, Mrs Knightly.'

'And what reason would he have to go prowling about at night down into a dark cellar?' She gave him an old-fashioned look. 'It wasn't an accident, was it?'

'There's cause for concern,' he admitted at last.

The big kitchen clock he'd noticed on his first visit here just then reached the hour and struck a loud, bossy four. 'Goodness is that time?' she exclaimed. 'And that Prue not here yet to help with the vegetables!'

She'd no sooner said it than Prue walked in, bringing with her a breath of the cold outdoors. She smiled as she hung her coat up on the back of the kitchen door. 'Brr, it's cold out there. Reckon there'll be another frost tonight.'

'Then a good hot soup's what we'll be wanting.' Mrs Knightly began bustling about, giving instructions, sending Prue for vegetables from the adjacent scullery. Reardon stood up, thinking of what Kate Ramsey had said to him. 'I'll not trespass much longer on your time, Mrs Knightly, but just one more thing . . . did your nephew by any chance come to visit you the night Mr Penrose died?'

'Gracious, I'd no time to be entertaining visitors that night! We had a supper party on, don't forget.'

'I'm talking about after the guests had gone home? Did Adrian come to visit you then?'

'That time of night? I've told you, I was tired and after we'd finished tidying up and Prue had gone home, I went straight to bed.'

Maybe the shadow Kate Ramsey had seen along the lane had been imaginary, after all.

Phyllis Knightly had never been blessed with children, but she'd always been happy with her situation at Bryn Glas. Firstly, working as a maid and then after she'd married, working in the house and helping the nanny to look after the Llewellyn children, while her husband worked as farm manager. And later, after his death and when everything had changed, she'd become housekeeper. Later still, when all the family had gone, her job had become more that of a caretaker, which she hadn't minded in the least – the house had been almost like her own. She lived here alone except for weekends and the odd times when any of the family came to stay, but empty or not, it wasn't in her nature to leave rooms undusted and uncared for, even if unoccupied. She kept everything like a new pin, smelling of Mansion polish and lavender. When Pen, always her favourite, had come back to live here permanently, things hadn't changed much – he liked the homely sort of meals she cooked for herself and was happy enough for her to keep things as they'd always been.

His decision to marry Anna Douglas had come as no surprise

to her. She was fond of saying she'd known both of them since they were knee high to a grasshopper, and thought it was the best decision he'd made in years. Everyone knew two women couldn't wring one dishcloth, but she wasn't worried about Anna coming here as the new mistress; there'd be no problem. She was in fact looking forward to her retirement, and already had her eye on the nice little house presently occupied by old Philips, who was ninety-two and told her every time she visited him with a bit of cake or a rice pudding she'd made for him, that he couldn't last much longer and didn't want to.

But now . . .

She lifted the sleeping cat and flopped into her chair. The wicker creaked as she sank heavily into it with the cat on her knee and stroked his black fur. Prue worked quietly at the sink, scraping carrots. The rich, nutty smell of the baking loaves came from the oven. It was one of those times she most enjoyed, a quiet well-earned sit in her ordered kitchen after a strenuous day, with the smell of good wholesome cooking filling the room.

'Oh, Silas, what am I to do?' she whispered in the cat's ear, tears now rolling down her face unheeded. Silas merely shifted his position, kneading his claws into her soft lap, and settled and closed his eyes again. Mrs Knightly wiped her eyes.

How far should you go in telling the truth?

TWENTY-ONE

After the hot kitchen, the cold outside, with its sharp fore-taste of frost in the air, was a welcome relief.

The light was fading fast and the two young lads working in the garden were packing up their tools for the day. Reardon raised a hand in salute as he passed them and felt their eyes following him, wondering what had brought him out there so late. The fact was, he wanted to clear his mind and mull over something Mrs Knightly had just said, and how it could be connected to the scrap of paper Gilmour had found in Murfitt's bookshop; a note Murfitt had begun but maybe changed his mind about. He needed to speak to Huwie Llewellyn, but for a few minutes that could wait.

Reaching the wall that seemed to mark the boundary of the property, he leant against it, looking back at the house. The lads had gone and the house crouched long and low against the hillside rising behind it. In the gathering dusk, it had a surprisingly menacing look, its windows lit here and there but with no signs of life showing behind them. The house that held a murderer. Perhaps a murderer twice over. The second time was easier, they said, yet it was more likely then that mistakes could be made. It was in spotting them where the skill lay, or maybe the luck. He grunted, turned his back on the house and was just resting his elbows on the wall before it occurred to him that as the safety measure it had surely been intended, the wall was now less than adequate, perhaps even dangerous. A few of the capping stones had fallen off and the roots of a stunted tree that had found purchase and unaccountably survived in the precipitous rock face had created an ominous bulge near where he stood. He looked down over the wall and felt dizzy. There were caves in the cliff, he'd heard, not visible from here, hidden by the scrub, and the river could be treacherous at times. It wound into the distance, a sinuous steel-grey band you could see if you leant far enough over the wall.

He let his thoughts wander, an unproductive activity that all the same often produced results, he'd found, but this time the flash of insight or inspiration he waited for didn't come. He looked out across the comely, rolling acres, green and lush even at this time of year, but shadowed now and *empty*. He hadn't met a single soul in the whole ten minutes it had taken to walk from Murfitt's shop to Bryn Glas, he now realized. He drew a deep breath of air into his lungs. Not above twenty miles away, back home, cold air like this gave you bronchitis, laden as it was with smoke and factory fumes. The wind, when it was in the right direction, stung your eyes and ears and blew smuts and soot into the clothes on the women's washing lines. And when it didn't blow, there was that ever-present smoke pall. He realized he was missing it: the cheerfully crowded streets, shops and familiar accents, noisy traffic, the foundries and smoke stacks that were a fact of Black Country life. And Ellen . . . He felt a sudden urgent need to see her, for at the very least a half-hour of normality. His vows for them not to meet vanished as though they'd never been. Excusing himself with the thought that in any case he had something to show her, to ask her advice about, with a last look at the serpentine river, he roused himself and went back indoors.

Walking down the corridor towards the study, he glanced through the upright struts into that room they used as a sitting room and saw Verity crouching there. Her mother had succeeded at last in prizing her out of her little dormer room like a winkle from its shell, but it hadn't made much difference to her mood. She seemed to spend all her time huddled up to the fire, in the same position as she was now. The fight had gone out of her once more, the spark of animation she'd shown when Reardon had spoken with her outside Kate's cottage was extinguished. She sat there alone. Where were all the others? Dressing for dinner no doubt, if Claudia Llewellyn had anything to do with it. Somebody should remind them they were out in the sticks, not bloomin' Mayfair.

'Hello, Verity,' he said, going through into the room and joining her.

'Oh, hello,' she answered drearily. She was wearing the same shapeless dark garments she'd worn before, and she looked as though she'd been crying. The news of Murfitt's death must have upset her more than he would have anticipated. He was wondering how best to broach the subject when she did it for him. 'Have you caught him yet? The one who killed Adrian?'

News travelled in this place faster than a ferret down a rabbit hole. First Mrs Knightly and now Verity, both of them knowing it had been no accident. But it was no use denying what eventually must come out if he wanted answers to questions. 'I'm sorry, you were a friend of his, it must have been a shock.'

'A friend?' she came back, rather violently. 'Who told you that? The only time he was a *friend* was when he needed me to drive him around! When that old Tin Lizzie of his wouldn't go.'

He was taken aback. Yet she had been crying, and if it wasn't for Murfitt, who was it for? She would of course still be grieving for Pen, the uncle she'd thought so much about, but she'd surely got past the floods of tears stage by now? It made him feel sorry for her and he didn't pursue, for the time being, what he suspected might be an unprofitable, if intriguing line. 'I'm sorry if I got it wrong, but all the same, you might feel able to answer a question that's puzzling us a bit. We're interested in a coat of his that appears to have gone missing. Would you know if he's got rid of it recently? A dark green one?'

'Oh, that coat!' She added scornfully, 'His prize possession. He'd never have got rid of that, never. He said it had belonged to his father.'

His father?

'The old man had had it specially tailored for him years ago in London. Green loden cloth – you know, the sort they wear in Austria, with a Persian lamb collar. It had his father's name or something embroidered on the inside.'

Green loden overcoat, with a fur collar. The last word for the dashing Edwardian gentleman, worn with a homburg or a top hat and a silver-topped cane. Bespoke London tailoring like that was expensive, built to last, and it was often passed on, he knew – men's fashions didn't change that much, after all, and there were still coats around like that. They cost a fortune and were made to last a lifetime – that of the original owner and anyone he passed it on to.

'His name was inside, you said?'

'Well, I never actually saw it. Adrian only mentioned it to show off, when he told me the coat had belonged to his father.' She sounded far too bitter for such a young woman.

After a moment he said carefully, 'Then you didn't know he was illegitimate?'

'Adrian? What? Really?' She went silent, and began to look very troubled. After a moment or two she said, 'That would explain a lot, I suppose. He had a huge chip on his shoulder about families and money and that sort of stuff. He was very mixed up, you know, apart from that pacifism thing.' She began to cry.

'Miss Lancaster, please. I hadn't realized you were so attached to each other.'

He judged it better not to risk putting his foot further in and presently she recovered herself sufficiently to scrub away at her wet face with her handkerchief, before saying, in a subdued voice,

'No, I've just told you, we weren't. We weren't attached. *I* was fool enough to think we were, perhaps, once, but not lately. And Adrian, never. I mistook his interest. He used me, like I said.'

Reardon was caught in a dilemma. He ought to take advantage of this opening to find out if she knew more, but he had doubts about whether she really did and in any case found himself loath to press her. If Murfitt had been as mixed up as she said he had been, then this young woman was even more so. He was saved from making a decision by the entrance of her mother.

His hope that Ida would be able to help calm down the situation was short-lived. Regarding the woeful appearance of her daughter with rather less exasperation than was usual, she went straight up to her and took her hand. Verity looked alarmed at this unaccustomed sign of affection, as well she might. 'Verity dear,' Ida said, in tones usually reserved for imparting the death of a loved one, 'I'm so sorry to have to tell you this, but it's Huwie . . .'

'What about Huwie? What's happened?'

'Well, you see –' she looked apologetically at Reardon – 'he's gone.'

'Oh,' said Verity.

'The thing is, Vee . . . now you mustn't get upset . . . he's taken your car.'

If Verity was beside herself with rage – and she surely was, her fury having miraculously dried up her tears – then Reardon was even more angry. Mainly with himself, for not having sought out Huwie immediately after seeing Mrs Knightly. But he didn't have to blame himself for long. Ida soon told them that he had left before breakfast. The Baby Austin had passed Prue, arriving for work, but she'd been in a hurry and hadn't looked at the driver. No one had noticed Huwie wasn't around until Theo, wishing to speak to him, had found his room empty and his belongings gone. Uncanny, almost a repeat performance of Verity's disappearing act, Reardon thought.

No one seemed particularly concerned that he had once more taken himself out of their lives, but they were united in indignation about the motor car. Something that had been regarded with amused tolerance in the family – Verity's little toy – had now caused Huwie to become a target for their condemnation.

'That's probably the least of it,' Theo said sourly. 'We'd better get Mrs Knightly to check the spoons and anything else of value. Though I can't really see what there is to be worried about. He'll come out of the woodwork sooner or later if he wants his share of Pen's money.'

No one refuted this. Huwie, without much effort, seemed to have the ability to alienate everyone he came into contact with. What Reardon was finding hard to understand was why none of them was asking *why* he'd disappeared so abruptly, just as a second murder had been discovered.

'You really mean there isn't much chance of getting my car back, inspector?' Verity interrupted, not intending to be sidetracked. 'You can't let him get away with it!'

'We-ell,' he temporized, not liking to be caught wrong-footed. Didn't she realize how many Baby Austins there were on the roads? It was the cheapest little model in Britain and for anyone who could just about afford to buy and run a motor, it was far and away the most popular choice. In this case, the anonymity it afforded as a getaway vehicle couldn't be faulted. Huwie had almost certainly headed back to London and the odds on finding the motor – or him – were about the same as backing the winner of the Grand National. But Verity wasn't accepting that.

She said, very sharply, 'There must be *something* that can be done to find it, you're the police, after all.'

Nevertheless Huwie had unwittingly done her a good turn. Where everything else had failed, the theft of her beloved car had had a truly electrifying effect. There was colour in her cheeks and a sparkle in her eyes that didn't bode well for Huwie, should he ever turn up again. She sounded almost like her mother.

'We'll do what we can,' Reardon said weakly.

But whatever was to be done, it was too late to do anything that night. He took himself back to the Fox, his mind churning.

They met as Gilmour, feeling like the Second Murderer in *Macbeth*, was fastening a reproachful Tolly back into the kennel behind the Fox, avoiding the dog's eyes. 'No joy with Miss Bannerman, then?' Reardon asked.

'You could say that,' Gilmour answered. 'She's gone.'

'*What?* She's gone as well? Gone where?'

'Who knows? But it looks as though it's for good. She left with all her luggage – in a chauffeur-driven car, according to her neighbour. Er – did you say "as well"?'

'We'd better go inside. I need a drink.'

Beside a roaring fire in the bar, over pints of bitter drawn by Fred, he told Gilmour about the missing Huwie, what Ledgerwood had uncovered about the burnt paper in the grate, and the information Verity had given about the missing loden overcoat. 'Ledgerwood was a bit scathing when I suggested the towels might have been burnt, so I wouldn't even suggest the coat could have gone the same way. It looks as though we might have been right, that our lad took it away when he left.'

'Our lad being Huwie?' Gilmour said. 'He'd still have to dispose of it – especially if it has a name in it.'

'If it has, you can bet on it that name won't be Murfitt.' Nor Llewellyn. Mrs Knightly had been adamant that Penrose Llewellyn hadn't been Adrian Murfitt's father. But then, Mrs Knightly, he was certain, hadn't been telling the truth about everything – or not the whole truth.

At the moment the question was academic. Neither of them, Pen or Adrian Murfitt, were here any longer to tell. And Huwie, who might have known, had disappeared. Sadie Bannerman gone, too. Huwie had left of his own free will, and so had Sadie – Reardon hoped. But was it coincidence that the two had shaken the dust of Hinton from their feet on the same day that Murfitt's body was discovered? They hadn't gone together, though. Mrs Tansley, Sadie's neighbour, would hardly have mistaken the motor in which Sadie had driven off for Verity's Baby Austin, much less Huwie Llewellyn for a smartly dressed chauffeur.

'We need to find Huwie, and Sadie, I suppose – though she'd every right to leave if that's what she wanted. She's an unlikely suspect for killing Murfitt, anyway – she might have bashed him on the head in a temper, but to break his skull like that she'd have had to give it more clout than I imagine she's capable of,' Reardon said, translating Dr Emerson's 'considerable force'. 'Any more than I can see her having the strength to drag him to the top of the cellar steps and heave him down.'

'Not to mention cleaning up after she'd done it,' Gilmour

added. 'She wouldn't know one end of a scrubbing brush from the other, believe me.'

'We've no reason to question her, in actual fact, though I'd liked to have talked to her. She said she came from London, didn't she? Fat lot of help that is.'

'We have her address, though.'

'We have?'

'There are copies of the letter Pen sent her when he offered her the job, and the one from her accepting it.' Gilmour was looking smug. The hours he'd spent with those papers hadn't been entirely wasted.

'Well done, Joe,' Reardon said, a bit winded, 'then that leaves us with the elusive Huwie. I don't suppose there were any convenient copy letters between him and his brother as well? All right, don't answer that . . . We do have the address he gave us but there's not much hope that he'll be there, even if it was authentic.'

'I dare say not,' Gilmour said slowly, 'but that note we found, the one Murfitt screwed up and chucked away: *"Huwie, I have decided. . ."* They knew each other, didn't they?' He was reaching for the appropriate folder, growing animated. 'That antiquarian bookshop Theo said he dealt with. Wasn't it in the Charing Cross Road?'

'Yes, or near enough.' Reardon's heart lifted as he saw where Gilmour was pointing and realized the address of the shop and the one Huwie had given as his own were identical. It could mean nothing, probably just Huwie automatically covering his tracks, he cautioned himself, rubbing his face until the ridges of his scars beneath his fingers made him aware what he was doing. All the same . . .

'Supper's ready, I think,' Gilmour said, interpreting signs from Fred at the bar.

Mrs Parslowe was wasted on Fred and the Fox. In another life she might have been cooking for visiting princes and potentates at the Savoy. But after a manful attempt, Reardon braced himself to face her over his failure to do proper justice to her oxtail stew and dumplings and announced he was going to see his wife. He left Gilmour to make up for him as a queen of puddings arrived, a triumph crowned with an airy meringue, and prepared to leave for Kate Ramsey's house.

'I'll take the dog with me, give us both some exercise.' This at least earned him a modicum of forgiveness from Flo, who had taken a fancy to Tolly and thought it a crying shame he should be chained up outside on a cold night like this. But Fred, once he'd got a decision stuck into his thick head, was not to be moved. That dog wasn't to be allowed a paw inside the Fox.

The walk was brisk enough to clear his head and as the road was empty as usual, Reardon felt it safe to let Tolly off the lead to work off some of his surplus energy. He was relieved to find him obedient when called to heel as they reached the cottage and that he hadn't rolled in anything unspeakable. The women had just finished their meal and were sitting by the fire with a tray of coffee. It took Ellen about ten seconds to uncurl herself from her favourite position on the hearthrug and cross the room. He gave her a husbandly kiss and warmed himself in her smile of welcome. 'Well, you two look very snug in here.'

There was a cosy, girls-together atmosphere that made him see with a sudden pang how much Ellen might miss evenings like this, with all those clever, like-minded chums she'd made in her previous life. She was London born and bred; the offer of a well-paid teaching job had brought her to Dudley and marrying him had kept her there. He was afraid that being a Black Country policeman's wife, without the career she'd been trained for, didn't offer much in the way of recompense. But he didn't know what he could do about it.

Kate went to fetch another cup. 'And who's this?' asked Ellen, stretching out a hand towards the dog.

'Tolly, short for Autolycus. Snapper up of unconsidered trifles, apparently,' Reardon said apologetically, hoping he'd got it right.

She laughed and held out her hand. Tolly needed no more invitation. She rubbed between his ears and when she resumed her place on the hearthrug, he sat beside her and put his head on her knee, gazing at her with ardent adoration in his eyes while she went on stroking him. After a while, soothed and with the edge taken off his exuberance for the time being by his walk, he settled to sleep in absolute bliss, waking up only to nudge her with his nose whenever her hand stopped stroking.

'I've seen him before. Doesn't he belong to that fellow who owns the bookshop? Adrian Murfitt?' Kate asked. Taken aback slightly, Reardon realized that the papers left strewn across the table probably meant the women had been working in the cottage all day and had failed to hear the news about Murfitt. Kate, who hadn't known him personally, but had been into the bookshop once or twice, was particularly shocked when he told them, as much at the thought of what was happening to quiet, uneventful Hinton as at the murder itself.

'Do you think it has something to do with Pen Llewellyn's death?' she asked.

'There appears to be some connection,' he said cautiously, and since they were bound to hear of it, he told them of Huwie's disappearance with Verity's motor car and why he himself was angling for a trip to London, in an effort to trace him. He didn't add his pessimistic view that nothing would come of it. 'Miss Bannerman has left unexpectedly, too,' he added.

'Perhaps they've eloped,' Kate said carelessly. 'Oh, how crass of me! But those two! No, forget I said that.'

'Kate, is there something I should know about them?'

'No. What I mean is, I don't know Huwie at all. I only met him that once, though he struck me as being . . . well, not the sort of person you would trust very far.'

'And Miss Bannerman?'

'Oh, Sadie. I didn't know her much better, I must confess, but I always wondered what she was doing here. I know she was Pen's secretary, but for someone like her to come and work here in Hinton . . . a bit odd, wasn't it? I mean, it's hardly the sort of job you'd choose to enhance your career prospects.'

'The same thing, more or less, applies to Adrian Murfitt.'

'Yes. And they both came here about the same time.'

'Hmm.' Not wanting to discuss the whys and wherefores of the case, which would be asking for it to be going round and round in his head all night, he slipped a hand inside his jacket and passed across to Ellen the poems Murfitt had been writing. 'Tell me what you make of these.' He watched her as she read them carefully, a little crease of concentration between her brows. She was wearing a jumper the colour of autumn leaves that he particularly liked her in. As she handed the papers to Kate, she caught him looking at her and smiled, looking more like herself than she had for weeks. Maybe it hadn't been such a bad idea for her to come here at that.

'What do you think, Kate?' she asked after a minute or two.

'I'm not sure.'

'Not very good, are they?'

'There are one or two that have something, but . . . oh well, one man's meat, you know.' She paused and pulled a face. 'All right, since the poor man's dead, it can't hurt him if I say I don't think they are . . . but it's only my opinion.'

'Mine, too, I'm afraid,' Ellen agreed. 'But as you say, poetry is very subjective. One thing I do think, though. There's a lot of anger in them.'

'He was angry about a lot of things that had happened to him,' Reardon said. 'I suppose it was one way of getting rid of it. It didn't seem to help him like anyone very much.'

'He liked his dog, though. What's going to happen to poor old Tolly?' asked Kate. Tolly pricked up his ears.

'His nice warm kennel's waiting for him.'

'I don't mean just now.'

'There's no future for him at the Fox, with Fred Parslowe around, that's for sure.' He explained the situation regarding Tolly and Fred.

Ellen looked shocked. 'Well, we can't let that happen, can we?' she said, looking at Reardon. 'Not when we have Gypsy's basket waiting at home. Which naturally had never even entered your head when you brought him here.'

Gypsy was their mongrel puppy who'd been killed under the wheels of a milk float when she ran out into the road. And of course he hadn't expected Ellen to think of taking Tolly on as a replacement. Of course not.

TWENTY-TWO

The enviable location of Bryn Glas did much to add to its attractiveness. Anna knew, however, those practical Tudor builders had almost certainly chosen the site for prosaic rather than romantic reasons, for the shelter the hill afforded, with its face to the light, rather than the magnificent outlook its principal windows commanded. Enough land surrounding the house for self-sufficiency in the days when it was a farm: a few rows of peas and beans, potatoes, a cow and a pig, perhaps, plus the extensive adjacent hilly acres where sheep could roam. A house like this, however, was nowadays expected to have something more than a one-time farmyard surrounding it. A garden would be required by any potential buyers, though would it now include the ambitious knot garden of Pen's imagination? Wouldn't keeping it clipped and in shape be too time-consuming to maintain, a Tudor conceit that wouldn't be appreciated?

'Are you sure you want to go on with the idea?' she'd brought herself to ask Theo once more. Now that he'd had time to think it over he would almost certainly have said no, if the decision had been his alone, she was sure, but Ida was all for it and the now-absent Huwie had unexpectedly given the scheme his approval. They had both been aided and abetted in this by Claudia who waved away discussion, saying languidly that although she personally didn't care one way or another, it would be an attractive feature when the house was put on the market.

Outside the windows at the back of the house, a narrow stream that ran down the hillside to join the river below had been diverted at one time and dammed to make a small pond out of what Anna had thought might have been the original sunken garden, but it had long ago silted up, the dam had given way and the stream now followed its natural course. At some point, the space the pond had occupied had been roughly filled in, perhaps to allow more room for farm carts to turn around or for some other mundane reason. Farmers, even now, didn't usually see the sense in wasting land that could be more usefully used in other directions on merely ornamental purposes. The pond had still been there when farming had been abandoned by his father, said Pen. He had particular memories as a boy, of lying in the grass at the edges, watching dragonflies skim its surface, though precisely when it had been filled in he couldn't remember, or why. Whatever the reason, it had left a sizeable but bumpy space in front of the windows, separated from them by a few square yards of old flagstones, before the gradient became steeper, eventually stopping at the wall above the giddy drop to the river.

As a garden, it was half-hearted to the point of non-existence. The addition of low, clipped knots filled in with herbs and flowering plants would add the character and interest it lacked, Pen had enthused, and although Anna had been doubtful of its appropriateness in such a context, she hadn't said so. The two young farm lads who were presently working as her assistants, at the moment unemployed because of the seasonal nature of farm work, were glad to have this job. Eamon Brannigan was one of a large Irish family who had for some reason fetched up in Hinton, a young giant who laughed and talked so much no one else got a word in edgeways. He was a cheerful presence and everyone liked him, despite the fact that he was wont to regale the world at large with not always tuneful renderings of 'O'Rafferty's Pig' and the like when he was wielding his pick. The much quieter Ned Clifford, Prue's brother, was tall, gangly and thoughtful, a sensitive lad who always had a book with him to read whenever he got the chance. Accustomed to hard farm labour, they were making good progress in the first digging of the hummocky ground.

The morning after Huwie's disappearance, Anna was taking a breather from calculating the number of box plants, hundreds certainly, that she would need to order for the low hedging which would set the Celtic knot pattern Pen had finally decided on. Crossing her arms against the cold she clutched her clipboard to her chest as she considered what flowers would complement and give colour to the traditional but duller herbs to be planted within the hedges: the lavenders, sages, thymes, rue and so forth. Deep in thought, the shout from a few yards away so startled her she almost dropped the clipboard.

Ned was standing as if God had sent a thunderbolt and struck him rigid, looking down at the freshly turned red earth. As Anna joined them, Eamon backed away. His face was white under its weatherbeaten tan. 'Jesus, Mary and Joseph,' he breathed, crossing himself.

'What's the matter, Eamon?'

Wordlessly, he pointed downwards. The sun gleamed on something white, only partly visible under a thin layer of disturbed soil, but unmistakably a skeleton, laid out flat. She could see clearly what looked very much like the top of a skull.

Ned managed to find his voice. 'We came to that big rock,' he said unsteadily, pointing to a great slab of sandstone on one side. 'When we managed to move it, we saw it.'

Pulling herself together, Anna said, 'I think the police are still here, in the office – one or other of them, at any rate. Go and tell them, Ned, will you? Don't say anything to anyone else.'

He nodded, and seeming glad of the action, sloped off at speed round the corner. Anna took the other boy's arm and led him to a wooden seat that stood by the dining-room windows. For all his strapping physique and extrovert personality, Eamon was far more shocked than Ned. 'I have to go,' he said, looking towards the turned earth and beginning to shake. 'Sorry, Mrs Douglas, but I can't stay here.'

'Eamon, I think you should, until the police have spoken to you.'

Their jackets had been thrown on the seat and she picked up the nearest one and placed it round his shoulders. Superstition ruled in the Brannigan family. His mother was reputed to have the gift: she could see spirits and the wee folk; she never let her children wear green or bring branches of mayflower into the house and she'd seen a crow hanging around their garden for days before Pen died. Anna forced herself to be calm. This might not be what they imagined. She had worked on the land during the war, doing her bit, and seen what a plough could turn up – pottery shards and glass bottles, sometimes ancient coins. Bits of old farm machinery and even, once, the grisly skeleton of what turned out to be a monkey, a source of absolute wonder that no one had ever been able to account for.

When the study door burst unceremoniously open, Reardon was engaged in a difficult telephone conversation over the usual crackly line with Superintendent Cherry, trying to persuade him it was necessary for both himself and Gilmour to make the trip to London. He listened with half an ear as Ned burst in, but Cherry was on the point of giving rather grudging consent and he flapped an in-a-minute hand towards the boy. Gilmour, however, heard him out and left at a run, arriving at the scene with Ned not two strides behind him.

The commotion had by now brought others out of the house, too. Everyone but Eamon stood on the bank of earth that had been thrown up around the turned-over area, staring down. Gilmour too looked at what lay half-concealed below until, after a moment or two, something about the arrangement of what he could make out began to seem not quite right. He turned to Mrs Knightly. 'Do you have a brush – a soft one?'

She nodded to Prue, who sped away and came back with a small, soft-bristled hand brush. 'Will this do?'

He probably shouldn't be doing this, Gilmour thought as he knelt on the soft earth, but if he was right . . . Very gently he brushed away the light covering of soil to expose the rest of the skull and then sat back on his heels. It took a moment for everyone else who had been following his actions to realize what they were seeing. There was a stunned silence. Then Ida, her hand to her mouth, exclaimed, 'Oh, my God, it's Rory!'

'He was our dog. A beautiful creature, an Irish wolfhound.' Theo's lugubrious face looked more mournful than ever.

'He was bigger than a donkey,' Ida remembered, 'one whisk of his tail might break your leg – or sweep everything off a table, come to that. He was always Theo's dog, really, hardly left his side, but everyone loved him.'

'Not everyone,' Theo corrected sharply. 'Though he was the gentlest, most sweet-tempered dog in the world.' For a man so little inclined to show his emotions, he was clearly upset by the discovery of the dog's skeleton. It wasn't hard to believe him one of those who liked animals better than people.

'So how did he come to be buried there?' Reardon asked them, asking himself how was it Theo hadn't known the grave of such a beloved dog was in the very place where they would be digging. 'Suppose one of you tells us when and how he died?'

Ida shrugged. 'Theo's the one to tell you. It must be over twenty years ago and I for one wasn't here when it happened, nor was Pen. We'd both married and left home by then. You were a late-starter, weren't you, Theo?'

'Claudia and I were in fact just about to be married. But . . . Look here, it was all a very long time ago and in any case I fail to see why it's necessary to drag up totally irrelevant stories about dead pets.'

'These family quarrels can be the very devil, can't they?' Reardon said.

Theo fixed Reardon with a basilisk stare. 'And just what made you say that, inspector?'

Reardon wasn't sure himself. Except for that 'not everyone' from Theo just now, which he thought was a dead giveaway. 'Your brother, Huwie, left home after some sort of contretemps between you. I think it had something to do with your dog's death.'

'And if it had . . .?' Theo drew in a deep, angry breath. 'Inspector, my other brother's death is the unfortunate reason you're here, but I fail to see why a decades' old family disagreement which didn't involve him is any concern of yours.'

Reardon was fast losing patience. 'Yes, we *are* here to investigate that death. And now another. Murder regrettably includes washing dirty linen, Mr Llewellyn.'

Theo was silent for so long Reardon thought he was going to refuse to answer. Ida nervously took her cigarette case from her bag and offered black Sobranies all round but only Theo took one, after a moment's hesitation. The smoke curled over the table and Ida finally burst out, 'Oh, do explain, Theo. We shall be here all day, otherwise.'

'It was something and nothing, that just got out of hand,' he said at last. This was so obviously not true, it must have sounded ridiculous to him also. At any rate, he suddenly abandoned the stonewalling and began speaking rapidly. 'I was home from London for the weekend, preparing to leave. It hadn't been a very comfortable weekend – the usual rows between my father and Huwie. He'd left school about two years previously . . . trying his hand at various jobs and not staying long in any of them, showing no signs of settling to anything. He'd brought an old school friend to stay that weekend, someone he'd been at Uplands House with, and they'd been out rabbiting. It was a hot day and we – my parents and I and two or three friends who'd joined us for lunch – were sitting outside taking coffee before I left. The two of them came back in tearing spirits – I think they were half drunk, in fact. Huwie didn't dare to drink too much in front of my father but no doubt they'd had a bottle with them. When they joined us they were cock-a-hoop because they'd bagged half a dozen rabbits and a few pigeons and Huwie tossed the bag down, silly fool, instead of disposing of it before they came to sit with us. Rory was a wonderful hunting dog – he had a gentle mouth, though he'd chase anything that ran. And . . .' He took a deep drag of the cigarette he'd only half-smoked, then squashed it out.

'And?'

'You can guess the rest. His natural instincts were roused. He went sniffing round the bag of course . . . grabbed it and was off with it before he could be stopped. He wasn't so young any more but he still had a turn of speed. The chap who was supposed to be a guest simply picked up his gun and shot him, dead.'

'Shot him? That was overreacting, surely?'

'Yes. But to give the young fellow his due, he was absolutely aghast at what he'd done. I think he'd picked the gun up instinctively, meaning to frighten Rory off – but a *dog* doesn't recognize that kind of threat. I've told you they were probably drunk but that was no excuse, and I . . . I didn't stop to think, I just saw red – and knocked the blighter down. He just lay there, looking positively sick and kept repeating he was sorry, but Huwie came for me like a fury. It was ridiculous, or so it seemed afterwards. Two grown men, fighting like street urchins. At the time, it seemed anything but that. I . . . well, I'd been good at boxing at school, and I only felt it was time somebody taught my stupid little brother a lesson he wouldn't forget.' A dark look crossed his face. 'God knows what would have happened, if it hadn't been for my mother. She jumped up – I think she had some idea of separating us – and then she just . . . collapsed. After that . . .'

It was lucky that Gerald Fairlie was one of the guests, Theo continued when he'd gathered himself. He still hadn't fully qualified, but he'd known enough to get Mrs Llewellyn upstairs and administer her medication. Theo had gone up with them and didn't come down again until after he'd seen his mother settled. By that time, neither Huwie nor his friend was to be found. 'I didn't in fact see my precious brother again until he came here for Pen's birthday party.'

'And Murfitt?' There was a silence. 'It *was* Adrian Murfitt

who was the guest, wasn't it?' Murfitt, whom Mrs Knightly said
had been sent to school at Uplands House, where Huwie had
also been a pupil. (The same school, incidentally, where Kate
had taught, though not at that time.)

'Yes. Yes, it was. How did you know?'

Gilmour said, 'We found a note from him addressed to your
brother.'

'But my God, you surely don't believe I've harboured a grudge
against him all these years until I could get rid of him?'

'People have been known to do that.'

'Except that I'm not one of them. Murfitt in fact had the grace
to write me a letter of apology afterwards, which put an end to
the matter as far as I was concerned.'

'So you forgave him?'

'It was a terrible thing to have happened, but it wasn't calculated, the drunken impulse of a moment, and I believe he deeply
regretted it. It was my brother I couldn't forgive,' he said coldly.
'If he hadn't interfered, my mother would not have collapsed.
He disappeared that same day and made no effort to contact her
afterwards . . . She was never herself again, never quite recovered.
As it was, I had to leave for London almost immediately, so my
father saw to Rory's burial. In fact, I was glad of that, I preferred
to forget the whole thing, as long as I didn't have anything to do
with my brother – or his friend – ever again.'

'But you did have dealings with Murfitt later, when he was
working in that London bookshop. How did you feel about
meeting him again?'

He shrugged. 'It was a long time ago. As I said, he'd made
his apologies.'

'And you'd forgiven him. Of course. But not forgotten?' He
didn't deign to reply. 'Have you any idea why your brother should
have disappeared again?'

'Has anyone ever known why Huwie does anything?'

'You say your brother Penrose wasn't present at this fight you
had, but he must have been told about it – and the part Murfitt
played?'

'Of course he knew.' Ida put in. 'We all did.'

'We know he sponsored Murfitt's bookshop here in Hinton.
Under the circumstances, wasn't that rather strange?'

For the first time there was no aggression in Theo's response. He spread his hands, and Reardon felt he was genuinely at a loss.

Gilmour and Constable Kitchin from Wyvering had spent most of the afternoon canvassing the residents in the outlying parts of Hinton. Nearly all those they spoke to admitted to seeing Murfitt at some time or other and most of them remembered the dark green loden cloth topcoat he had taken to wearing when the weather had turned cooler. It was a distinctive coat and if it had turned up anywhere unexpectedly it would have caused comment, so it had either been destroyed already, or was being kept out of sight until it could be disposed of. Gilmour had gleaned nothing they hadn't already learnt about Murfitt – most people's recollections of him were vague, since he hadn't stirred much out of his shop and few had exchanged words with him, unless they had been customers – and the rumours which had circulated about him had ensured there were not many of those. His death had been an unenviable end to a solitary existence, his only acquaintances being his aunt, Mrs Knightly, and the two unlikely young women, Verity and Sadie Bannerman. Which in itself was intriguing, thought Gilmour.

The afternoon was drawing in when he returned to Bryn Glas to make his unsatisfactory report to Reardon and found that Cherry had in fact just rung back to sanction the trip to London for the next day. Reardon was making plans for how they should each make use of the time there. He viewed Gilmour's lack of progress with a shrug. 'No more than I expected.' He gathered up his papers and announced he would like to call in on Dr Fairlie on their way back to the Fox.

'Shouldn't we make an appointment? He's probably out on his rounds.'

'We'll take a chance.'

On their way out, Gilmour left Reardon to walk to the car while he delivered back to the kitchen the tea tray that Prue had earlier brought into the study. As he was pushing open the kitchen door with his knee he heard raised voices and met the unusual sight of Mrs Knightly and Prue facing each other, their faces flushed. They both looked upset.

Prue was saying, 'Look, I'm sorry, I'm so sorry, but I just can't bear thinking about poor Mr Llewellyn, and not knowing . . . If there's any chance it might help to find who did it—'

Simultaneously, they saw him standing there in the doorway. Prue gave the housekeeper an odd look, half-pleading, half-defiant, and threw another, almost stubborn one, at Gilmour. Mrs Knightly turned away and began taking plates from the wooden drying rack by the sink. With her back to the room, she said, 'Go on then, tell him, seeing you're so set on it.'

'Mrs Knightly, they have to know. It can't hurt anyway, not now.'

Hurriedly, Prue almost snatched the tray from Gilmour, jerked her head for him to come in and then said again, almost pleadingly, 'I have to, Mrs Knightly, I'm really sorry, but I do have to tell.'

Mrs Knightly didn't reply. She took the plates she'd stacked and put them in a cupboard and then suddenly turned to put her arm round Prue's shoulder. 'Oh, don't go on so, girl. You're right, it can't hardly hurt now. But better from me. You'd best sit down to hear this, sergeant.'

Gilmour chose to prop himself against the table, while she picked the old cat up from what he evidently thought of as his rightful place in her basket chair. He settled on her knee and automatically her hands moved to stroke him. 'All right . . .' she began hesitantly, and then went on rapidly, as if determined to get out what she had to say before she regretted it. 'When we first spoke, Mr Reardon asked me who was in the house the night Pen died. I told him there was only the family and me. Well, that wasn't exactly so, I'm afraid. But it won't get you any further in finding out who killed poor Pen, because it was only my nephew who was in my room and I know he couldn't have killed anyone.'

Gilmour only just stopped himself from punching the air. This was it, then. What had seemed to be an affair confined solely to the family had suddenly gained another dimension. Not only the family here that night, all of them swearing they'd seen and heard nothing. Except for the movement Verity had heard, of course. Which must have been Murfitt coming up the stairs from the housekeeper's room. Reardon would want to hear this but

Gilmour was reluctant to stem the flow by going out to fetch him. 'What was your nephew doing here?'

His wish was suddenly answered when, in the sometimes uncanny way he had of being in the right place at the right time, Reardon put his head round the door at that precise moment, looking irritated and wanting to know what was keeping Gilmour.

'You need to hear this, sir.'

'Oh?' Reardon took in the tension in the room, the women's agitated faces, Gilmour's barely concealed elation. Abandoning his impatience, he joined them, drawing out one of the straight-backed chairs from under the table and straddling it.

Ten minutes later, they had it. Murfitt had come down to Bryn Glas that night and stayed out of sight in the house-keeper's room. No one else had known he was there except for Mrs Knightly herself and Prue, who had taken in to him a share of each course of the celebration feast. 'There was no harm to it,' Mrs Knightly said. 'Just a bit of whatever was left over and a sit by the warm fire. He used to do that, you know, just come and sit with me of an evening. He was good that way, came down to see me two or three times a week.' Her lips trembled. She had been fonder of him than she had admitted, perhaps even to herself.

If he'd been in the habit of calling on his aunt here for a decent meal, it certainly explained how he'd managed to put up with the discomforts of his own living quarters.

'And sometimes he'd forget to go home,' remarked Prue, evidently not a paid-up member of the Murfitt admiration society, but with an apologetic glance at the housekeeper. 'More than once, I've come in to do the fire early next morning and found him still here, asleep on the couch.'

'If he was, there was no harm,' repeated Mrs Knightly. 'But he didn't spend *that* night here. He never stirred out of my room until he went home just before I went to bed, and now . . . now, look what's happened to him. Now he's been . . . murdered, by the same person as murdered Pen.'

'Mrs Knightly, we don't know that.' But Reardon couldn't put any certainty into it. Supposing Murfitt had killed Pen – for a reason not yet apparent. Someone knew this and had then killed Murfitt – someone who either wanted revenge for Pen's death . . .

or because he might have stumbled across the real killer? It was understandable why Mrs Knightly had been so anxious to keep from them that he had been in the house that night, knowing he was bound to be a suspect. Even though it was allegedly against his principles to kill. And why should he want to kill Pen, the man who'd done everything he could to help him?

'Thank you, both of you,' he said, standing up.

'I don't know what good it's done. He didn't kill Pen.'

'What time did he leave?'

'Just after the doctor.'

'And there's nothing else you wish to tell us, Mrs Knightly?'

'What else is there to tell?' She began stacking crockery again.

They were lucky. Dr Fairlie was at home. He opened the door himself and when Reardon had introduced Gilmour and asked for a few minutes of his time, he led them into a small sitting room, excusing himself for a moment or two and inviting them to take a seat while they waited.

Instead, Reardon took advantage of his absence to examine the photographs ranged on the upright, closed piano, particularly one he took to be of Fairlie's parents: his mother, fair-haired and rather bored looking, as though she would have been happier astride a horse than sitting with a baby on her knee. Fairlie resembled her rather than his father, Henry Fairlie, severe and distinguished looking, with a hand resting on the back of his wife's chair.

Before he came back Reardon, who always took notice of such things, had time to study the rest of the room – chair covers frayed and thinned to the softness of silk, an ornate plaster ceiling with pieces missing from the cornice and a watermark on one wall like the map of Italy. An oriental rug, almost worn to the threads, its once glorious colours faded, was laid on ancient floorboards, a foot wide, the polish overlaid with a thin film of dust. On the way in, he'd noticed the front door, peppered with the exit holes of woodworm. Fairlie House was not in good order, but then, Dr Fairlie looked like a man who didn't notice such things; a plain, sensible man with no frills, born into a lifestyle which didn't suit him. A lifestyle he evidently couldn't afford to keep up with – not unfamiliar these days, a once affluent family fallen into bad times. Who looked after him? Someone should.

The answer came almost immediately with the entry of Fairlie himself carrying a decanter and glasses, followed by the same untidy woman who acted as his receptionist, bearing a tray with sandwiches. 'There you are,' she said, plonking the tray on a table. 'And if there's nothing else, doctor, I'll be on my way now.'

'Thank you, Myra. Everything's fine. Mind how you go. No more falling over.'

'I'll be careful. And I've got my torch this time.'

'Mrs Jenkins,' Fairlie informed them, 'managed to trip over and nearly broke her ankle the other day, going home. If I didn't know you better, Myra, I'd be tempted to think you'd been at the bottle,' he added with rather heavy-handed humour.

'More likely it was that man! Appearing like that out of nowhere and scaring the living daylights out of me.'

'Which man was that?' the doctor asked with a frown. 'You didn't say anything about a man before.'

'That Murfitt, him from the bookshop. I won't speak ill of the dead but you ask me, he was up to something, sneaking about – well, look how he's got himself murdered!'

She looked all set for a gossip but Fairlie, switching on a lamp said, 'Thank you, Mrs Jenkins.' She rolled her eyes and left.

'He doesn't seem to have been a popular man, Mr Murfitt,' Gilmour said.

Fairlie shrugged and waved a hand towards the sandwiches and decanter. 'You'll excuse me, I hope, if I eat while we talk. I have evening surgery in half an hour. Will you join me?'

They accepted whiskies but waved away a sandwich. 'Thank you, sir, but Mrs Parslowe's dinner awaits,' Gilmour said.

'Then you won't want to spoil your appetite.' Fairlie poured himself a large measure and attacked the sandwiches himself with relish – a case of the cobbler's wife being the worst shod, if this was his usual evening meal, which seemed likely enough.

'Well, I suppose this latest bad business is why you're here?' he asked after the first bite or two. 'If there's any help I can give . . . John Emerson has made me au fait with the details.'

'Just one or two points. For a start, tell us what you know of Murfitt?' Reardon asked.

'I didn't know him at all. I must confess I'm not much of a reader and haven't the time for it these days, anyway – dull chaps, doctors, I'm afraid! I never went into the shop, but I believe I've seen him around once or twice.'

'You met him when you were younger, though.'

He stopped in the act of taking another sandwich and frowned. 'Did I? If I did, I don't remember. How do you make that out?'

Reardon reminded him of the incident when the dog had been shot. He added carefully, 'I think you might know more about the quarrel that followed than you implied when we last spoke. You were there, weren't you?'

'Ah.' He looked slightly put out. 'Yes, well, I didn't think it necessary to mention it,' he admitted. 'Raking over old bones never does any good, you know. So, he was *that* fellow, was he? Good God! Well, of course I remember what happened to poor old Rory. Caused one helluva to do. I was home for the vacation and I'd been invited over there to lunch. But I didn't remember the culprit. Of course, it's a long time ago and our acquaintance was brief, to say the least, and anyway, I was more concerned with what was happening to Mrs Llewellyn. She wasn't in good health, but she tried to separate them, Theo and Huwie, when they came to fisticuffs over it. The shock could have killed her.'

'Lucky you were there, then,' Gilmour remarked.

'Yes. I wasn't yet out of medical school but I knew enough to make sure she was all right – she had to be got to bed, take her medication and so on. When I eventually went downstairs again, after I was satisfied she was settled, and no apparent harm done, I found Huwie and his friend had prudently got themselves out of the way, and the other guests, a local couple, had left, too. There was only Theo and his father, but such a tense atmosphere I judged it better that I left them to it and went home, too. I had to go back to medical school the next day and forgot all about it.'

Having finished the sandwiches, he went to pour himself another large scotch. Returning to his chair he said, 'Are you telling me that was the cause of the big trouble between Huwie

and Theo? I always thought it was something that happened later.
Though I suppose I might have guessed, if I'd given the matter
much thought. Theo thought the world of that dog, and he was
in one heck of a temper. And Huwie always knew how to slide
out of trouble.'

'Apparently so, even if it meant never coming back to Bryn
Glas again – or not until he arrived for Pen's birthday party. And
now he's disappeared again.'

'The devil he has!' This was obviously news to him. He stood
up again, taking a stance by the fire, pulling his pipe out of his
pocket and proceeding to fill it from an oilskin pouch. He looked
very tall, rather gaunt and tired in the shadowed light from the
lamps. 'You're saying he had something to do with Murfitt being
killed? Huwie? The Huwie I met at Pen's supper party?' He made
a doubtful face. 'Well, if you want my opinion, I suppose
anything's possible but—' He stopped abruptly. 'My God, who
would have thought . . . it's damned peculiar, isn't it, that Murfitt
should choose to be here, in Hinton? After that trouble with Theo?'

'Apparently they'd settled their differences. Both Theo and
Pen eventually became reacquainted with him through the anti-
quarian book business.' Fairlie shook his head in amazement.
'Would it surprise you further to know that it was Penrose
Llewellyn who financed Murfitt's bookshop?'

'What?' Even more taken aback, it took him some time to
reply. 'Yes. Yes, it damn well would,' he said at last. 'Unless
there was something in it for him.' He added hastily, 'That sounds
harsh, but I have to say Pen's good nature often depended on
whether it suited his own purposes.'

'But not always, surely? I've heard he spent time with an
apparently disagreeable old woman, Mrs Brewster, for instance.'

'That was different. Little boys can become very fond of their
nannies, you know.'

'His nanny?' Reardon blinked.

'Yes, really,' Fairlie returned wryly. 'Nanny Sumner – or Nanny
Muriel, as they called her. Late in life, after her nannying was
done, when everyone thought she was a confirmed old maid, she
married Thomas Brewster. His first wife had died in childbirth,
leaving him with the baby – that's Carey – so I suppose it was
a mutually convenient arrangement.'

'So Muriel Brewster was Carey's stepmother.'

'She was. Which makes Carey's devotion to her all the more commendable.' His sandwiches finished, he stole a covert glance at his watch. Reardon took the hint and nodded to Gilmour. They stood up. 'You lead a busy life, doctor. Thank you for your time.'

'There's always something, yes.' He smiled. 'But no one forced me to take up general practice.'

'It's a vocation, I'm told.'

'If that means I wouldn't trade it for anything else, I suppose it is. Yet people seem to think I ought to be living the life of a lord.' He added wryly, 'You've only to look around you to know why I don't.'

'Haven't you considered moving to somewhere more manageable?'

He looked down his patrician nose. 'Giving this up? Good Lord, no. This house has been in my family for as long as Fairlies have been around, inspector. I rather feel it's one's duty, as my father and his father did, to keep it up.' Suddenly embarrassed that he'd been caught in an apparently unguarded moment, he ushered them to the door.

Reardon was silenced. We live in a modern world, and not the past, he thought. But, like his own view of that, which in saner moments he admitted could be rose-coloured, Fairlie's was one he was entitled to.

Carey was more or less camping out in the house now. Jack had found a dealer willing to take the old-fashioned furniture she'd grown up with and because she'd accepted whatever was offered, it had been taken immediately. Upstairs there was now virtually only her bed left, and downstairs a wicker chair, a couple of straight-backed ones and the kitchen table, all of which would be given to Martha Tansley further along the lane when Carey left. Mrs Tansley had been very helpful, offering her services and getting rid of Muriel's personal possessions – her few bits of jewellery, her good coat and sensible shoes, her serviceable frocks. And also – Carey made a face – her nightgowns, trimmed with scratchy crotchet work and the brown wincey petticoats, the long woollen combinations, the thick lisle stockings. Glad of the help when it was offered, Carey hadn't enquired too closely where all the items had gone. Mrs Tansley was an incurable busybody, but basically kind.

The main problem had arisen over selling the house. Buyers for such property, in a place like Hinton, were non-existent. Anna had suggested that rather than leave it empty until a buyer should magically turn up, it might be rented to a young Hinton couple who were expecting a baby shortly. Carey had agreed, though without the lump sum from the sale of the house her future plans were going to be more restricted than she had anticipated. Anna, horrified at the thought of her staying in the house under such primitive conditions, had pressed an invitation to stay at her house but Carey had no wish to spend her last days in Hinton in such close proximity to a man whose affection for her was, at the most, brotherly. She needed to become used to distancing herself from him, rather than forging closer links.

Now only the last task remained: sorting the contents of a drawer, most of which she'd already discarded. Only a couple of photograph albums were left, plus several loose snapshots and a bundle of letters tied around with a frayed blue silk ribbon. She threw some more coal on the fire, made herself some tea and began by putting aside the one photo she wanted to keep. This was a sepia snapshot of a man with a kind face whom she'd always known she would have loved had she ever known him: her father, the man who had died when she, Carey, was a child of two. It wasn't until she was thirteen that she'd been told Muriel wasn't her real mother. Perhaps Thomas Brewster had married her because he had imagined that as the Llewellyn boys' nanny she must be good with children. It was interesting that the leather album was crammed with photographs of 'her boys' as Muriel had called them, and scarcely any of Carey herself. Well, she could live with that. It hardly came as a surprise. There were only a few snaps where Ida featured, too. Perhaps Muriel hadn't liked little girls.

Now for the thick bundle of letters. All of them, Carey saw when she untied the ribbon, were from her darling, her baby, Huwie, addressed to Muriel as 'his dearest Nanny Moolie'. They began with letters from school which were mostly tearful complaints about bullying and being beaten, the hatefulness of sums, the awful porridge at breakfast that made him sick and please would she ask his mother to send a cake and some sweets and new socks as some fellow had pinched four pairs of his. Over the next years at school, the letters changed but the tone did not, and they ceased abruptly when he left school. Until they'd begun again, three or four years ago. Letters written by a child were precious, and although it was difficult to imagine Muriel as sentimental in any way at all, it was understandable they'd been kept. But it was less understandable to keep the ones written by a man who took no more trouble than to write as if he was submitting a health or weather report and to hope she was well, too . . . Still, he had written.

And then she came to one that brought her heart into her mouth.

Half an hour later, the panic hadn't subsided. Here in her hands was a potential time bomb and Pen, the only one who could have advised her what to do about it, was no longer here. Who else could she trust? None of them at Bryn Glas: Ida, Claudia, nor Huwie himself, and least of all Theo, from whom she'd always shrunk. There was indeed one person she would have trusted her life to, but now he was the last one she could go to.

TWENTY-THREE

Although they were not dissimilar in size, the London premises of Everard Forster, Rare Books, were otherwise as unlike the Hinton bookshop as its owner was unlike Adrian Murfitt. Not on the Charing Cross Road itself, but situated in a short side street, the shop had a handsome frontage with the name gold-painted on black above its old-fashioned bow window, in which only a few handsomely leather-bound volumes gave any indication of its purpose. Two lollipop bay trees in pots stood one either side of the glossy black front door, which was locked. To be admitted, you had to ring the bell and wait.

Forster himself, a hugely fat man whose width filled the

doorway, answered the summons. Possibly in his fifties – though with all that fleshiness it was hard to tell – he was immaculately suited. Reardon immediately wondered if his tailors charged him double: that amount of grey pinstripe would have made two, conceivably three, normal-sized suits. His shoes were highly polished ox-blood, and the knot of a discreet maroon tie was half-hidden under the third of his three chins. Reardon followed the faint, pleasantly mingled smell of bay rum and Vinolia soap as he was waved inside. After he had examined his warrant card and without asking what his business was, Forster courteously gestured him to a chair with hands that were surprisingly small, white and carefully manicured, with an onyx ring on his left pinkie. His throaty voice was cultured, though he breathed heavily, with a slight wheeze.

This was an *establishment*, Reardon had decided as soon as he stepped through the door into a hushed silence, never in any circumstances to be called a shop. There were few books on display – fewer even than in Murfitt's shop – but all of them were housed in tall, dignified, glass-fronted bookcases. So discreet was the overall ambience you might have been forgiven for thinking you'd strayed into some gentleman's comfortable library. Polished parquet surrounded an oriental carpet in subtle tones of faded gold, aged leather chairs with brown velvet cushions stood on it; framed woodcuts and antique maps hung from a picture rail above wood-panelled walls that were painted a dull green. Soft-shaded lamps graced occasional tables. There was a lectern supporting an open book and a desk pushed unobtrusively into one corner, as if to deny that anything so infra dig as 'trade' went on here.

Forster listened carefully and without any visible emotion to what Reardon had to tell him, as circumspectly as he could, about Adrian Murfitt, but when he'd finished, the sound of wheezing had become noticeably louder in the small, quiet room. It suddenly stopped and for a horrible, disconcerting moment Reardon thought Forster had actually died. Then it began again, louder and quicker and this time with a whistle to it. His vast bulk collapsed back into his chair, he began to gasp between breaths and his knuckles showed white as he clutched the chair arms. Reardon had already sprung up to go to his aid, but the disagreeable necessity of having to grope under those chins to loosen his collar was averted when he saw with relief that Forster was coming round. His breathing became less stertorous and he was trying to lever himself upright. Reardon helped him. 'Are you all right, sir?' Plainly not, but what else did you say in the circumstances? 'Can I get you anything?'

A manicured hand flapped denial. 'It's nothing. Used to it,' Forster told him on a still-whistling breath, then pointed in the direction of a small table at the back of the room. 'Brandy.' And with an immense effort, added, 'You, too?'

'A pleasure,' Reardon lied, simply in the interest of keeping the man alive. But it seemed Forster was not for the other world yet and Reardon was going to be spared having yet another corpse on his hands. At his direction he poured what was evidently the remedy of choice for his attacks and was immensely relieved when it did the trick and he saw colour returning to the pendulous cheeks. 'But shouldn't you see a doctor, sir?'

'Won't do any good. A minute or two . . . we can talk then.'

Reardon took as small a sip as he decently could from the meagre contents of his own glass and hoped there'd be a chance of disposing of the rest soon. He couldn't see any convenient plant pot, so barring accidentally knocking his glass over and spilling the contents on to the possibly priceless Persian, he would either have to leave it or drink it. He loathed brandy – or at least the blinding headache it always gave him. 'I'm sorry to have brought you such bad news, sir. We can leave the rest if you don't feel up to it.'

'A shock, yes,' Forster admitted. 'But these things . . . best got over with. How did it happen?'

The murder of someone you'd known was appalling news for anyone to receive, but the strength of Forster's reaction to it made Reardon wonder just how well he had known Murfitt. Not knowing the nature of their relationship made him very careful how he told the story, or as much as he felt the man needed to know about how Murfitt had died. Especially was he careful not to let him know the conditions in which he had lived. Forster was obviously a fastidious man and Reardon guessed that to hear such sordid details would be additionally painful.

After another silence, Forster said, 'And now you need answers to questions, I suppose. That's what you're here for.' His voice had taken on a slightly sardonic note. His affliction did indeed seem to be something he lived with: he was recovering fast.

'If you feel up to it.'

Forster inclined his head and motioned him to go on. 'What do you want to know?'

'You could start by telling me how you came to employ Mr Murfitt?'

'Employ?' The word appeared to taste strange on his tongue. 'He was down on his luck when we were introduced by . . . a friend he'd met during the war. I presume there is no need to tell you what happened to Adrian in those years? Yes, well, I never held that against him . . . Every man to his conscience, though not everyone believed that, did they, at the time or afterwards?' Forster spoke in fits and starts but he was gaining more strength by the second. 'He was finding it hard to get work, I needed someone to help out here – as you see, my health isn't all it should be. He was with me for four years, nearly five. We found each other . . . mutually agreeable.' After a moment he added, 'So much so that I gave him to understand he could expect to take over from me when I go.'

The way things looked for Forster, that might not have been too long, Reardon thought. And a nice little inheritance a place like this would have been for Murfitt. Which made the fact that he should have thrown away such an opportunity and taken up that miserable existence in Hinton all the more puzzling.

'You're wondering why he left,' Forster said astutely. 'But I'm not sure I can tell you – I'm still reeling from the shock, myself. The opportunity presented itself to set up on his own, you see, and he seemed to think it was the chance of a lifetime. A man called Penrose Llewellyn – you know of him?' Reardon nodded. 'I couldn't understand it, to be honest. For one thing, Adrian wasn't a fool, but mostly, I wanted to know why, if Llewellyn was set on investing in a rare book business, he had to do it out in the sticks. It didn't seem quite . . . it seemed not quite in line with his other business interests. Adrian said the question of where the shop was didn't matter, and of course, to a certain extent, he was right. But why would Mr Llewellyn put money into a set-up like that in the back of beyond, for someone he scarcely knew? To be honest, I had my suspicions. Something fishy about it.'

Probably more than he dreamt of, thought Reardon. There was something decidedly whiffy about the whole business. It was conceivable that Penrose Llewellyn might well have provided the wherewithal to set Murfitt up – as long as it didn't hurt his pocket too much – but why would the astute businessman he had been all his life have thrown money away on someone he scarcely knew? The bookshop operation was never going to make anyone's fortune – perhaps might never have broken even.

'Have you ever been to Hinton Wyvering, Mr Forster?'

When he smiled, Forster's eyes almost disappeared in folds of fat. 'Happily, no. The countryside, as someone or other once said, is very promising, at a distance. I prefer to keep it that way.'

'But you knew Mr Llewellyn. He bought books from you, I understand?'

'I know both the Llewellyns, yes, I deal with them quite often. Theo has been a client for many years. It's always been a pleasure to deal with him.'

'And his brother, Penrose?'

'I haven't had so much to do with him. He's impatient, not like his brother. He buys books like . . .' He paused to take another sip of brandy. 'For all the wrong reasons. He is not a serious collector.'

And that had obviously damned him in Forster's eyes, if not in Murfitt's. It was also evident in his use of the present tense that he hadn't heard of Pen's death, and why should he, unless Murfitt himself, or Theo perhaps, had informed him of it? In view of Forster's reaction to being told what had happened to his friend, Reardon was inclined to delay telling him this further news for as long as possible.

The other man was watching him, warily, it now seemed. 'Do you know yet who it was – the one who was responsible?'

'Not yet, that's why I'm down here. We hope to find something in Mr Murfitt's background that might help us to trace the culprit. Tell me, do your premises here contain a flat, Mr Forster? An attic flat, perhaps?'

Forster blinked. 'There's only the floor above this one, where I live. Why do you ask?'

'We're looking for the other Llewellyn brother, Huwie.'

'Another? I was under the impression there are only two.' His tone noticeably sharpened as he added, 'What has all this to do with me?'

'Well, you see, it's rather odd that you don't know Huwie Llewellyn. He gave us this as his address.'

For a moment Reardon thought the man might be going to have another attack. 'Does . . . does he have something to do with Adrian's death?'

'I don't know, but we need to contact him fairly urgently. Our problem is that he's disappeared, leaving only this address. But if you can tell me where Mr Murfitt lived before he went to Hinton, it's possible we might find Mr Llewellyn there.'

Forster didn't reply. His lips pursed as he looked down at the onyx ring, twisting it on his finger. He shifted in his chair, his flesh wobbling. 'Adrian lived here,' he said at last. 'We shared the apartment above.'

There followed a longer silence.

'There is something else you should know,' Reardon said. 'Penrose Llewellyn is also dead.'

'Is he indeed? Well, I'm sorry to hear that, but I believe he wasn't a well man. I understood that was why he retired to Hinton Wyvering.' Forster looked more closely at Reardon. 'My God, are you going to tell me his death was suspicious, too?'

'I'm afraid that's very much what it looks like.' He became aware of the street noises outside, the tick of a clock somewhere in the background as the silence lengthened.

'I told him no good would come of it,' Forster said at last. 'But when did anyone listen to good advice when they were bent on destruction?' Destruction? That seemed a bit strong. Forster, seeing his look, waved a hand again. 'Not physical destruction, God knows, I never thought it would amount to that.' He sighed and Reardon waited to hear what else he had to say. Under all that blubber was a kindly, sensitive and sensible man.

'Adrian was a rather secretive person, you know. He didn't tell me things – personal things. It made him difficult to live with sometimes. I knew little of how all this business with Pen Llewellyn had arisen and even less of his background. He had a chip on his shoulder for some reason . . . I imagined he was in some way disadvantaged. He certainly had no money, though I know he'd had a university education.'

Reardon was hearing again the same thing Verity Lancaster had said – a chip on his shoulder. 'Did you know he was illegitimate, Mr Forster?'

'No, but it doesn't surprise me.' He looked into the distance. 'I never really believed, you know, that it was Llewellyn who suggested opening the shop. I think it was Adrian who persuaded *him*. He could, I'm afraid,' he added carefully, 'be rather manipulative.'

Like Pen himself, then. But – *persuaded*? From what Reardon had learnt of Pen, he had not been easily persuadable. He remembered something else he had to ask. 'Do you by any chance know anything of a loden coat Mr Murfitt owned?'

'Yes, of course.'

'With a fur collar?'

Forster heaved himself from his chair and crossed to the desk in the corner. He opened a drawer and fumbled inside for a moment, returning with a snapshot. Silently, he handed it to Reardon. It was very clear and the subject was Murfitt – though such a vastly different Murfitt from the man Reardon had met in Hinton that he was momentarily unrecognizable. His hair was brilliantined and sculpted into smooth waves and he sported a small Hollywood style pencil moustache, shaped like a circumflex. He was pictured leaning negligently against the side of a sleek motor car, with one immaculately shod foot on the running board. His elbow rested on the open window and dangling from his hand was a check tweed cap similar to the one Reardon had last seen hanging on the kitchen door in Hinton. The long, fur-collared coat he wore fitted like a glove. Reardon studied the handsome, film star face for a long time. 'May I borrow this, sir?'

'No.'

The reply was unequivocal, but after a moment, Forster relented. 'All right, take it, as long as you let me have it back.'

Reardon promised and gave him a receipt as added assurance. As he took his leave, Forster said heavily, 'I've spent years of my life building this business up – the goodwill, my reputation. I thought it would go on after I'm gone, that Adrian would continue it . . . It's been my world and I always thought it was his, too.'

'You didn't – er – change your mind about leaving it to him when he left you?'

'No. Why would I do that? We didn't quarrel over what he'd done. It was his decision, and I didn't own him. In any case, I was always sure he would come back, when he'd come to his senses. I was wrong – over that and perhaps a lot more. It seems we shared a relationship, but not a life,' he finished sadly. Grief welled up in him suddenly, causing him to turn his face away.

Reardon heard the click of the lock as the door closed behind him.

They had parted to go their separate ways after arriving in London, Reardon saying drily to Gilmour that since he knew her so well, he would leave Miss Bannerman and her explanations to him.

The street where she lived was a yellow London-brick terrace of three-storey houses with flat windows and black-painted area railings. Like most of the other houses in the street it had been converted into flats. The card by the door listed the name Bannerman as being on the first floor. There was no bell but the door opened at a push and there was a flight of steps facing him. At the top was a door. Gilmour was sure he'd come to the right one when he saw it was painted a bright canary yellow.

He was in luck – sounds of activity issued from behind the door, but the person who answered his second loud knock wasn't Sadie Bannerman. She was a little, bent old woman who spoke in a barely audible whisper which Gilmour interpreted as being that Sadie Bannerman didn't live here any more. He showed his qualifications and quietened her alarm by explaining that he had recently met Sadie and was anxious to get in touch with her again.

Five minutes later he was nursing a cup of tea by the gas fire and the woman he now knew to be Sadie's grandmother sat in the chair opposite, regaling him with a lot of information he didn't want about how long she'd been here and what she thought about the other tenants of the house. But Gilmour was patient. She was nowhere near as decrepit as she had at first appeared. He soon discovered her whisper was due to the fact that she was hard of hearing and, like many deaf people, she wasn't aware that her own voice was barely audible. Gilmour raised his and kept his ears attuned.

The flat was small and cluttered with too much old-fashioned furniture and ornaments, every one of which had a lace doily to protect the highly polished surface it stood on. The claustrophobic feeling was heightened by the gas fire being turned up much too high, but Mrs Bannerman was friendly and talkative and they were getting along fine. Once she'd been assured her grand-daughter wasn't in any sort of trouble (which Gilmour devoutly hoped wasn't a lie he would need to be forgiven for) she waxed eloquent on the subject of Sadie – halfway to America by now, she said proudly.

'What?' So much for Sadie Bannerman then. It had taken all Reardon's powers of persuasion to be granted permission for both of them to come to London – and now . . . well, the days of Inspector Dew, following and apprehending the wife-murderer, Crippen, across the Atlantic were long gone, had they ever been likely to apply to such as Gilmour. Even if, however unlikely, Sadie did turn out to be a murderer.

'She's got a wonderful job waiting for her over there in New York, my clever little lass,' Mrs Bannerman told him proudly. 'Always was bright as a button, and I shan't half miss her, but as I've always drilled into her, you have to take your chances where you find 'em in this life, don't you agree?'

'You're not wrong at that.'

'I've had her since she was five years old, my daughter dying and the poor child never knowing who her father might have been, if you get my meaning.' She gave him a speculative look from her bright eyes and decided to go on. 'Well, see, her mother being as she was, despite being brought up right and proper, I've seen to it that my little Sadie didn't go that way.' Her eyes were worried as she stirred her tea. 'To tell the truth, I was worried about her, living on her own up there in that place nobody's ever heard of. She's not used to being alone and doing for herself. She's a good girl but she can be a bit . . . well, feckless, at times.

What's she been up to that you've come looking for her?' she asked suddenly.

'Nothing, I hope, Mrs Bannerman. I expect you know that Mr Llewellyn, the man she'd been working for, had died.'

'Yes, she told me that.'

As briefly as he could, he explained as much of the facts as he thought she needed to know. 'We only need to talk to her. I know the job in Hinton was only a temporary one, but she left it without leaving a word, you know.'

'I expect they told her to go,' she sighed.

'They?'

'That law firm she works for. It was them as sent her up there to work for that Mr Penrose and them as got her the job in America. Thought a lot about her, they did. "Gran," she says, "it's a wonderful chance for me over there. Before long I'll be sending for you to join me, just you see if I won't." I didn't say anything. I let her think one day I would.'

'What law firm are we talking about, Mrs Bannerman?'

She told him. He noted it down without much surprise.

'It doesn't make any sense at all,' Reardon said, tucking into Welsh rarebit in the Lyons Corner House where they'd arranged to meet and compare notes, 'for Murfitt to leave a cushy number like he had with Forster. He was living very comfortably, thank you very much, and with high expectations for the future and then . . . he just throws it all away. Why? And assuming Forster was right, how did he manage to persuade Pen – if that's the right word – into going along with him?'

Despite the large noisy room being so crowded, they'd managed not to have to share a table. They were both speaking with lowered voices, though their conversation was unlikely to be heard above the café music and the continuous loud babble of talk echoing around them.

Gilmour said, 'He must've been putting the screws on him for something.' It was unlikely that a complex and sometimes contradictory character like Pen Llewellyn had led a blameless life, they both knew that. Though it was questionable what misdemeanour, big enough to induce blackmail, could have reared its head at this stage.

'*Just Molly and me, and Baby makes three,*' sang the crooner from the rostrum, while a young woman at the next table hummed along and tapped her feet. '*We're happy in my blue Heaven!*'

Good for them, thought Gilmour, finishing his own rarebit and pushing his plate away. And happy was more than he'd say for the boss, who sounded as preoccupied as he looked. He knew that look. Something was going through his mind, but it was no use asking what, he'd only mention it when he'd thought it through. It was as though he didn't like what he was thinking, either, and didn't want to believe it, but if he'd got to the point where he was arguing against himself, that was all to the good. Gilmour wasn't without a few ideas himself, but they were refusing to come together as yet.

'Did you get anything on Huwie, sir?'

'Everything but his present address.' After leaving Forster, Reardon had made his way to Scotland Yard, hopeful that a man he'd met at a conference some years ago and kept in touch with, a DI Patterson, might have some answers for him. Which he had, but unfortunately none of them were helpful. 'You were right about him never being in the army, though. He missed conscription through convenient incarceration at His Majesty's Pleasure.'

The Nippy who was serving their table appeared and asked if there was anything else they wanted. She was middle-aged, and her white cap, pulled well down over her brows, didn't hide the lines of tiredness on her face. She looked as though her feet were aching. Reardon smiled at her. 'Well, we might have one or two of those nice cakes,' he said, following Gilmour's straying glance towards the nearby display stand of pastries. There was an hour yet before their train and plenty of time to linger.

She smiled back. 'I'll bring you a nice selection. More tea?'

'Yes, please.' She left and Reardon resumed: 'Huwie's been a naughty boy, one way and another. He's done time, as well as that two years in the Scrubs during the war for handling stolen goods, and since then he's been in trouble on and off for small-time stuff, petty theft and so on. But he seems to have kept his nose clean for the last year or two. At any rate, Patterson wasn't able to help with his present whereabouts.' Depressingly, it seemed as though Cherry's doubts about the necessity for their visit to the capital might have been justified.

The cakes arrived, more tea was poured. 'So what had Miss Bannerman to say for herself, then?' Reardon asked.

'Miss Bannerman,' Gilmour said, 'is somewhere on the high seas, even as we speak, swanning around on board ship to the US, to take up work in New York.'

'America?'

'And guess who's sending her there? The people she works for – Theo Llewellyn's law firm. She was working for Pen on loan, as it were. Seems Theo recommended her when Pen needed a temporary secretary.'

'Well,' Reardon said, swallowing a suddenly indigestible piece of chocolate éclair. 'Theo was up to something, if that was so. He does nothing without a reason.'

TWENTY-FOUR

While the two policemen were still in London, letters from Harper, Kingdom and Harper had been received by those who were to benefit from Pen's will.

Theo had deliberately not told his brother and sister that drawing up the will had been taken out of his own hands, though he'd known for some time. *'No hard feelings, old sport, and thank you for what you've done, but it makes more sense to have everything, personal and business, under one blanket so to speak.'* Incensed by Pen's insensitivity, he had nevertheless kept his feelings in check and then, after much thought, he'd wangled that sharp young woman Sadie Bannerman in here where she could supply him with information – which she'd done admirably. His eyes had been opened, as far as Pen's business assets were concerned, and his expectations had risen because, even in his darkest moments, he had known Pen would never forget his family – which in all fairness he had not. But . . .

So much inner rage smouldered in him that he felt as if he

might burst into flames any moment. This confounded new will was insult added to injury – old, never forgotten injuries, such as when Pen had stolen Cora from under his very nose; and the wounded pride when he'd dipped a toe into the waters of speculation, nearly drowned and had to be rescued by Pen. Now, not only was *that woman* to share in the benefits, but Pen's most valuable books were to be sold (a detailed list of them appended, so that none should accidentally go missing) and the proceeds added to the already considerable amount Pen had recently donated to the cottage hospital in Wyvering.

Anna Douglas. A hefty lump sum – and worse: Bryn Glas had actually been willed to her. Obscurely, though he would have had the house sold and pocketed the proceeds before the ink was dry on the contract if he'd had his way, this outraged Theo – more even than the money, or even the sale of those books, for God's sake. Bryn Glas, the Llewellyn family home, which should have been his by rights.

All his scheming, watching, waiting, plotting, gone for nothing. Well, scarcely that, but nothing like he had hoped for, and depended on. Everything he'd done for Pen. All those years of bending the knee. If he had been anyone else other than Theo Llewellyn, he would have howled in sheer frustration.

'She's gone without her *Sunflowers*,' Gilmour remarked, making conversation the morning after they'd returned from London. He sat with his legs stretched out, his hands shoved into his pockets, silently willing Reardon to open some discussion on where the previous day's events had left them, and what they were to do next to get things moving. He was starting to worry, wondering if he was actually going to make it home before the baby arrived. 'Sadie, I mean.'

A letter from Mr Harper, which had been waiting for Reardon this morning, had done nothing to lift his preoccupations of the previous day. But the name Sadie and the mention of the picture roused him to leave his brooding contemplation of the surprising contents of the letter, which had detailed the general terms of the will, and shift his gaze to the bright splash of colour on the wall. 'So she has.'

'She couldn't have been all that bothered about it,' Gilmour

said. 'Or maybe it wasn't hers at all. Maybe she said it was because
she'd just taken a fancy to it. It's the sort of thing she would like.'

It suddenly occurred to Reardon how few pictures there were
in the house at all, and yet somehow, even in such a large house,
they weren't missed. Well, linenfold panelling was its own embel-
lishment after all. Yet Pen Llewellyn had allowed this painting
to grace his office wall, incongruously modern, where he saw it
every day. Simply because it was cheerful, as Sadie had said,
sunflowers in a yellow vase, a reminder of hot summer days?
He eyed it more closely, trying to admire it. He knew he stood
accused of being a Philistine, but all these modern works of art
looked to him as though some junior-school child had been let
loose with his Christmas present paint box. This one was maybe
better than some, but he still didn't get it. And despite her claim
to it, Sadie had evidently thought it wasn't worth bothering about
in her hurried departure.

Without stopping to think why, he went to lift it from the wall.
Something was stuck to the back with adhesive tape that had the
grubby look of having been lifted many times and came away
easily. Underneath, a key. The safe key, it had to be. It would be
interesting to see if the old will was there, though it wouldn't
be needed, after all, in view of this new one. Comparisons between
the two might be enlightening, all the same. In the end, however,
hiding the key seemed a rather pointless ritual for Pen to have
gone through. The safe was disappointingly empty.

'Half a mo' though,' Gilmour said, 'there *is* something here.'
Almost hidden in the top right-hand corner, fixed to its roof, was
a small separate drawer compartment. That was locked, too and
the safe key looked far too big. Exasperated, he tried it anyway,
and hey-presto, the drawer opened, revealing a little cloth bag.
Silence fell as he tipped out four greyish bits of the same sort
of sea-washed glass which sat on the window sill of Verity's
bedroom. Except that these were dull and dark grey, with a pitted
surface, about the size of a hazelnut.

'Have you ever seen rough diamonds, Gilmour? Black
diamonds?' Reardon said at last.

Diamonds? 'No – er – have you, sir?'

'Never. But dirty bits of stone wouldn't need to be kept in a
safe.'

While they stared, a tap on the door preceded the appearance of Mrs Knightly. Reardon looked up. 'Yes?'

'Oh, I'm sorry if I'm interrupting,' she murmured, uncertain at the unusual sharpness in Reardon's voice. 'I just wondered . . . if you could spare a minute or two, Mr Reardon? I'd like a private word with you. But it will do later if—'

'That's all right.' He left Gilmour to put the stones back and followed her into her sitting room. A little embarrassed, she gave him a tissue-wrapped parcel. 'It's nothing much, but I . . . I just thought you might like these.'

The argyle socks she'd been knitting for her nephew were revealed in all their completed Scottish glory: lozenges of red, outlined in white on a dark green background. 'Please take them. They won't be needed, not now.' She sat down and picked up some sewing, her face hidden.

'That's . . . very kind. Thank you.' He folded the gift back into the paper. He hadn't the heart to tell her that never under any circumstances did he wear socks of any colour other than plain brown, black or grey, with the very occasional concession to lovat green.

She nodded and went on sewing – a darn in some piece of white linen that needed careful, tiny stitches, fine thread and close attention. 'There's something else,' she said, keeping her eyes on her work. 'I can't get it out of my mind . . . what's happened to Adrian. You asked about why he'd come to Hinton. Well, you see, when my sister Pattie died – it was only about a year ago – he found something.' She raised her head and their eyes met. Her face was puckered with distress. 'I think you've worked out what I'm trying to say, haven't you? But, please – it's dangerous to jump to conclusions. Adrian . . . he couldn't have killed Pen, if he's been killed as well, could he?'

He looked at her, attempting to sort out the flawed logic while he waited for her to continue. But whatever else she had been going to say remained unsaid. She started and didn't appear to notice the bright drop of blood that appeared on the linen; her gaze was fixed on what was outside the window, her mouth open. 'Oh my goodness me, look what the wind's blown in! I must let Verity know.' Throwing down her sewing, she hurried from the room.

It wasn't, however, the wind that had propelled Huwie Llewellyn down the drive of Bryn Glas, but Verity's Baby Austin, the door of which he was just shutting.

'I don't see the problem, Ma,' Jack was saying. He stood by the mantelpiece, resting his elbow negligently along it, but his fist was clenched. 'It's a matter of principle.'

Anna stared at him, uncomprehending.

'I should go,' Carey said hastily. She'd come across to Anna's house on winged feet to share with her the wonderful news – amazed to have been remembered at all in Pen's will, and with an amount far beyond her wildest dreams. Left with a generosity that would give her time, and space, to think about her future. The letter had come, almost making her forget, for the moment, that other letter from Huwie which Muriel had kept, the one that gave her such a plunging, gut-wrenching feeling whenever she thought about it. Should she show it to Anna? Or should she take it to the police? She knew the answer, really, but could barely contemplate what that might mean.

And now, arriving here, being called to enter in answer to her knock, she'd stepped into what looked very much like confrontation. Between *Anna* and *Jack*? She took a step back towards the door but Anna stopped her.

'Just a moment, Carey, dear. I can guess why you've come, and I do want to hear about it, but first, Jack is just about to explain why he should refuse the very generous legacy Pen has left, and I think you should hear what he has to say.'

'Yes, please. Please stay, Carey,' Jack said. He was unusually pale, the skin looked stretched across his cheekbones. Carey hesitated. She did not want to be here. Family rows were no concern of those outside. But she saw no escape when they were both so intent on her staying.

Abandoning his post by the fireplace, Jack found a chair and assumed his usual pose, hands in pockets, legs outstretched. 'You can't, either, can you?' he asked his mother gently. 'Bryn Glas . . . the family . . .'

'His family,' Anna answered, with more than a hint of sharpness, 'have been more than adequately paid what they were owed.'

'But me? He owed *me* nothing. Did he?' Jack said steadily.

Anna gave him a long, searching look, then sat down, very suddenly, on to the old sofa near the kitchen range, as if her legs had given way, reached out and pulled Carey down beside her. Jack sat up straighter and began to say something but she silenced him with a flutter of her hand. When she could speak she said, 'Am I to understand you think Pen had some . . . some obligation towards you?'

'No!' He ran a hand through his already rumpled hair. After a moment he said, 'Well, all right, at one time, yes, I did, but only for a while, when I fancied myself old enough to understand . . . thirteen years old and a man of the world. *Uncle Pen* who used to come and take me to the football match, or the zoo . . . Uncle Pen who paid my school fees. Who else, when you were always so hard-pressed for money?'

Carey thought that if a feather had floated on to the carpet, you would have heard it.

'Your school fees, Jack, were paid for by a trust left by your grandfather, you know that,' Anna said faintly at last.

'That was something I learnt later, but by then it didn't matter. I'd grown up a bit and I saw how stupid I'd been – the way you talked about my father . . . his photograph . . .'

'Yes, you must have seen how very much like him you are.'

Carey, poised for flight, wondered if they'd forgotten she was here and would they notice if she crept out, but Anna's hand was tight on hers. Jack's glance fell on her and he seemed to guess what she was feeling. 'Please stay, Carey.'

Anna's face still registered shock. 'There's such a lot you don't understand, Jack, so much you don't know about Pen, about either of us, so please, just listen for a moment.' Agitation was making her trip over her words, she who was always so calm. 'Your father and I were so young when we married, he hadn't yet qualified as a surveyor and we'd scarcely a penny between us, but we had just two years of perfect happiness. He died very suddenly, when you were only a year old. They said it was a brain tumour. He was just twenty-three – a very wonderful young man, charming, and so clever and so full of promise. I blame myself. I should have spoken to you, explained more, but I've always found it painful, very hard to speak of him.' She rubbed her hands together as if they were very cold. 'And you believed that I . . . that Pen and I . . . were lovers?'

'It wasn't up to me to judge.'

'How little you know me! Pen was only, ever, the very best of friends. He'd been fond of Charles and he supported me so much through the bad times. He would have helped financially, too . . . he begged me, but I wouldn't allow it. Later, after Cora died, he began to ask me to marry him, but . . . I'd loved once – and after someone like your father, how could I ever marry anyone again? Then, so many years later, coming back here to live, I gradually realized I did love Pen – though in a quite different way, and I saw I'd wasted all those years when I'd had no one. And now . . . I thought you'd be happy for me, though lately, I've sensed some – some reserve towards Pen.' Fear leapt into her eyes. 'But I never for one moment thought you hated him.'

'Hate? Pen? God, I didn't hate him, I *liked* him. I think I loved him when I was a small boy. He was my hero.'

Their eyes met. 'If that's true you've no right to refuse his wishes now that he's dead, any more than I have. He had no children of his own, but he loved you, too, and don't you ever forget it.' She released Carey's hand at last and stood up. 'Now I have things to do.' She paused. 'And as a matter of interest, I happen to agree with you about Bryn Glas. As for the money, we'll see. But perhaps a graceful acceptance on your part would at least be an apology.' She left the room.

He hesitated only a moment. 'Don't go, Carey, I have to sort this out but I must see you,' he threw over his shoulder as he followed his mother and closed the door behind him.

There was no point in staying any longer. He had fences to mend which might take some time and she . . . Shaken by what had happened, Carey let herself quietly out of the back door. The letter she had brought with her stayed in her pocket.

'You were out of order, leaving without letting us know, Mr Llewellyn,' Reardon was saying. 'Taking Miss Lancaster's car, what's more.'

'Only borrowing it,' Huwie replied with an irritatingly ingra-tiating smirk. 'A change of clothes, you know, bit of business to attend to.' He was wearing the same disreputable suit he'd worn previously, and looked seedier than ever.

'So you always intended to come back?'

'I had to return the car, didn't I?'

Did that mean a touch of panic, a change of heart when he realized what light his departure, and the theft of the car, would put him in? No, it had to be something more imperative for Huwie Llewellyn to return and put himself voluntarily in the firing line of questioning.

'Are you sure the real reason you disappeared hadn't anything to do with Adrian Murfitt being killed?' Gilmour asked.

'Murfitt has been *killed*? That's a shock.'

'When did you last see him?'

'Years ago. They told me he was working here, but we never actually got to meet.'

'That's surprising, when he was such a good friend. At least he was until he caused that quarrel with your brother. The one that made you leave the family fold.'

'Oh, *that* again!' But he was wary, not knowing how much they knew.

'Why did you suddenly come back after all that time?'

'I've told you – and it *wasn't* to kill my brother.'

'If you want to convince us of that you'll have to come up with something better than wanting to wish him a happy birthday.'

He sighed exaggeratedly, but perspiration had sprung up on his upper lip. He wiped it with the back of his hand and fished in his pockets for a crumpled pack of cigarettes and matches. Gilmour obligingly supplied an ashtray.

'Let's get on to why you both landed up here, in Hinton, you and Murfitt. And don't expect us to believe it was a coincidence.'

He puffed furiously, thinking, while Reardon, who had never smoked since the operations on his face, resisted the urge to waft the smoke away. He'd suffered worse in the interests of getting witnesses to talk. And talk Huwie did, at last. Whatever he'd been doing these last days while he'd been away from Bryn Glas had unnerved him, to the point where he now decided he needed to get something off his chest. Once he was started, in a mixture of self-justification and spite towards Murfitt, he was off like a railway train.

The two had known each other since their schooldays, he repeated, but after that weekend at Bryn Glas which had caused a disruption with his family (glossing it over with fine disregard for the exact truth), they'd hardly seen each other. Then, about six months ago, they had met again by chance, in a London bar. Huwie, then engaged in some unspecified but clearly dodgy business, had hardly recognized Murfitt, who had fallen on his feet and was working in the rarefied world of antiquarian books, well in with a man who was favourably disposed towards him. They had a drink together and Huwie learnt that Murfitt, through his work, had met up with Huwie's brothers again. The incident of the dog had amazingly either been forgotten, or tacitly not mentioned.

Murfitt had been in a strange mood. Huwie hadn't expected him to want to pick up on their old friendship, but after a few more drinks, Murfitt had become confiding about what he was doing, and told him that circumstances had made it necessary for him to go and live in Hinton. In fact, he was trying to persuade Pen to invest some money in setting up a bookshop there. The trouble was, Pen wasn't inclined to accede.

'Did he give a reason for needing to live here?'

'No, and I didn't ask.' He lit another cigarette from the first and threw the stub into the fire.

'But you managed to come up with something that would finally persuade Pen?' Reardon caught Gilmour's eye, and he brought the cloth bag from the safe. At the sight of the diamonds sliding on to the desk, Huwie's eyes bulged and he turned the colour of putty. 'I see you know what these are, Mr Llewellyn. Unimpressive, aren't they, to say what they're worth?'

'Oh, Jesus Christ.'

'Who do they belong to?'

'They're mine.'

Reardon laughed, braced his hands on the desk and leant back.

Huwie shifted. His eyes slid to the grey pebbles and stayed fixed, as if mesmerized. 'I sold them to Pen, as an investment,' he said at last, 'but he never paid me for them. He said he wanted to make sure they actually were diamonds first.'

'Huwie, you've never owned a diamond in your life. Where

did you get these? And where does the murder of Adrian Murfitt come into it?'

'It doesn't,' he said desperately. 'They'd nothing to do with that, nothing.'

'Convince us.'

He lit another cigarette, this time with hands that shook as he tried to work out a convincing lie. And at last, as if such was beyond him, he gave in. 'All right. I'll tell you how it was. You'll see then I'd nothing to do with killing anybody.'

He had been doing small-time jobs for a man posing as a South African wine merchant, who was in reality smuggling diamonds into the country. When he had met Murfitt and heard his story, Huwie saw his own chance. He knew Pen could never resist the lure of making a bob or two, and diamonds, like gold, were a good investment, so he convinced his boss to sell the stones to Pen, with some substantial commission in it for himself. It had taken him some time to persuade the man but in the end he had agreed. Huwie arranged to meet Pen in London and the stones were handed over, though Pen had insisted they'd have to be authenticated before money changed hands. In the meantime, in exchange for the opportunity, he'd finally agreed to finance Murfitt's business in Hinton, and had in fact kept to that part of the bargain. But he had hung on to the diamonds too long and the patience of the man who was selling them had given out. Huwie had come to Bryn Glas to demand the money must be handed over.

'And you killed him because he was still refusing to pay, then took his keys to search for the diamonds.'

'No! It was nothing like that! If you really want to know what happened . . .'

'We do, Huwie. We do indeed.'

'All right. That night, when we'd had supper, Gerald went upstairs with Pen, and the other guests left a few minutes later. We – my dear family and I, that is – were understandably a bit nonplussed at what we'd just learnt about old Pen getting married, as you might imagine. We stood around talking, but there didn't seem much point in it and after a bit we all went up to bed. I undressed but I knew I wouldn't sleep, so I went downstairs into the dining room for a nightcap. I left the door open and didn't switch the light on – I could see well enough with the light from the hall.'

'And you saw – what?'

'I poured myself a scotch and then I heard Fairlie saying goodnight to Pen before he came down the stairs. I stayed where I was – I'd already drunk a lot that night and I didn't need his disapproval. Just as he got downstairs, Mrs Knightly came into the hall and they spoke. After a moment or two, she went back into the kitchen, but he didn't leave . . . he went into her room, the housekeeper's room. I thought that damned odd until I heard him speaking to someone, but it was nothing to do with me so I went back upstairs. I heard Fairlie's car drive away a few minutes later.'

'Did you recognize the voice?'

'Yes, I did, after a bit. It was Murfitt. I couldn't think what the hell he was doing in the house but I didn't want to have anything to do with it.'

'So you waited until you thought Pen would be asleep, after which you went along to his room to get the keys to his safe. But he was still awake, you argued and in the course of it, you killed him.'

At that he jumped up and banged his fist on the desk. 'What have I told you? *I did not kill him.*'

'Sit down.'

He stayed where he was, glaring, but then sank down like a deflated balloon. 'I did go to his room, I'll admit it, but it was hours later, around three o'clock. I wanted to make sure he was asleep, but when I went in – well, he was already dead, wasn't he?'

'But you still took the keys?'

'And a fat lot of good they did me – and I did return them, later on.'

Reardon eyed him. 'You went into the room and searched it with your brother lying dead. You did nothing about it and left him, left someone else to find him in the morning?'

'He was dead, for God's sake! What sort of a fool do you think I am, letting myself in for being the last person to see him alive? I could see there'd been a struggle and who was going to believe me? Not my family, not you lot, I'd have been a ready-made murderer as far as everybody was concerned!'

*   *   *

For so long it had been there, always at the back of Ida's mind, the knowledge that when Pen died, her financial situation would improve. 'When' he died, the 'when' always somewhere hazily in the unimagined future. Hypothetical, speculative, what if, a sort of pipe dream you didn't really dare to pray would come soon – because that would actually have meant Pen dying. Life without Pen, his faults notwithstanding, wasn't to be contemplated. It was only now he'd gone that she saw how much she was going to miss him, how much it already hurt. All the times he'd come to her rescue, financially and otherwise, came back to her, reproaching her a hundredfold. Especially how good he'd always been with Verity. Too late now to confide her worry about the child to him, even if it would have meant one of his brisk, sometimes abrasive and unwelcome strictures on her own inadequacies.

She pinned a smile on her face and climbed the stairs to her daughter's room, ready to congratulate Verity on her own legacy, the money Pen had left her.

She found her curled up like a foetus on her bed, white as milk, her face contorted with pain, clutching her belly. Ida hurried to the bedside and tried to take her hand, but it was clenched and unreachable. 'Vee, what is it? Whatever's the matter?'

Verity groaned and curled up tighter as another spasm of pain caught her. When it subsided she said, through gritted teeth, 'I'm losing a baby, that's all.'

'What?' Ida sprang away from the bed, as if stung by a hornet. 'Don't be ridiculous!'

The pain momentarily easing, Verity struggled to a half-sitting position. 'Ridiculous, why? That's what can happen, can't it, when you—' She moaned again.

'When you sleep with a man? *Verity?* Who? When? Where?'

'Ironic, isn't it? All this money Uncle Pen's left me, and now I'm not going to need it, when I've been so desperate for it. If he hadn't died, you'd never have known. He would have helped me before it came to this, I know he would.'

Despite being rigid with shock, Ida said sharply, 'Stop that. I won't listen to that sort of talk.' Verity was quite beyond her understanding, most of the time. But this was something she very well understood. Her racing mind fastened on ways out. 'Pay attention,' she snapped. 'I know what I'm talking about. I lost three babies before you were born.'

Verity shot up straight, nearly knocking her head on the low, sloping ceiling. 'You did what? I didn't know that!'

'There's a lot you don't know about me, Vee.' Not only about the failed pregnancies, but also about the serially adulterous husband and why he'd absconded, for which Verity, knowing nothing of what her idolized, charming father could really be like, had always blamed her mother. Ida had never disillusioned her, unable to destroy her dreams. 'It's of no consequence now,' she went on, dry and brisk, 'and you've been a very silly girl, but first let's be certain you really are pregnant.'

Questions came next, a list bombarded her: Have you been sick? Have you seen a doctor? What about this, that and the other? And above all, how long?

'Seven weeks,' said Verity.

'Seven weeks?' Ida breathed again. 'Well, then. There can be all sorts of reasons to account for that. Stress, worry, anything . . . we must get Gerald Fairlie to have a look at you.'

'No!' The cry was so sharp, coming with another pain to double her up, that Ida's antennae bristled. Then her hand went to her mouth.

'Merciful God, that's not who it is, Vee?' she almost whispered. 'Gerald Fairlie?'

'Are you out of your mind, Mother?' Verity began to laugh hysterically. *'Gerald?'*

Then who? But Ida knew that was a question which wouldn't be answered, even if she asked it. And her mind refused even to consider that man with the dog, whom Verity had swerved to avoid on the day she, Ida, had arrived here. The man who had now been murdered.

In any case, by now she was almost certain Verity had been worrying herself sick over nothing. She longed to rock her silly child in her arms, as she had when she was a baby. But the most she could produce without embarrassment was a brusque injunction: 'Come along now, this won't do. You don't need me to tell you've been stupid, bottling it up and making things worse. But

you soon won't need me to tell you you've been worrying yourself
over nothing, just you see.'

'Are we expected to believe him?' Gilmour asked.

'Against everything that's saying I shouldn't, I'm sorry to
say I do. To a point. Huwie Llewellyn's an even bigger fool
than he appears if he expects us to believe that twaddle about
the diamonds.' Reardon picked up the four stones, rolled them
in his palm like dice and then tossed them back on to the desk.
'If his Mr Big isn't laughing his head off at having fooled him,
or fobbed him off, whatever, while he does a probable disappearing act, I'll eat those nice new socks I've just been given.
Somebody like that, entrusting Huwie to negotiate that sort of
deal? And Pen Llewellyn going along with it? Come on! Why
did he think Pen wasn't paying up?'

Gilmour frowned. 'OK, so Pen knew these were only bits of
any old stone—'

'Which we'll assume they are until we know different.'

'Yet he still agreed to set Murfitt up with the bookshop. Who
then goes and kills him. What sort of sense does that make?'

'We don't know he did, do we?'

'Then what was he doing here that night? OK, he didn't stay,
as he sometimes did. Mrs Knightly let him out after the others
had gone – but if he was the same man Mrs Ramsey thought she
saw, he'd still have had time to slip upstairs and kill Pen before
he left.'

'True,' Reardon replied. 'But in that case, who killed *him*?'

'Somebody we don't know about yet. Somebody who has no
connection to Pen?' The suggestion hung on the air like a wet
blanket.

Reardon picked up Mr Harper's letter and flapped it. 'They
all benefit from Pen's death. Even Carey Brewster. And Jack
Douglas, who has an ambivalent attitude towards Pen, to say
the least, suppose his mother had known what he could expect,
for instance, and told him? He left that night with her, Carey
and Mrs Ramsey, but there was nothing to stop him coming
back and doing the job later. Mrs Douglas has a key she uses
to let herself in.' He let a few moments pass. 'But maybe we
shouldn't be looking at those likely to gain, rather anyone who'd

lose. Not financially, but maybe in some other way. Someone
like . . . Fairlie?'

Fairlie?

There had never remotely been any reason to suspect him; he
had no motive, he didn't profit from the will, he and Pen were
supposed to be the best of friends and were apparently on good
terms that night, and besides, Pen had been alive when he left.
'That would have meant *he* had to have a key as well – and that
he came back and finished him off . . . unless . . .'

He broke off, tracing a pattern on the desk with his forefinger.
'Look . . .' he began again, after Reardon had let several minutes
pass. 'This may sound ridiculous, but what about . . . well, smoke
and mirrors? What the eye doesn't see . . . He didn't need to
come back, did he?'

'Good lad!' Reardon said approvingly, and Gilmour sighed.
He might have known he wouldn't have got there first. 'You're
right. He was heard to say goodnight to Pen before closing his
door . . . Verity's room was only a few steps away – I suppose
Fairlie spoke loudly enough to hope someone would hear, and
Huwie, downstairs in a room just off the hall, certainly did,
and Mrs Knightly. There was no reason why Murfitt, too,
shouldn't have heard. But which of them heard Pen reply?
They wouldn't, would they, if Fairlie was speaking to a dead
man?'

It was possible. 'Yes, but why should he, of all people, want
to kill Pen? Unless . . . unless he knew something dire about his
health that no one else did and . . . helped him to die?'

'Well, from my first conversation with Fairlie, I wouldn't rule
out the possibility, if he thought it necessary. But I don't think
so, Joe. Much more likely some argument sprang up and it was
done in the heat of the moment. If it was premeditated, as a
doctor he'd surely have chosen a more subtle way of dispatching
him, wouldn't he?'

Gilmour thought it over. 'Something to lose, you said?'

'The penny dropped when I saw this.' Reardon took out of
his wallet the snapshot of Murfitt in his previous incarnation
which Everard Forster had lent him. 'Compare this with the
photos on Fairlie's piano of his father and there's not much doubt
the reason he came to Hinton was to stake his claim.'

Gilmour whistled as he looked at the photo. 'You're right. But how does Pen's murder fit into this?'

'I don't know yet, but in view of what happened to Murfitt, we'd better work on the assumption that it does.'

TWENTY-FIVE

C arey reached Fairlie House at that grey, melancholy hour between daylight and darkness – *entre chien et loup* – when even the familiar feels threatening and frightening. The bare winter branches of the elms behind the house stood black against a cold, greenish sky, a band of gold still visible at its rim. The evening star, hanging above the gravestones in the churchyard where generations of Fairlies slept, only added to the sense of loneliness.

She'd timed it correctly: Gerald himself was assisting the last of his patients out of the door and down the steps, sending old Mrs Garson on her on her way with a smile. Myra could be heard, clashing about in the dispensary. He greeted Carey in surprise but led her into the house without question.

Inside was scarcely warmer than outside and the fire in the back room was low. He put more coal on and Carey said, 'I have a letter I'd like you to read, one sent to my mother.'

He took it from her. His expression didn't change as he read it. She waited but he still said nothing. 'Is it true?' she asked eventually.

'Isn't that immaterial? You believe what it says, don't you?' he said flatly.

She drew in a breath. That Adrian Murfitt was Gerald's half brother? What else could Huwie's letter mean, if it was to be believed? He'd told Muriel that Adrian had proof positive of that. She wished Gerald would light the lamps; she couldn't read his face properly with only the flickering light from the replenished fire. But he seemed not to notice how dark the shadowy room was. He sat, unmoving, and even when she spoke again, he didn't answer. Her heart began to beat rather fast and she made a hesitant move to go, but he motioned her to stay.

'It was the coat,' he said at last, still in the same monotone. 'My father's, the one he used to wear when he came to see me at school, the one he cut such a dash in. Do you remember him at all? A handsome chap, my father. I couldn't discover what had become of the coat when he died. Then *he* came here, Murfitt, wearing it, as bold as brass. Kept on coming, insisting he was my father's son . . . wanting his share, was how he put it. I told him there was nothing left *to* share, nothing except the Fairlie name, and he laughed and said that would do. That it was his by rights, anyway – he had his birth certificate and his mother's marriage lines . . . and since his date of birth was six months before mine, he should be acknowledged as the rightful Fairlie heir. Even though he'd never even *seen* the man he said was his father, the man who'd always taken care to visit his mother only when his son was not there, away at school or otherwise. The coat he'd left behind on his last visit had never been claimed because he'd died, suddenly, before he could return for it. Murfitt took it off and showed me – the embroidered red and gold coat of arms and the name Fairlie on the scroll beneath.'

This was more than Carey had bargained for. She'd been hoping he'd deny the letter, say it was nothing but lies concocted by Murfitt, passed on by Huwie. Reading her thoughts, he went on, 'I'm trusting you, Carey. I know you, at least, my darling, will understand.' The proprietary endearment shocked her. She closed her eyes for a moment. 'It was mine by rights, you see – only a coat, but it mattered to me because it was such an essential part of my father, but Murfitt refused to hand it over. I was by no means prepared to accept what he said: he must be a fraudster who'd got hold of these so-called proofs somehow. I told him I needed time, he couldn't expect me not to take legal advice as far as proving the validity of his claim went – my mother died when I was a baby, I never knew what the relations between her and my father had been, though he was a man attracted to women . . . but I could not – would not – believe he had been a bigamist, that his marriage to my mother had been a fake. Waiting wouldn't do for Murfitt, though, he

wanted immediate recognition. He'd somehow struck up a
rapport with Pen, got him on his side and persuaded him to try
and talk me into acknowledging Murfitt, even if he was my
father's bastard. Pen knew more than anyone what a drain Fairlie
House is on me and he insisted that selling it was the only
sensible and right thing to do. To sell my inheritance, and to
share the proceeds with Murfitt, who wouldn't then make any
claims on the Fairlie name.' He gave a bitter laugh. 'Pen always
thought he knew what was best for everyone, didn't he? And
when he saw persuasion was getting him nowhere, he began to
use coercion . . .'

'Coercion?'

There was no answer. It was as though he'd been talking to
himself, as though the spate of words had been forced out of
him like champagne from a shaken bottle, and now the bottle
was empty. How impossible it must have been for him to face
the truth – not only that his father, a Fairlie, his idol, had had
feet of clay, but had even possibly been a bigamist. Suddenly
he stood up, peered at his watch and said abruptly, 'Well, work
doesn't stop. I have an urgent call to make on a patient. Come
with me and we can carry on talking in the car.'

This was something she positively did not want to do, but
she knew there was more he was desperate to say . . . and
possibly to no other living person than herself would he have
willingly admitted what she'd already heard. For the sake of
what he'd always done for her, this man she'd known all her
life, she couldn't refuse.

They left the house. For a moment, after he shut the door, he
stepped back, facing it, then he went into the surgery to collect
his bag, opened the dispensary door and exchanged a few words
with Myra before leaving her to lock up.

As Reardon and Gilmour hurried to leave Bryn Glas, Verity
called out from the sitting room. This time she wasn't crouching
miserably over the fire but sitting next to her mother. She was
actually smiling and the papers they were poring over together
suggested they'd buried whatever hatchet had been between
them. 'Have you seen Carey?' she asked. 'She was here looking
for you earlier, said it was urgent.'

'I don't suppose she said what it was about?'

'No. She just asked to use the telephone, and then left in a hurry.' She gave him a worried look. 'I thought she seemed a bit upset.'

There was only one other telephone in Hinton, and since that was where they were bound . . .

Myra Jenkins was just leaving when they arrived at Fairlie House, after calling at Lessings Lane on the way and not finding Carey there. 'Surgery's closed and if you want the doctor, he's just left.'

'Was Miss Brewster with him?'

'She was, as a matter of fact. He was on his way to see a patient – old Mrs Ghyll. She hasn't been well since her husband died last week. There hasn't been an emergency call, not that I'm aware of, but he tore off like his tail was on fire. Is there something wrong?'

'Jump in the car, Mrs Jenkins, we'll give you a lift home. You live not far from the Fox, I think?'

'A few doors along. Well, thanks, I wouldn't say no.' Gratified by the offer but with her avid curiosity unsatisfied by the silence that hung in the car, she sat bolt upright on the back seat as Gilmour drove back into Hinton.

'You're lucky it hasn't taken longer, considering what a bad fracture it was.' Jack had been told yet again by the specialist doctor who was monitoring the progress of his broken leg. 'Give it another week or two.' Another week or two, not long to him, maybe, but Jack was finding it hard to be patient. But since he couldn't go back to his job without being certified fit for work, he'd gritted his teeth and kept on with the recommended exercise routine, which included two daily brisk walks, one of which invariably seemed to take him past Carey's house. He'd developed a nagging worry about Carey, ever since she'd made her decision to leave Hinton, though he'd kept it to himself. Now, however, it was he who needed reassurance. She'd made it plain by not waiting for him yesterday that she thought he'd been acting like a jealous schoolboy over his mother's attachment to Pen. He knew she was right. He was a bloody fool to have let it rankle, even if it had been subconscious.

He found her house in darkness. She was probably with Kate Ramsey, he told himself – a virtually empty house was no comfortable place to spend an evening alone, but for some reason he still felt obscurely worried.

By the time he arrived home, the police car had just drawn up outside the Fox, Myra Jenkins had alighted and was coming towards him. She looked disappointed that no one but him was around to see her arriving in state. 'They're looking for Carey Brewster,' she said when they met, waving back towards the car. 'You haven't see her, have you?'

'Not recently.'

'She's probably still with Dr Fairlie then, so that's all right.'

'Yes.' He bade her goodnight, watched until she'd let herself into her house then hurried towards the Wolseley, with an urgent feeling that it was very far from all right.

'She's gone off with Fairlie?' he said into the car.

'If you mean Miss Brewster it seems she has.'

'Something's up, isn't it? It's important that you get hold of Fairlie – and Carey?'

'Yep,' Gilmour said. 'I'm just working out the way to get to a place called Pyldene. The doctor's gone to see a patient there . . . maybe you can point me the way.'

'Why has he taken Carey with him?'

His sense of urgency communicated itself to Reardon, adding to his own unease. There was no reason to believe Carey was in any danger – if she meant as much to him as everyone said. He had to remind himself sharply that there was in fact nothing against the doctor so far, except Reardon's own unprovable suspicions. And yet . . . Could they afford to ignore that, and the fact that Carey had wanted to contact them urgently, that she'd seemed upset . . .?

'Pyldene's out of the way. I can direct you there, but better to show you.'

Reardon made a decision. 'Right. You know the route – you can navigate. Or better still, you can do the driving.'

Gerald, steady, unflappable Gerald, was driving erratically and at an almost reckless speed: the headlights slicing into the blackness ahead. Carey wasn't dressed for riding in a heater-less car

on a freezing night and despite her woolly gloves, her fingers as
well as her toes were soon numb. Icy draughts insinuated themselves around her ankles, her neck. She huddled into her coat,
shivering and pulling her collar tighter, and the car swerved
unnervingly as he reached back into the dickey, hauled out a
tartan car rug and tossed it on to her knee. He hadn't even paused
to put on a coat or driving gloves before leaving, but he didn't
appear to be feeling any discomfort. And despite what he'd said
about talking as they drove, he hadn't spoken since they left
Fairlie House; his gaze stayed fixed on the empty road. She was
afraid to break the silence; it was less unnerving than her fear
of what she might hear if she did.

She tucked the rug tightly around her legs and feet, trying not
to dwell on his driving and the way her nerves were jumping.
'Who's the patient you have to visit, Gerald?' she made herself
ask at last.

'What?' He took his eyes off the road and threw her a quick,
sideways glance. The car did a kangaroo hop, the needle on the
speedometer flickered and then went up to a dangerous thirty
while she gripped her seat. 'Oh, old Amos, Amos Ghyll.'

Not for the first time that evening, her insides did a gut-
wrenching plunge. On her left, the hillsides rose, close and
dark, hugging the side of the road. She didn't want to think
of how close they were on the other side to the cliffs above
the river. Where was he taking her, and why? It was no professional call he was making on Amos Ghyll – the old man, a
well loved Hinton character, had died last week, everyone knew
that. She closed her eyes, but they flew open when she heard
him say suddenly, 'I've done things that were wrong, Carey,
but that doesn't mean I've done them for the wrong reasons,
you must believe that. It shouldn't have happened to Pen. It
wouldn't have happened if he hadn't lied to me about writing
a confession.'

The car bucked and jerked and the noise of the engine made
her acutely aware of the silence of the night outside wrapping
itself around them, the absence of any human habitation for miles.
Was it possible that her breathing had actually stopped for several
minutes?

'Do you remember the night your mother died, Carey?'

Muriel? What had Muriel to do with Pen writing a *confession*? Confession of what?

'How could I have forgotten?' she managed to say. The night when all those last months of increasing agony for Muriel had finally ended. Carey had nursed her through those last weeks of constant pain, though worn to a shadow herself with all the sleepless nights . . . and then, that night, Pen had arrived, searched her face and insisted she must get some rest while he sat with Muriel or there would be another patient for Gerald in the family. She'd had no will to do anything but obey, falling almost immediately into an exhausted, bottomless sleep. 'You came that night, Gerald, making a call on your way from somewhere else, and found Muriel had just died. But you and Pen let me go on sleeping, for hours longer.'

'You needed it. There was nothing that already hadn't been done.'

With a sudden wrench, he pulled off the road and bumped along over the rough grass and heather that covered the spur of cliff jutting out over the river. She knew where they were headed: it was a well known vantage point, offering magnificent views across the wide valley below and the rising Welsh hills in the distance, you could see it from Bryn Glas. Somewhere far below was the river, making a sharp oxbow bend round the escarpment into flatter land beyond. The place was known locally as the Old Man, so called because the rock which formed it resembled, at a distance and with a lively stretch of the imagination, the bearded profile of a man.

Before they reached the seat at the end, Gerald stopped the car. The engine died and he turned off the headlights. There was nothing to see ahead, they were isolated in a black void. After a moment he began to speak again. 'The night Pen died . . . what happened was . . .'

'You don't have to tell me this, Gerald.' Her mouth was dry.

'But you of all people have the right to know,' he insisted. 'That night . . . I called in to give Muriel her morphine, and found Pen sitting with her while you slept. She didn't need it, she was dead when I arrived, minutes after he'd put the pillow over her face. He was still agitated but he made no bones about what he'd done: you couldn't take any more, he said, you or Muriel. Nor did I feel any compunction at signing the death certificate. Neither of us, I have to say, felt any remorse, and at no point was it ever mentioned between us again – not until we went upstairs together the night he died and he issued what was tantamount to an ultimatum, said he was prepared to make public and confess what had happened if I wouldn't "do the honourable thing" as he put it . . . in other words if I didn't agree to go along with this bee he had in his bonnet about Murfitt's "rights". He was bluffing of course. Even a man in his state of health wouldn't voluntarily put his own neck in the noose. But it made me angry that he'd chosen to interfere in what was no concern of his.' He stopped, leant back and closed his eyes. After a while he went on, a note of desperation creeping into his voice: 'He wouldn't listen to me so I took hold of him and forced him to look at me . . . It wasn't deliberate, I . . . I just went too far. I'm a doctor, I should have known better. God knows, I hadn't meant him to die. I tried desperately to bring him round but . . .' He stretched a hand out and grabbed hers and even through her gloves she felt a scalding heat coming off him. 'Please believe me, Carey.' She pulled her hand away as though burnt. She felt sick.

'And then, there was Murfitt . . .' He went on, but Carey had had enough.

Without even thinking about it she wrenched the door open and tumbled out of the car, catching her foot against the running board and almost falling. She ran, stumbling among the heather roots and tussocky grass, back towards the road, her numbed feet and legs stiff with cold and inaction and not working properly at first. Her breath was coming in great sobs, she willed herself not to think of footsteps pounding behind her . . .

The night sky was as black as a witch's heart above the tortuous rock-sided road to Wyvering. Jack was hunched over the steering wheel, anxious not to miss the turning to Pyldene. Suddenly in the tunnel of blackness, the beam of the headlights revealed something pressed against the rocks – no, not some-*thing* but some*one*, a person, desperately waving their arms. Jack let out a profanity from his service days, stamped on the brakes and was out of the car before the other two realized what was happening, racing forward, no trace of his limp evident. They too were out of the car in a moment, but then Reardon's hand fell on Gilmour's arm. The car's headlights showed Jack with his arms wrapped around Carey as if he would never let her go.

Almost incoherent, she was helped into the back of the car with Jack beside her. It was Gilmour's turn to take the wheel and follow the track Carey had indicated. Fairlie's car stood lonely and silent, the only alien object on the headland, empty save for his bag on the passenger seat, open with some sort of book protruding from it. Of Fairlie himself there was no sign. The cliff top was treeless and bare of anything except grass, rocks and clumps of heather. There was nowhere he could have hidden himself, nowhere to go except over the cliffs and into the river below.

EPILOGUE

Reardon sat with his feet up, by his own fireside. Ellen in the chair opposite, was writing Christmas cards and letters on the small table drawn up to her chair, while Tolly was curled up at her feet in Gypsy's old basket. He didn't know why he still needed the sheaf of papers on his knee that he'd been reading yet again. He knew it by heart, a typed copy of the book Fairlie left deliberately displayed before he had abandoned his car. The case was closed, loose ends tied up, but the dark memory of Hinton still haunted Reardon. Three unnecessary deaths: an old man, a young man who only wanted what he saw as rightful recognition and a good doctor.

Fairlie's body had been recovered down river the next day. He hadn't drowned; the jump down the cliffs and on to the rocks had killed him before he'd hit the water.

The book he'd left was a quarto-sized exercise book with board covers and the handwriting covering the pages was no doctorly scrawl, but a neat and careful hand, almost copperplate. It was a journal of sorts, written up sporadically, only when something of interest or worth recording had occurred. The first entry that concerned the case had been dated four months previously:

> He came here again, last night. Each time his demands have become more insistent, though he says he is prepared to wait – but not indefinitely. Meantime, he seems to take perverse pleasure in prolonging the torment. First it was the coat, and now the documents he claims he found when his mother died. Until now, I have been able to disregard what he calls evidence but this last . . . I cannot, I will not, allow the name of Fairlie to be smirched by some Johnnie-come-lately who may, or may not be, who he says he is.
>
> After he had taken himself off, I was sent for to see old Amos Ghyll, who was dying of emphysema. The end

was very near, and though there was no need, I stayed to see it through with his wife, who had sat by his bed for three days. Downstairs a son and a daughter also waited, united in grief. The old man, honest and God-fearing, had been an agricultural labourer, the couple had been married for over sixty years and had brought up a family of six in this tiny cottage, yet they had survived all the vicissitudes of a hard life: sickness and unemployment, the loss of a daughter to childbirth and one of their sons in the South African war.

And in that room, in that modest, loving home, as the quiet hours passed, something extraordinary occurred. I cannot explain what happened to me, I only knew that in some way the night watch had vouchsafed a glimpse of the way life should and could be lived. There is no future for me now, but in the presence of death, I saw the chance – not for redemption, or forgiveness . . . never that . . . but perhaps a last chance to do what Pen had wanted, to right a wrong.

I sat with Mrs Ghyll until her husband breathed his last. When I left I drove, not towards home, but to the bookshop on the Townway, resolved to make what good I could of it.

I parked my car in the alley behind the shop. The back of the premises, where Murfitt lived, was all in darkness. I prepared to knock, my hand on the knob, but it twisted under my grasp and the door opened. It seemed he'd soon learnt our country ways, not bothering to lock his door. As I stepped inside, the dog, who slept in the shop with the kitchen door shut, began to bark. Not knowing where to find a light, I stood in the darkness until Murfitt came down the steps and opened the door into the kitchen. The beam of the heavy metal flashlight he was holding shone right into my face.

'What the hell are *you* doing here?'

'I want to talk, Adrian.' He turned the lamp on and the kitchen was revealed in all its tawdriness and Murfitt in his pyjamas. Hearing his master's voice, the dog had evidently been reassured and had grown quiet.

'Haven't you left it a bit late?' he said. 'Maybe I don't want to talk to you.' Shivering, he lifted the coat – the

green loden coat! – carelessly hanging from a hook behind
the door and shrugged himself into it, then walked to the
fire, poked it to a blaze and put the kettle on. He took a
mug from the cupboard and drew the teapot towards him.
After a slight hesitation he reached up for another mug.

'I don't see why we shouldn't settle this thing amicably
between us, somehow,' I said as we drank the tea.

'What? You've changed your tune! Too late. What I want
I can get without you.'

The spirit of conciliation I arrived with, my good intentions, evaporated. Looking at him, wearing the loden cloth
coat as if it were his right, I remembered the first time I'd
seen it, myself at eight years old and my father, tall and
handsome, striding into my aunt's house – the astrakhan
collar turned up, a dashing figure, coming to drive me and
my mother home to Fairlie House. To me, it was a symbol,
that coat, of everything I admired about him, the father I
worshipped, and to see Murfitt wearing it . . . and to know
that Pen, too, would still have been alive if it were not for
him. My actions were quite outside myself, I wasn't aware
of how murderous the rage consuming me was as I snatched
the torch Adrian had left on the draining board and hit him,
hard, at the point on the temple which I knew was most
vulnerable. Instantly, without a sound, he staggered, fell to
the floor and lay silent, blood pouring from the wound on
to the coat. I raised the torch and hit him once more, then
again, twice. It was over in a few seconds. He died quicker
than Pen.

After that I went upstairs and found what I needed
among his personal papers: his birth certificate and the
marriage lines that told the abominable, shameful truth.
He had indeed not been lying about his mother's marriage
– a no doubt hasty and foolish act of remorse on my
father's part. I took the lot downstairs and burnt them in
the grate.

It wasn't until I saw the amount of blood pooled on to
the floor tiles that I almost panicked. My own clothes were
covered in blood and the immediate surroundings were
spattered. I needed to get the body out of the way and tidy

up. The clarity of mind that comes in an emergency is an amazing thing. Remembering I'd attended the previous occupant of the shop who had once fallen down some treacherous cellar steps that led from the shop (and been fortunate enough to have suffered little more than a wrenched shoulder), I saw the possibility of making Murifitt's death look like an accident. That dog was making a racket again and as I opened the door it launched itself at me. I had to let the body fall to fend it off but fierce as he is, he's only a small dog. I grabbed his collar and forced him into the storeroom, shutting the door. The noise he made was terrible and I was afraid it would wake the neighbourhood before I could get away.

I was about to drag Murfitt to the stairs when I realized he was still wearing the coat. It was useless now, soaked as it was with his blood, but not only had it the tailor's label sewn into the inside, it had the Fairlie coat of arms and name, too. I removed it, rolled it into a ball with the towels I used to clean up and took it away with me. It went on to a garden bonfire and cost me more to see it burn than it had to roll Murfitt down those cellar steps.

I am not a religious man, but if you should read this, Carey, and believe that God will have mercy on my soul, I beg you to pray for me. Until now, I have always lived honourably, tried to lead a good and useful life, but without you by my side, what have I to lose?

Reardon had seen to it that Carey certainly did not read this, with its subtext of blame. It wasn't Carey's inability to accept him that had caused Fairlie to take his own life rather than face the music and be hanged for his crimes. It was seeing his over-weening family pride and his father's reputation in shreds, and by no means least, the damage to his professional reputation. The pity of it was another wasted life. Wasted? But Fairlie had murdered twice over and colluded in another. None of them in cold blood, but he was a killer just the same.

Ellen sealed up the reply she'd just written to a newsy letter from Kate, who was presently sorting out loose ends in Hinton, then coming to spend Christmas with them before taking up that position she'd been offered with the NCW. The Llewellyns, without too much apparent regret, had put Bryn Glas on the market and left, she had written. Anna, with all her friends gone from Hinton and Jack and Carey making plans to marry, was going to shut up her house and make a long-promised visit to a cousin in New Zealand.

The telephone rang and Ellen left the room to answer it. Reardon waited for the inevitable summons to some emergency, but he heard her laugh, and it was some time before she came back, with two glasses and a bottle she'd been keeping for just this occasion.

'It's a girl,' she announced. 'Elizabeth. Elizabeth *Ellen* Gilmour. To be known as Ellie. Seven pounds and another little copperknob, just like her father.'

'Good news. But Joe was hoping for a boy.'

'Never mind that. If she's half the man her father is, she'll be all right.'

Reardon raised his glass and drank to it. 'He has his moments,' he said.

He picked up the typed papers, tore them across and dropped them into the blazing fire. A moment of his own had just come. He watched the sheets of paper curl up and finally disappear like the memory of green Shropshire hills shrouded in darkness. He raised his glass again. 'To Ellie,' he said.